KILLER LOOKS
By
Karen Diane Oliver

Killer Looks

This is a work of fiction. Names, characters, organizations, places, events and incidents are either products of the author's imagination or are used fictitiously.

Text copyright ©2018 by Karen D. Oliver

To my husband, Randy.
Thanks for being there.

Killer Looks

Killer Looks

Chapter 1

Lauren Sedgeway awoke and opened her eyes slowly, feeling the tiny grains of sunshine that scratched and clawed at them, leaving them wounded. As she blinked, the healing tears came, bathing her eyes in sweet relief. God, she hated Arizona.

She stretched, rolled over and squinted at the time on her cellphone. Shit, David would be here in 20 minutes with the divorce papers for her to sign. And she'd look like hell. Not that he'd notice. And not that it mattered. Just time for a quick shower and a toothbrush before he arrived his usual 10 minutes early. It was one of his character traits that annoyed her the most. Not exactly grounds for divorce, but she didn't need any. He was the one who wanted out of the marriage and finally, without a second of thought, so did she.

As she got into the shower, she reflected momentarily on their life together. Maybe there was one memory worth keeping. One snippet of something exceptional. Nope.

Shower finished, she grabbed for her towel, pulled aside the shower curtain and, startled, found David standing in the bathroom, arms folded over his chest and leaning against the vanity.

"What the fuck! Get out of here, David. God, you're such an asshole," she said as she quickly wrapped the towel around her. She pushed him out the door and slammed it behind him.

"Lauren, I've seen you in the shower hundreds of times. What's your problem?" he asked from the other side of the door.

"You gave up all rights to seeing me naked when you asked for the divorce. I thought I had all your keys. How did you get in?"

"You still have the key under the fake rock in the backyard. When you didn't answer the door, I thought something might be wrong so I let myself in."

"The reason I didn't answer the door is because I was in the shower. And you're 10 minutes early. Had you been on time and not early, I would have been out of the shower and able to answer the door. Damn, you're annoying. Go wait in the kitchen. I'll be down as soon as I get dressed."

She was glad that this chapter of her life would soon be over. She would no longer have to follow David's job and live in places she hated. Like Arizona. David had gotten transferred here from Connecticut 5 years ago, and she had left behind a network of friends, her favorite bakery and a couple of pounds. She had had to contend with unbearable heat, road rage (hers), an affair (his) and the constant, relentless sameness. Maybe his affair hadn't done much for her self-esteem, but her life was now hers. Getting away from David, his trophy girlfriend, Miranda, and Arizona gave her a chance to live where she wanted, to do what she wanted. She was fortunate that she could work from anywhere. Being a book editor and sometime-author meant that all she needed was a computer and wi-fi to do her job, and she did it very, very well. So, she really didn't need David. Never had. But that didn't mean she wouldn't accept the generous settlement her lawyer had spent months wrestling from him. *Let's just call it a final kick in the nuts,* she thought. It was payback for the affair.

He was waiting in the kitchen with its dated orange peel walls and tile floors as she padded from the bedroom wearing a t-shirt and jean shorts. Signing divorce papers didn't warrant any special attention to her wardrobe. If she had to do this, she'd be comfortable.

"Let's get this over with," she said as he handed her the pen. A quick scribble on a couple of pages and it was done.

"I want to thank you for this, Lauren. I know we both want to move on with our lives," said David.

She just stared at him. Did he honestly think she signed the papers for him? What a piece of work. This was all for her. She was finally free of the bullshit he brought into her life. She didn't know about moving on, but she sure as hell was moving up.

As he walked out of the kitchen and out of her life, she felt nothing for him. Anything that had been there was gone. She had tons of planning to do and she was anxious to begin. First things first, though. She'd have to find another place for that fucking key.

Chapter 2

Two weeks after her divorce was finalized, Lauren prepped for her move. The boxes were packed, all fifty-two of them, and the movers would be arriving around 9 am to start loading. She had sold her house furnished so all that was left of her material life was in those fifty-two boxes, soon to be deposited at her new furnished rental home. She was headed to Montana. She and David had visited Glacier National Park and she'd fallen in love with the area. Because of that, she thought the beauty of Montana might inspire her new life. She loved trees, mountains and rushing streams. Of course, they'd traveled there in the summer months when blue skies, sunshine and mild temperatures added to the enjoyment of the trip. She knew she would also be facing brutal winters, road closures and more snow than she had ever seen in Connecticut. She would be far from the conveniences of a larger city, especially since she was moving to a very small, but wi-fi friendly town. But that was fine with her. At this point in her life she thought she just might prefer small town living for a change. The realtor had said that cellphone service was adequate, but her house was located in one of those "iffy" locations. She'd need to get a landline. She didn't even know anyone who still had a landline. *Welcome to Montana.*

The movers arrived three hours late so she had time to make some final phone calls. She had been renting back from the young couple who had bought her house, so she let them know she would be out of there by 4pm and would leave the keys and garage door opener in the kitchen. She had gotten the house in the settlement and had made a nice

profit from the sale. She had David's Land Rover, which
was now hers, and money in the bank. She called to
transfer her utilities to the new owners and then reached her
Montana realtor, Maggie Banks, on her cellphone just as
the movers were loading the last boxes.

"Maggie, it's Lauren Sedgeway."

"Lauren! Are you still in Arizona?"

"Not for long! The movers are loading the last of
my stuff and they'll be leaving in the next half hour. I'm
going to spend the night in Flagstaff since I'm getting such
a late start. I should be there in about 3 days, but I'll keep
you updated on my progress. Everything all set with the
house? Can you make sure I have plenty of firewood and a
stocked kitchen?"

"Sure thing. Everything will be there when you
arrive. Swing by my office and I'll give you the keys. You
might need directions, too, since you're on the edge of
town. Snow isn't due for a couple of weeks yet, so you
shouldn't have trouble getting here. The landlord said that
if you think of anything else you'll need, just call. We'll get
it taken care of."

"Thank you so much for everything. I'll see you
soon!" said Lauren. She ended the call and walked to the
driveway where the movers were closing up the back of the
truck. Fifty-two boxes filled with her past life were going
with them. Her new life would be in the car with her. She
had stocked up on water and food for the road, hoping to
shorten her travel time by eating as she drove. She had a
couple of blankets, a few small boxes, one of those survival
kits David had forgotten to take when he transferred the

ownership to her and two manuscripts she could read in the hotel room at night.

As she drove away from Scottsdale, she had nothing on her mind but her new start. She was intrigued by the idea of living in a small town, getting to know her neighbors. But still, she could be as isolated as she chose to be, especially when working. She wasn't one of those women who talked about "finding" herself. She knew who she was, what was important to her and what she could accomplish. She was fearless. It was her life with David that had fucked her up. She should have left him earlier, but she had gotten complacent. The editing and writing kept her busy and distanced from his demands, sexual and otherwise. The affair was predictable. His asking for a divorce was just a formality. They had been living separate lives for a long time and now she could live hers in Montana.

The trip was uneventful and three days later as she pulled up to the real estate office, Maggie Banks was waiting for her. She met her at the door and as she walked inside the small office, Maggie extended her hand. Lauren eagerly accepted it.

"Lauren, it's so good to finally meet you! We've got you all set up at the house. Looks like the snow's going to come in quicker than we thought, maybe even tonight."

"I guess I got here just in time. You said you had directions for me?"

"I do, but I've asked Cal Morgan to lead you out there, now that it's getting dark. Wouldn't want you to get lost."

"Cal Morgan?"

Killer Looks

"He's my husband's cousin. He does a lot of work for me in my business. Construction and handyman stuff. He doesn't live far from you so I asked him to get you there, maybe start a fire for you."

"Gosh, I appreciate that. It's been a long week and I'm ready for a night before the fire with a glass of wine."

"Hell, that's what I forgot to get," Maggie said.

"Oh, don't worry, I've got a couple of bottles in my car. Never travel without it!" she said as they both laughed.

The door to the office opened and a cold blast of air rushed in along with the most beautiful man Lauren had ever seen. He was tall, about 6'3" and his presence overwhelmed the small office. Piercing green eyes, black, silver-flecked hair, hard body and just enough swagger to make even Sam Elliot jealous.

God, please let this be Cal Morgan, Lauren thought.

"Cal, I want you to meet Lauren Sedgeway. Lauren, this is Cal."

"Ma'am, welcome to Wildwood," he said, tipping his cowboy hat to her. "Hope you had a safe journey."

Her mouth refused to open. All she could do was stare at him. Finally, she managed a smile and an "uh huh".

"I think we'd better get going," he said urging her in the direction of the door. "It looks like an early storm headin' our way."

Lauren turned to Maggie. "Thank you and I'll be in touch soon. Maybe we can get a cup of coffee sometime."

"I'd love it. Make sure you call if you need anything. Shit, what's wrong with my brain? I prepared a little welcome basket for you." She ran to her desk and picked up a lavishly decorated gift basket. "A couple of newspapers, a phone book, some Montana boysenberry jam, beef jerky and smoked almonds. Enjoy!" she said as she handed Lauren the basket as she was walking out the door.

"Thank you, I will." She followed Cal to the street.

"Lauren, this is me," he said, pointing to the biggest extended cab truck she had ever seen. Black and silver and powerful, just like its owner. "Just follow me and I'll get you there in one piece," he said, a slight smile forming on his face. She couldn't take her eyes off him.

Flustered, she fumbled for her keys, started her car and finally pulled up behind him. She tried to take notice of her route, but her thoughts kept drifting to him. Good thing Maggie had given her the written directions. She'd need to follow them to get back to town.

About 15 minutes later, he led her down a short side road and pulled up in front of a small cottage that bordered the edge of a pine forest. Hers was the last house on that road. She had noticed one other house driving in, but it was dark and she couldn't see it well. Her house was exactly as the pictures had depicted it and she was delighted. She pulled into the driveway, turned off the car and took a moment to take it all in. Cal helped her carry in her luggage, a few boxes and everything else that remained in the vehicle. Once they were inside, he quickly moved to the fireplace and started a fire.

"Cal, thank you so much. It should be toasty in here soon. I appreciate everything you've done."

"No problem. Is there anything else I can do for you?"

She couldn't think of a thing. Not a damn thing. He seemed distracted and anxious to leave.

"Well, if there's nothing else, I've got to get home to Phoebe," he said.

"Oh," she said, a slight hint of disappointment in her voice.

"She's about to deliver her pups and I want to be there when she does."

"Oh!" she said, probably a little too energetically. "What kind of dog is she?"

"A Rottweiler Pitbull mix."

That breed scared her, and an unexplained chill caused her to shiver. He noticed, misinterpreted her action and added another log to the fire.

"You'll have to add more wood to the fire to make sure it lasts all night. Before you go to bed, really stoke it and you should still have embers in the morning. If it does snow, I'll send someone out to plow your driveway in case you want to head back into town tomorrow. Have a good night."

"You too, and good luck with Phoebe," she said.

He walked to the door, opened it, closed it behind him, then ambled to his truck which he'd left running by the driveway. He hadn't expected to stay long. Just long enough to see if she'd be a problem. He didn't think so, but he'd have to get to know her better.

It came as a surprise when Maggie had rented her the place. No one had lived there for years and he'd been able to keep prying eyes away. But, she was too damn close. She was at the end of the road and his was the next house up from hers. She'd have to drive by every day. He'd have to be more careful.

Chapter 3

By the time Cal got home, Phoebe had delivered her pups. Four females and two males. He immediately drowned the pups, then threw them in the back yard for the scavengers to find. They'd be gone by morning.

He started to make dinner and thought about the night he was going to have. The girls were waiting for him. Eager to please him. They'd been in the playroom all day, getting ready. When the meal was prepared, he set the table for three. Soon they would join him. He opened the door to the basement, turned on the light and descended the stairs. The soundproof playroom with only two small windows was on the right and he unlocked the door and walked inside. Two cages and their occupants awaited him. Gaby's 6 x 10-foot cage butted up against the cement block north wall, and the 25-year-old was huddled on the small cot under a thin blanket.

He had built the cages himself out of reinforced chain link fencing. It had taken the better part of six months to get them just the way he wanted, including laying new concrete for the bolts in the floor. One cage was painted pink, the other purple. He wanted the girls to like their new homes.

Tess was in an identical cage opposite Gaby's, her green eyes defiant as he entered. At 35, she had been there the longest, almost 10 years, she guessed, and she was determined to escape. Given the chance, she'd break free or die trying. He unlocked Gaby's cage first, grabbed the chain that encircled her ankle and pulled. She cried out in pain, but quickly rose to her feet, her head down. She stood at the door of the cage, silent. He entered the cage and freed her ankle chain from the floor bolt, dragging her by the chain as he walked to the next cage. He unlocked Tess's door. She was already on her feet and walked to the door of her cage. She looked directly into his eyes, hatred for him evident on her face. He ignored her as he removed her chain from the floor bolt. He then grabbed both of their chains, attached them to a custom belt around his waist and led them upstairs to the kitchen, where he ordered them to sit. He detached the chains from his belt, then re-attached them to a bolt secured to the floor. It had been the same ritual every night, except for the rare time he had visitors. Then the girls were left downstairs and Phoebe was chained to the bolt in the floor, eliminating any suspicion about why the bolt might be there. The girls were never detected.

In the mornings, they were able to use the bathroom and shower in the room across the hall from the playroom. A tray of food was left in their cage while they showered. They would not have food again until their meal with him in the evening. They were unable to access the bathroom during the day so he placed a bucket in each of their cages. They would empty and clean the buckets before they showered and return them to their cages. Mostly, they slept. When they were awake, they talked about him, about escape and about what would eventually happen to them.

When Tess was taken and brought here, there had been another woman, Beth, in the cage that Gaby now occupied. She had told Tess she thought she was pregnant and when Cal had found out, Beth went to take her shower one morning and never came back. Tess was sure he had killed her and her baby. Gaby joined her two weeks after Beth disappeared. She never told Gaby about Beth.

Cal had prepared a beef stew and he gave each of them half a cup, a slice of bread and water to drink. He liked his women thin and weak, so he'd never let them overeat. Tess figured she'd lost at least 10 pounds since she'd been here and Gaby, maybe 15. But Tess was not weak. She was building muscle in her cage every day. She did push-ups, squats, crunches and ran in place for hours, building up strength and endurance. She had bad-ass written all over her.

The women each wore long, flowing white muslin gowns with nothing underneath. Their hair was long and braided, and a small hair tie secured the braid in place. Their periods had become synchronized during their captivity and when they occurred, they were given adult diapers to wear. He gave each of them birth control pills every morning. He had paid two prostitutes to secure prescriptions for him at a clinic in Helena. Five, crisp 100-dollar bills were enough to keep each of them refilling the prescriptions for him. After the incident with Beth, he wanted no more surprises.

When dinner was finished, the women cleaned up the kitchen, put away the dishes and were then led back downstairs to the playroom. At the wall opposite the cages, Cal had placed a king size bed, a rod hanging with dozens of pieces of lingerie from which he could choose for the women and a table containing sexual paraphernalia.

Tonight, would be a red night. The women disrobed, dressed in the red lingerie he had selected and joined him on the bed. It was the only time the chains were not attached to their ankles.

Cal was insatiable. His sexual appetites varied and the women were forced to perform sexual acts on him and each other. The rugged good looks that had lured them into this trap were still there, but when they looked at him now, all they saw was pure evil. Gaby had already given up all hope of ever escaping this prison, but Tess was more determined than ever to escape. All she needed was a plan.

Chapter 4

The manuscript was killing Lauren. There would be a lot to edit, but it looked like the story was a good one. She'd been at it for the better part of two weeks, sequestered in her cottage. Snow had come and then melted, then come again, but it had left the trees with only a light dusting of snow and her driveway clear. She was almost out of food and firewood, so a trip to Wildwood was in her immediate future. She was still in her pajamas, but left the comfort of the fire in the living room to refill her coffee cup in the kitchen. As she looked out the kitchen window that faced not the woods, but the back of the neighboring house, she saw the truck that she had followed here two weeks ago. It was Cal Morgan's. Maggie had said that he lived close to her, but she had no idea how close. Funny how she'd never noticed it before. She guessed that now that most of the leaves were gone, she was able to get a better view. She still had some firewood, but it would be an excuse to pay him a visit to find out where she could get more. His handsome face had flitted through her mind occasionally during the time she'd been here. But she was so busy with her new life that the face didn't stay there very long.

She didn't want anyone new in her life right now, but damn, that guy was hot. There was something dark about him that intrigued her and maybe scared her a little. But he and his good looks were just a mild distraction and nothing more.

Two hours later she was showered, dressed and ready to head into Wildwood. She thought that if Cal's truck was still there, she'd stop by to ask about that firewood. When she looked out the kitchen window, the truck was gone. She'd have to ask in town.

Directions in hand, she made the 15-minute trip back into Wildwood. It had a stagnant population of around 20,000 and it seemed to be designed to cater to tourists who came to fish in the summer and ski in the winter. She drove slowly through the town to get her bearings, found the market and then recognized the real estate office. She pulled up in front, hopped out and opened the door. Maggie was standing by her desk, looked up to see Lauren standing there and a big smile appeared on her face.

"Lauren! I was wondering when I'd see you again. How are you settling in?"

"I've been caught up in editing a manuscript and finally ran out of food and firewood. I know where the market is, but do you know where I can buy some more firewood?"

"I should have sent Cal out to check on you again. He'll bring a cord out to you as soon as I can get in touch with him. He's been a little reclusive himself, lately. You can pay him when he drops it off. There's a *Merchant First Bank* on the next block if you need to get some cash. One hundred dollars should cover it."

"Thanks, you've been such a big help to me. I didn't realize that Cal was my neighbor. I've been so focused on my work that I haven't thought to look out my windows. It wasn't until this morning that I saw his truck parked at the house up the road from me," she said.

"Oh, I guess I forgot to tell you just how close a neighbor he was. Cal's a pretty reclusive guy, though. He's busy with work, and you don't see him out much. Keeps to himself."

"What's his story? Sorry, if I'm being a little nosy, but a man who looks like that has to have a story," Lauren asked.

"Not sure I know the whole story. He's lived here all his life. Went into the service for a few years, but came back for good. About 15 years ago, I think," she said.

"No wife or girlfriend?"

"Nope, and doesn't seem to date, either. He's the most eligible bachelor in town, and then again, he isn't. No one's been able to turn his head. Are you up for the challenge?"

"Definitely not. I don't want any complications. I guess I was just curious."

"Hopefully, he'll be able to get that firewood to you tonight," she said, getting back on topic. "When you're ready to take a break, maybe you'll meet my husband and me at Smokey's Bar. There's live music on the weekends and we have a lot of fun. I'll introduce you to a few more people in town. Everybody's curious about you, too, you know. You're our first book editor," she said.

"Not much to tell, but I'd love to meet your friends. I'm starting to get cabin fever so I'll let you know when I can make it. Looking forward to it."

She learned her way around the town a retailer at a time. The market was surprisingly well stocked and she even found a couple of bottles of her favorite cabernet sauvignon. She set up a checking account at the local bank where she was able to deposit the $10,000 cash she'd brought with her. And she found a little bakery, a gem of a shop, that rivaled the one she had left behind in Connecticut when she moved to Arizona. Wildwood was magnetic.

Not surprisingly, when she arrived back at the cottage, Cal was already unloading a face cord of firewood and stacking it in piles by her front door, allowing her easy access on cold mornings. He tipped his hat to her when she pulled into the driveway, but continued his stacking without looking at her again. She unloaded the car and carried her groceries inside, putting them away while Cal finished with the firewood. A half hour later, there was an expected knock on the door. It was Cal. She opened the door to let him in and he stepped inside and stood there, hat in hand.

"Maggie said I would owe you $100 for this. Is that enough?" she asked.

"Yes, that's fine."

"Why don't you sit by the fire while I grab my purse in the other room?"

"Thanks, I'll do that for a minute if you don't mind."

She watched as he moved to sit on the sofa, and left to get her purse that she'd thrown on the kitchen counter. She pulled out a hundred-dollar bill and then wondered if she should tip him. Would that be expected or would he be offended?

He was still sitting by the fire, but stood up as soon as she entered the room. She reached out to hand him the money then figured she'd better say something.

"I've got a bit of a dilemma. I don't know if I should tip you or if you'd be offended by that," she said.

He laughed softly and said, "You don't need to tip me. My tip is included in the cost of the wood. But if you'd like to cook me dinner sometime, I might be agreeable to that."

She was taken aback. This was unexpected, and unsettling. From what Maggie had told her, he had no interest in female company, but here he was, being overtly friendly. She was attractive, but at almost 45, didn't think she would interest a man who looked like him.

She might have waited just a few seconds too long to respond to him, because he started to look uncomfortable, shuffling his feet from side to side as he settled his hat on his head. She noticed his discomfort and immediately smiled at him.

"I would like that! I'm a pretty good cook so how do you feel about octopus and sea urchin?" He didn't respond, but instead just stared at her, a look of surprise and then mild revulsion on his face.

"I'm just kidding. How about steak and wild rice, maybe a salad?"

"I guess that'll do," he said with a smile and a sigh of relief.

"How about Saturday, then? Around 5?"

"That sounds good."

"Ok, I'll see you then." By that time, he was at the door, opened it and let himself out. She could hear his truck driving up the road but he didn't stop at his house. *Maybe he was delivering wood to some other woman*, she thought, the double entendre making her giggle a little.

Saturday came, and with it the nervous anticipation of a first date. Except this wasn't a date. She was cooking a thank-you dinner for the man who delivered her firewood. He arrived promptly at 5, dressed in a button-down shirt, nice jeans and polished cowboy boots. He carried a slightly wilted bouquet of flowers that he immediately handed to her.

"I'll put these in water while you make yourself comfortable. We'll eat around 6 if that's ok with you?"

"Sure," he said with no elaboration.

When she returned from the kitchen, she brought with her a bottle of wine and 2 glasses, though unsure if he even drank wine. She was surprised when he accepted a glass.

He spoke first. "So, how are you feeling about your move here? About Wildwood? Think you'll be making it a permanent move?"

"I like it just fine. I'll have to see if I make it through one winter first, before I decide to call it home. I love this little cottage and I might consider buying it from the landlord if I elect to stay," she said.

She saw a slight change in his mood, a frown appearing and then disappearing as quickly as it had arrived. *What the fuck was that all about?* she thought.

"There are a lot of folks who come here thinking they're going to start over, but the tough winters finally get to them and they leave. Most of the people who live here have always lived here. Don't know anything else. Coming from Arizona had to be tough for you."

"Oh, I'm surviving ok. As long as I can get food and firewood out here, I'm pretty comfortable. My work keeps me very busy. I don't really have time for much else. I am getting together with Maggie and her husband, though. I guess he's your cousin, right? Anyway, I'm meeting them next Saturday at Smokey's. Maggie wants to introduce me to some of her friends and that might be nice."

"Maggie and Charlie's friends are ok, but it takes time to fit into their circle of friends. They're not real interested in outsiders."

She found it a strange comment, considering how friendly everyone she had met so far had been to her. She could feel herself fitting in just fine. He was the one who seemed to be the outsider.

She was anxious for the meal to be over. Cal was making her uneasy. She couldn't quite connect his good looks with anything sinister, but something dug at her gut. Maybe it was her writer's instinct. No, Cal Morgan was hiding something. She wondered if she would ever find out what it was.

Chapter 5

Gaby was losing it. She no longer spoke, just slept most of the day. When evening came, Tess had to almost feed her to get her to eat. Cal was angry at her lack of participation in their night games and Tess was afraid Cal would grow tired of her. She cared about Gaby and worried that Cal might harm her. She tried to talk to Gaby while Cal was gone, but Gaby was growing more unresponsive. It was as if she had given up. She had stopped speaking about her family, her past life. She sat on her cot, rocking back and forth for hours. The only time she stopped was when Cal came down the stairs. Then she froze.

Gaby knew her mind was retreating to another place, another time. It was more comfortable to be there than in this cage. She knew Tess was worried, but there was nothing she could do. She remembered a time when Cal meant everything to her. She had met him at a coffee shop in Butte. She had her car packed with everything she owned and was heading back to college for her sophomore year. She was a pretty girl and had no lack of male admirers, but he was different. He was older, sexy as hell with the good looks that would melt any girl's or woman's heart. And he had chosen her. They had sat talking at the coffee house for hours. He had invited her to his house in Wildwood for the weekend and she had readily agreed. His house was remote and the weekend romantic. He was attentive, loving and she was spellbound. When the weekend was over, she returned to campus, waiting for him to call. He didn't. She was frantic to see him again, be with him again. What had she done wrong?

Killer Looks

Her teenage girl's heart caused her to be reckless.
She had to know what had changed. Embarrassed, but
needing answers, she decided to drive from the campus to
Wildwood, to his house, and confront him there. She
slipped out of town, telling no one where she was going,
and arrived at Cal's door. He didn't seem surprised to see
her.

"Gaby, please come in," he said as he opened the
door that led to the kitchen, then locked it behind them. He
suddenly took her in his arms and she was relieved. She
had done the right thing, coming here.

"Can you stay for the weekend?" he asked her.

"If you want me to, yes."

He sat down at the kitchen table and motioned her
to join him. As she sat, her foot kicked a large metal bolt in
the floor, causing her to wince with pain.

"What is that thing?" she asked him, rubbing her
foot.

He ignored the question, then asked one of his own.
"Will your friends be expecting you back any time soon?"

"No, I didn't tell anyone I was coming here.
Besides, they'd think it was strange that I was dating
someone so much older than me. So, I didn't tell them
about you, either. They know I'm seeing someone, but have
no idea who."

"I see," he said.

He rose then, and she could see an erection through
his jeans. He did still care about her, she thought, a little
smile escaping her lips. He walked over to her, took her
hand and led her toward a door she hadn't remembered
seeing before. They'd spent most of the time in his

bedroom the last time she'd been here, so she wasn't surprised she hadn't noticed it then.

"There's something I want you to see. It's very special to me and not something I share very often. But I want to share it with you. It would mean so much to me."

She was thrilled that he considered her special enough to share something so important to him. There was a deadbolt on the door and he unlocked it. Then, when he turned on the light, she noticed a set of stairs leading to a basement. Still holding her hand, he led her down the stairs and they stopped in front of a door off to the right. Across from that door was another that led to a bathroom. She was curious as he took out a key to unlock the first door.

"This is what I wanted to show you, but I want it to be a surprise. I'll cover your eyes, ok?"

He covered her eyes with one big hand, holding her back tight against his erection, the other hand unlocking the door. As soon as the door was opened, she could hear a woman screaming.

"Run, get away!"

Suddenly he shoved her into the room and as his hand left her eyes, she could finally focus on what was in the room. The woman who was screaming at her was locked in a purple cage, her ankle secured by a chain that was bolted to the floor. She was shaking the side of the cage, still screaming for her to run, to get out. She didn't understand.

Cal's arm suddenly secured her around her neck and she struggled to breathe. She fought him, but couldn't get free. She was sinking into blackness.

Killer Looks

When she awoke, she was in the cage next to the one with the other woman in it. The woman had stopped screaming now, and just looked at her with pity. Gaby was dressed in a white gown and nothing else. Her ankle was chained to a bolt in the floor, just like the one she had seen upstairs. She started screaming, wanting to be let out. She pleaded, threatened and cried for hours. The other woman seemed to know what she was going through and looked at her with sympathetic eyes.

When she couldn't cry another tear, she asked the question that she was afraid she knew the answer to. "We're not getting out of here, are we?"

The other woman answered. "No, not unless we figure a way out. My name's Tess."

"I'm Gaby. How long have you been here?"

Tess hesitated, not wanting to tell her the truth, so she just said, "A long time."

Gaby started to cry again, looking around the room, perhaps looking for a way out. That's when she spotted the bed, sex toys and the lingerie. She wasn't stupid. She knew what that meant.

Gaby knew her family would soon be looking for her. When she stopped showing up at classes, someone would notify her parents. When her dorm room was searched, they would find her bed made, her suitcase missing, but no indication of where she had gone. How would they ever find her here? Maybe they could trace her cell phone. But she had made no calls on her way to Wildwood, hadn't even checked her email or social media. There was no signal way the hell out here anyway, so she had turned the phone off. She was pretty sure Cal had hidden or destroyed her car and her cell phone by now. She hadn't stopped anywhere, talked to anyone. She might as well have been a ghost.

Little by little she had withdrawn into herself. She was lead around by Tess and Cal, going through the motions, with no real sense of self. She had turned her mind off. She knew that Cal wouldn't put up with this for long. But she didn't care.

Chapter 6

It was Saturday and Lauren actually found herself looking forward to a night at Smokey's Bar with Maggie and her husband, Charlie. She stood in front of her closet looking for something appropriate to wear. She didn't exactly have the wardrobe for a Montana bar, but she finally settled on a pair of jeans, her push up bra and a T-shirt that said, *Age Gets Better with Wine*. If that didn't make a statement, she didn't know what would. Either Maggie's friends would love her sense of humor or she would be met with blank stares and fake smiles when she was introduced. Turns out they not only loved her sense of humor, but welcomed her to the community with open arms. Cal was wrong, she mused.

She first met Maggie's husband, Charlie. He was a deputy sheriff for the Montana Highway Patrol and a pretty intense guy, but he loosened up after a couple of beers. Mayor Babs Horne and her veterinary husband, Nathan, were about her age and they seemed fascinated by her job, wanting to know exactly what a book editor did. A brief explanation, and then they all focused on the band playing songs from mostly their generation. Not exactly oldies, but great music. She found herself singing along with the band all night long, drinking beer rather than wine, and having a hell of a lot of fun. Charlie's best friend, Jared Martin, also a deputy, joined them after the band's first set and she found conversation with him easy and interesting. She was pretty sure Maggie was trying to set her up with Jared which, surprisingly, didn't seem like such a bad idea after all. It could have been just the effects of the beer that made

33

her even consider it. She'd see how she felt about it in the morning.

Though the night was still young, Maggie and Charlie had to get home and Babs and Nathan left shortly after they did. That left her and Jared to shut down the bar. She was really having a good time with him and he seemed to be enjoying her company as much as she enjoyed his. They were in the middle of a conversation about some cases he would be working soon when she noticed Cal walk in. He walked up to the bar, ordered a whiskey, then leaned his back against the bar, his eyes fixed on her. She frowned, and Jared noticed.

"Hey, where did you go?" Jared asked.

"Oh, nowhere really. My neighbor, Cal Morgan, just walked in and he's standing by the bar, staring at me," she said.

"You're a beautiful woman. Shit, I hope I don't have to compete with him. I'd lose. I think of myself as a pretty good-looking guy, but…"

"Hey, don't sell yourself short. He may be hot, but there's something off about him. At first, he seemed very pleasant, even delivering firewood for me, but I get the distinct feeling that he doesn't like me living here. Or at least not as his neighbor. Seems the house I'm renting hasn't been occupied for a long time, so he's had a lot of privacy. I mentioned I was thinking of buying the place if I decide to stay in Wildwood and he didn't seem to like that. I'm not sure what to think, but he does make me uncomfortable. I know he's Charlie's cousin, but I'm keeping my distance from him. Looks like I'll need a new firewood man," she said, a hearty laugh escaping her lips.

Killer Looks

Jared laughed along with her, but another glance in Cal's direction stopped her laughter. He was still staring at her, and an uneasy feeling overcame her. Then, he tipped his hat to her, turned and walked out the door. Jared noticed her change of mood immediately, followed her gaze to the bar and saw the little vignette as it played out. It seemed innocent enough, but he knew better than to doubt a woman's instincts. They were usually right.

Jared offered to drive her home since she'd had a bit too much to drink, which was fine with her. He said he'd stop by in the morning before his shift and take her to her car. Smokey's was ok with her leaving it overnight, so she probably wasn't the only one whose beer-to-ability-to-drive ratio was a little out of whack.

The drive back to her place was filled with light-hearted banter and she found herself being drawn to Jared's amiable personality and intellect. It had been a while since she had laughed so much and it felt good. He was a history buff and she shared with him some of the historical novels that she had edited. One about the Civil War was particularly interesting to him and he had, in fact, read it. It had seemed that they had just gotten on the road when he pulled up in her driveway. He smiled at her, leaned over to kiss her, which she eagerly accepted, then went around to her side of the car and opened her door for her. When he walked her to her front door, he took her keys from her, opened her door, gave her another kiss and said he'd pick her up at 7 to take her to her car. She hadn't had this much fun in years, maybe decades.

She was ready for Jared the next morning and although she had a bit of a hangover, he showed no signs of one. He was dressed in his uniform and it surprised her a little at first. Last night he had worn jeans and a sweater, pretty casual stuff, but the uniform gave him a sexy, powerful persona and she was obvious in her appreciation of his appearance.

"Well, don't you look all official," she teased him.

"Just doin' my job, ma'am, just doin' my job!" he teased right back. "Are you ready to go?"

"I've just got to grab my coat and purse. I'll meet you at your vehicle."

She had left her purse in the kitchen by the window, and as she went to it, she caught a glimpse of Cal standing by his truck, but looking in her direction. *What was with this guy?* She was going to start complaining to him about *her* privacy. Enough was enough. She'd run it by Jared, but she was definitely going to say something to Cal.

As she sat in Jared's SUV, she tried to be cool about the previous night, but she found herself throwing sidelong glances at him. She liked this man, and at her age, there would be no game playing. She was pretty sure he liked her, too, so she took a shot at asking him over for dinner as a thank you for taking her to her car.

"Jared, mind if I ask you a question? A personal question?"

"Go for it," he said, smiling.

"I'm assuming you don't have a girlfriend, wife, fiancée or anything like that?"

He laughed a hearty laugh, before he answered. "No, none of those right now."

"Well, if you have none of those entanglements, is there anything that would prevent you from having dinner with me one night this week? You know, to pay you back for bringing me home last night and taking me to my car this morning."

"So, would this be a date?"

"Not a date, no, unless you wanted it to be which I'm fine with, but no, it doesn't have to be a date, although an honest to goodness date would be wonderful for a change. I can cook or we can go out. Either one works for me. What do you think?" She held her breath as she waited for his answer.

"I think I'd like that. How about tomorrow night, after my shift? I'm off at 7."

"That's great. I'll cook. Anything you don't like?

"Nope. Surprise me."

Well, that went better than expected, she thought. She hadn't read him wrong. And as far as she was concerned it would be a date.

Chapter 7

It had been a black night last night. Tess hated black nights. That usually meant Cal was irritated about something and he took it out on her and Gaby. Those were the nights he used whips, bondage and pain to satisfy his needs. Something had changed to make him like this, but she had no way of finding out what that was.

Tess shouldn't be here. Every instinct in her body had told her there was something wrong with Cal. She was streetwise, a fighter and should never have succumbed to his manipulations. She didn't, at first. She was working as an escort, a high-priced one, in Jackson Hole, where her classic beauty and shapely body gave her leverage. She could pick and choose the men she spent her time with and her favorites all had money, lots of it, that they were only too happy to share some of it with her. Her boss got her cut, but Tess was able to put aside enough money on her own to start over, to get away from that life. She liked the idea of the anonymity of New York City, where she could blend in, reinvent herself. It was expensive, she knew, but she had a hefty bank account.

Then she met Cal Morgan. Not through her occupation, but at a coffee shop. She was standing in line, ordering a skim latte when he reached in front of her for a cd on the counter. He was incredible looking. She was sure he was a model or an actor. They were everywhere in Jackson Hole. On second thought, he was older than she first thought, so probably an actor. As he leaned in, his head turned to look at her and he smiled. Perfect white teeth, green eyes, hot body.

But she looked away, grabbing for her coffee. She was leaving for New York. The last thing she needed was some guy fucking that up. As she left the coffee shop, she saw him standing at the curb, arms folded over his chest and leaning against an extended cab truck. As soon as he saw her, he approached her, hat in his hand.

"Ma'am, I want to apologize for being a little forward back there. I'm here for a couple of days from a small town in Montana and you are the most beautiful woman I have ever seen. Frankly, you took my breath away. I just wanted to tell you that. You have a nice day."

She was dumbfounded. He turned and walked away from her, got into his truck and drove across the street to the market. Shit, that was her next stop and she was bound to run into him again. She'd just run in, get what she needed and hope to miss him.

No such luck. He was talking to a cashier as she walked in and he tipped his hat to her and smiled again. This time she smiled back. No sense being a bitch. She could do a little small talk, especially with someone who looked like him.

"Where in Montana you from, cowboy?" she said in her best western movie dialog.

"Why little missy, I hail from Wildwood." He gave it back to her as good as she gave it. She laughed and he joined in. The ice was broken.

"Name's Cal Morgan," he said, extending his hand to shake hers.

"Tess Baldwin."

"Nice to meet you, Tess Baldwin. Here I go being forward again, but may I buy you dinner tonight? I'm leaving tomorrow for home and I'd sure like some company. Good conversation, a good steak, nothing more than that. No pressure, I can take no for an answer, but I sure hope you say yes." The cashier watched the repartee between them, fascinated if not a little jealous. "Go on honey, he seems like a nice guy," she said, causing Tess to consider it.

She said yes to dinner and then, later, to spending the night with him in his hotel.

The next day, she had a client in the evening, but spent the rest of the day with him. Over coffee that morning, she revealed a little about herself, but never about her true occupation. She told him she was in sales. He didn't know her body was her product. He was interesting, a good fuck and pretty to look at. But it was coming to an end. She was moving on and he was headed back to Montana. She had taken a taxi to the restaurant the previous night, and planned on taking one home. He insisted on driving her back to her apartment on his way out of town. Stupidly, she let her guard down. She had a rule that no man would ever know where she lived and she'd never broken it. Until now. That was the last thing she remembered before waking up in the cage in his basement.

Chapter 8

Jared got to the station around 7:30, a half hour early for his shift. Enough time for a cup of coffee and a day's overview from his captain. Lauren had been waiting for him promptly at 7 this morning and he was surprised by the feelings she stirred in him when he saw her again. He remembered last night, a little skewed by the couple of beers he had had, but by the time they left Smokey's he was stone cold sober. He'd had fun. The warm kisses were a bonus. And he had found her fascinating, articulate and incredibly intelligent.

Only his closest friends knew just how intelligent *he* was. Charlie had seen Jared's Mensa International membership certificate hanging on the wall of his home office about two years ago and had started calling him Einstein when they were off duty. Jared didn't flaunt his intelligence, but didn't apologize for it either. He had tested with The Flathead County Sheriff's Office Detective division to join their team of detectives and this was his last week in a uniform. He was being assigned to the cold case team. Actually, he *was* the cold case team. He already had some 30 folders on his desk which he'd started to study. One case in particular interested him. A missing college student, Gaby Parmenter. She'd been last seen on the campus of the University of Montana at Missoula almost 8 years ago. Only about 50 miles from Wildwood. Most of the cases on his desk just needed some follow-up investigation and they seemed solvable with a lot of hard work. But Gaby Parmenter was a different story. She had just disappeared. Her car was missing along with a suitcase and a few clothes, but there was no paper trail through her bank, cell phone, credit cards or traffic cameras. She was just gone.

Charlie came in a few minutes later and his sheepish grin directed at Jared said it all.

"So, seems like you had a really good time with Lauren last night. I assume you drove her home. Anything happen you want to tell me about. That you *don't* want to tell me about?"

"I had a great time with her. First interesting woman I've met in a long time. I like her. Want to get to know her better. We're having dinner at her house tonight. You know, to pay me back for taking her home last night and dropping her at her car this morning."

"You spent the night with her?" Charlie bellowed.

"No, you asshole, I picked her up this morning at her house, then drove her to her car."

"This dinner tonight. Is it a date?"

"I'm not sure. She said it doesn't have to be a date, but she'd like it if it was so I guess by the end of the night, we'll both know for sure."

"I can't remember the last time I saw you with a woman. One that made you happy, at least. She sure seems like a pretty sharp lady, and not bad to look at either."

"I'll agree with you there. Her looks are intriguing, but it's her mind that first drew me to her. She's easy to talk to. Plus, we have a lot in common."

"Yeah, I could tell, she's got brains. Most guys look at tits and ass, but you, my friend, are all about gray matter. I guess there's someone for everyone. Seriously, I hope you have a good time tonight and that this thing between you two plays out long term. You're a good guy, Jared, and you need someone like her in your life."

"Hey, aren't you getting a little bit ahead of yourself? It's one date."

"Yeah, yeah, I know, but you won't have me to keep an eye out for you now that you'll be a DCI agent. I sure will miss you on the roads with me, though. Shit, I've got to roll," he said checking the time.

"Me too," he said, following Charlie out the door, and heading to his own patrol vehicle. "Let's have a beer soon, ok?"

Jared found himself looking forward to his not-a-date date with Lauren. He'd taken a quick shower, donned some jeans and a shirt before putting on his leather jacket and driving to her house to arrive by 7 pm. As he was coming up her road, he happened to glance in the direction of Cal Morgan's place. Lauren had said he made her uncomfortable and that wasn't the first time he'd heard that about Cal. Maybe it was his time in the service in Iraq or that incident with his mother, but there was something about his reclusive nature that caused some speculation in town. No one got close to Cal Morgan, and for the most part, nobody wanted to.

Jared pulled into her driveway, turned off the ignition and getting out and locking the Jeep's door, he walked to her front door, a bottle of cabernet sauvignon in his hand. When she opened the door, she was a vision in black. She was wearing a pair of tight, black skinny jeans, a black V-neck cashmere sweater that showed a tasteful amount of décolletage, silver jewelry and a pair of leather boots. Quite a departure from the faded jeans and t-shirt she

had worn last night. He noticed her hair next. Last night it
had been secured in a ponytail, but tonight loose waves
cascaded over her shoulders, the brunette color tinged with
flecks of gray. On her, it looked good. And he had a
sneaking suspicion she knew it, too. Her makeup was
subtle, classy and the coat of mascara on her lashes
emphasized her hazel eyes. He took a minute to admire her,
to breathe in the flowery scent she was wearing, before
extending the bottle of wine to her.

"Thanks, Jared. I'm so glad you could make it. I've
made some lemon chicken with fingerling potatoes and a
salad, so I hope you're hungry." God, that sounded so
cliché, like something out of an untalented scriptwriter's
mind. What she had wanted to say was that he was fucking
hot, in or out of uniform, and she was dying for more of
what they had shared last night. Shit, she was almost 45
and acting like a hormonal teenager. She was at the height
of her sexual prime and a potentially hard cock had just
walked through her door.

"I've got to admit, I called Maggie about the wine,"
he said. "I wanted to get something you'd like."

"It's perfect and thank you," she said. She looked at
him, paused for a minute, then continued. "We're being
ridiculous. There's no need to be so formal or
uncomfortable. I like you, I think you like me, so let's
break the ice."

She grabbed him then, kissed him passionately on
the lips and moaned when he returned her kiss with similar
passion. They went on like this until the timer on the stove
told her the potatoes were done.

She pulled away from him, flushed, unsteady on her feet and moved into the kitchen. Satisfaction and sexual tension were at war in her body, and when she looked back at him, saw him adjust himself in his now too-tight jeans. She guessed it was going to be a fine night after all.

The next morning, she awoke to find Jared next to her, his broad back the first thing she saw as she opened her eyes. She moved slightly, then watched as he turned over to face her, a broad smile on his face.

"Sorry about burning the chicken last night," she said, saying the first inane thing that came to her. It had been a long time since she'd awoken with a man in her bed.

"I think I was as much to blame as you were. We salvaged enough so we didn't starve, did we?" he said.

"I was starving for something, but it wasn't chicken. Even went back for seconds." she said rather playfully.

He let out a loud laugh and hugged her to him. It had been easy like this all evening. She was amazing. Direct, funny and playful, but, at times, their conversations took on a more serious tone. They talked about her life's work and his upcoming promotion. She was impressed that he was going to be working cold cases, and he found her knowledge of the investigative process to be equally impressive. A great editor had to know a little bit about a lot of subjects, she told him, but she had to admit that her favorite genre to edit was true crime. She was fascinated by the criminal mind.

"Look, I have to drive to Flathead County today to meet with my new supervisor. Are you interested in taking a drive? We can have lunch there after my meeting."

"Ooh, is this like meeting the parents? It's a big step in our relationship, you know." She was trying to keep it light, not trying to read more into it than it was. This would be the third day in a row that they had spent together. Truth was, she liked spending time with him. But a relationship had been the last thing she had expected here in Wildwood.

He laughed again. "I love your sense of humor and it sometimes catches me off guard. I know you're in the middle of editing a book, but can you take a break? I'd like your company."

He'd said, *I'd like your company*. Not some company, *your* company.

"Sure," she said.

"I'll take a shower, head home for some things and meet you here in an hour. Work for you?

"Uh, huh," she said. The sun was just throwing out its first beams of light. She heard him go into the shower, run the water and she rolled over for 5 more minutes. When she woke, he was gone and she had to scramble to get ready. He'd be here in half an hour.

Chapter 9

He watched the deputy sheriff's car leave Lauren's house around 7 am. Shit, it wasn't bad enough that she was living there, now she was fucking a cop. A cop who might become more than an infrequent visitor and a possible danger to his way of life. When he was on this road alone, away from prying eyes, he was sure his secret was safe. The playroom was mostly soundproof and his method of securing his captives in the cages was foolproof. The girls couldn't be heard and they couldn't escape. But a cop saw and heard things other people didn't. That had him worried.

The girls were not girls anymore. Gaby was approaching 30. She was becoming a problem and he was getting bored with her. He would replace her soon. Tess was older, but she had a fiery spirit and even though he could see she hated him, he was excited by her. The day would come when he would have to replace her, too, but that time was farther off.

He had hoped that Lauren would tire of the winter storms and isolation, but she seemed to thrive on it. Now that Jared Martin was interested in her, he didn't see her leaving any time soon. She hadn't been curious about him, hadn't even gotten close to his property, but he knew that could change in a heartbeat. Something would happen and she'd be on his doorstep in a minute asking for help. He didn't want her wandering anywhere near the house. But he couldn't be here all day, defending his solitude. It was time to build a fence.

He wandered to the basement to let the girls out of their cages. Tess was first today, and as she showered, he watched the soap run in rivulets down her firm body. He didn't give them their privacy and they were so used to him standing and watching, that they no longer thought to hide themselves from his gaze. She still gave him an instant erection and he looked forward to tonight. It would be a white night.

Gaby sat on her cot and watched as Tess was led back into her cage. Gaby jumped up immediately and walked over to the door of her cage. Cal quickly reattached Tess's chain, then, pulling his keys out of his pocket, he locked her door and unlocked Gaby's. He led Gaby away and she quickly showered. Cal watched her, too, but her emaciated frame did nothing for him. She would participate tonight and then he would dispose of her. There was always another girl.

He would be away from the house more often now. He'd gotten a new remodeling job and it would take the better part of 2 months. The homeowners had wanted it done before Christmas so he was on a tight deadline. Building the fence would be slow. It was already late October and there wasn't much light when he got home from his day job. He'd be working on weekends, putting up one slat at a time. The ground would freeze, too, putting even more urgency into the task. Building a fence in the middle of a winter season would be impossible so he needed it done before permanent winter blustered in.

He had not talked to Lauren since he'd had dinner at her house. He had come on too strong, intimating that Montana was not the place for her and that she'd find it hard to fit in. She had become uncomfortable and the dinner had ended quickly. He'd seen her around, throwing her looks he could see made her uneasy. That was good. The more she tried to avoid him, the safer he would be.

You think you're going to be safe? I'll find you, you know. Just like I always do. You can't hide from me. I know where your favorite hiding places are. Your sisters told me. They always tell me everything you do. You think they're your protectors? You're wrong. They only tolerate you like I do. Let's see how you like what I'm going to do to you next.

He couldn't get her voice out of his mind. His mother. Her voice would reverberate into his consciousness and the hatred would come. She'd been dead 28 years, but he'd never been able to separate himself from the abuse she inflicted on him and his sisters. She had lied about them. His sisters. They did try to protect their baby brother. But each of them left the house as soon as they could, to get away from her. When his last sister left, he was alone with her. Still too young to leave. He was only 12, but at 5'8" and 145 pounds he didn't look like a little boy any longer. And he was beautiful, in spite of what his mother told him. She began to look at him differently. And when she took him into her bed, she knew exactly what she was doing. Soon, so did he.

His mother, Caroline Morgan, was a pillar of the community. After his dad died in Vietnam, his mother got her law degree and then was appointed to the bench after 20 years of practicing law. As a Federal Judge, she was well respected by the legal community, earning a reputation as a fair and impartial adjudicator. However, she was hard-lined when it came to handing down sentences, especially to young male offenders. Her rulings were swift and often harsh. There had been complaints, a threat of censure, but nothing ever came of it.

Cal lived with her in that house until the day he turned 17 and joined the Marines. She had adopted a 10-year-old boy, Adam, who had come through the foster care system a year after he left. When Adam was 12, he shot his adoptive mother, the judge, then turned the gun on himself. Cal and his sisters came back for the funerals, talked to police, but never shared what they knew must have happened. Adam had found the only way he could to stop the abuse that Cal never could.

Cal had been weak. His mother knew that and used it to her advantage. But she was gone now, and he was in control. In control of his life and in control of the women who were now his captives. No woman would ever rule his life again.

Chapter 10

Lauren had some coffee brewing in the kitchen while she was in the shower and after getting dressed, applying a little makeup and putting her hair in a ponytail, she prepared two cups for the road. She was anticipating a bit of awkwardness at first, but then she thought they'd find that easy rhythm that seemed to work so well for them.

She heard Jared pull up outside, expecting to see him in uniform and in his patrol vehicle. But instead, he was in a suit and driving his personal vehicle, a large charcoal SUV. He was on his cell phone, so didn't get out of the vehicle right away. Shit, she was underdressed. Maybe she had time to put on a casual dress instead of the jeans and sweater she currently wore. She ran upstairs, kept the sweater, but replaced the jeans with tights, a wool pencil skirt and boots. She was just coming down the stairs when he knocked on her door.

She walked to the door, opened it and was met with his smiling face. After appraising her appearance, he pulled her into his arms, greeting her with a passionate kiss. So much for awkward.

"Well, hello to you, too," she said, an impish smile appearing on her face.

"I've been wanting to do that since I left this morning. Too soon?"

She laughed. "Just fine." She grabbed her coat and the two cups of coffee, handing one to him. "I made a cup for you. Black, okay or do you like it sweet and creamy?" she said with a sultry edge.

He looked at her and smirked, appreciating the delivery of her last comment. "Black's fine. You ready?"

The drive was about an hour and it gave her time to ask about his new position. "You'll be working with cold cases? Tell me about that," she said.

"The county has a backlog of cold cases and no one's looked at them in quite a while. Mostly missing persons, but there are a couple of murders in the files, too. They will be my sole focus, but I may be pulled into other cases if there's a connection to any of mine."

"There is this one girl, Gaby Parmenter, who disappeared from her campus about 8 years ago. Just vanished. She's either been dead since she was taken, or she might be a victim of a sexual predator. You know, a human trafficker or one of those guys who wants a sex slave. I'm figuring she must be dead, since someone's bound to have noticed something a little strange about a neighbor or relative by now. But you never know."

"How do you even begin since it's been so long?" she asked.

"Start with the family, college friends, roommates, ex boyfriends, anyone who knew her. There's always something someone knows, but they don't think it's relevant or important. It's my job to pull it out of them by asking the right questions."

"Sounds fascinating. You're smart, so I think you'll be very successful." The banter continued with a discussion of her book edit, which was now done for the moment and sent back to the author for revisions.

When they got to the County offices, Jared dropped her at a coffee shop while he met with his supervisor. As she sipped her latte, she contemplated this thing, whatever this thing was, that she had with him. She was not looking for a relationship, especially with a detective, but she found him captivating. He was smart, which was huge for her. He was funny and attentive. Two more checks in the positive column. Ok, the sex was good, too. Actually, it was great. But, and it was a big but, it was only day three. Shit, she'd need to reel in her emotions, put up her usual wall and ultimately scare the guy away. That was the plan. But she'd enjoy it while she could.

On the drive back, she was more pensive than usual. A disquieting memory of Cal Morgan had caused the change in her. The memory slipped in, and stayed. It was something Jared had said about strange neighbors and missing persons. But she was being an idiot for letting her imagination get the better of her. Cal Morgan was a little strange, but that was all.

Chapter 11

He had made it to the hardware store yesterday and his fence slats would be delivered tomorrow. He wondered what Lauren would think when she saw the fence going up. Hopefully, she'd be pissed, not curious. He thought about it. She'd be pissed.

He had seen the way she had looked at him when they first met. How most women looked at him. He used his looks to his advantage, and would need to use them again soon when he began looking for Gaby's replacement. Lauren's interest in his looks had waned quickly, especially when he'd made every effort to make sure she stayed away from him. He needed to make sure he didn't go too far, make her suspicious instead of just uncomfortable. He decided he'd be cordial the next time he saw her in public. Especially if she was with the cop.

She's going to find out about you, you nasty boy. She's a smart one. Don't think you can get away from her prying eyes. They'll see right through you.

His mother's voice invaded his present again. She talked to him more often now. Ever since Lauren had arrived. He was strangely attracted to Lauren, but repulsed by her at the same time. It was her strength that caused him to revert to that 12-year-old again, to those same feelings of powerlessness he had felt in his mother's presence. Yet, he was somehow drawn to her. What would it be like having her in one of the cages?

His thoughts of Lauren evaporated and he focused on Gaby instead. It was almost time for the girls' showers and he knew Gaby's time with him would soon be over.

Killer Looks

Tess would shower first, and once she was back in her cage, he would take care of Gaby. She didn't matter. He would dispose of her quickly and, tonight, would take her body where he had taken Beth's. No one would find them.

He left the kitchen and his fifth cup of coffee and walked to the basement door. It was still dark this early November morning and the girls would complain about the cold again. He'd take the space heaters down to the playroom and the bathroom later today. Maybe when he got back from disposing of Gaby's body.

Gaby's body. Once, curvy and luscious, but now painfully thin. Had he done that to her? No, she had refused to eat. She could have kept most of her curves if she'd just eaten what he placed before her. He'd caught Tess grabbing bits of food from Gaby's plate when Gaby refused to eat. He wouldn't punish Tess, though. Those extra calories kept her body in a desirable condition.

As he descended the stairs, he heard silence. He'd need to wake them up. He unlocked the door, hit the light switch that controlled the illumination of the one single bulb in the center of the room. Both women stirred, then rolled over on their cots to look at him.

"Tess, you go first today."

Tess stood, grabbed her bucket from the corner of her cage and walked to the door, a look of loathing on her face. He unlocked the door and her leg chain, attached it to his belt and led her to the bathroom. She emptied and cleaned her bucket, then he attached her chain to a bolt by the shower and he left to get her breakfast tray. He had left a clean white gown for her. She would be done with her shower when he returned, and he regretted that he would not have time to watch her today. But he had to prepare for Gaby.

As he reentered the bathroom, Tess had finished her shower and was standing with her bucket in hand, waiting for him. He smiled at her. She glared at him. He'd have to tame that feistiness, he thought. He led her back to her cage where her breakfast was waiting for her, opened the door, attached the chain, then locked the door as he left.

He then looked over at Gaby, cowering on her cot. He walked to her cage, unlocked the door and her chain, then she picked up her bucket and followed him out of the room, attached by her chain to his belt.

Gaby entered the bathroom, emptied and cleaned her bucket, then disrobed, ready to step into the shower. She did not notice a clean gown and he had not brought her breakfast tray when he had brought Tess's. She started to panic and found his gaze locked on her.

"I'm sorry, Gaby," he said, approaching her. She screamed and tried to run, but her chain kept her confined to a small run radius. He started pulling on her chain, drawing her in, but even with her adrenaline strength at full capacity, she was no match for him. He grabbed her, finally, and wrapped the chain around her neck. As he looked into her eyes, he saw the life leave them. It was the look he had wanted to see in his mother's eyes, but he'd been too weak. So, he would pretend that Gaby was his mother.

Gaby's lifeless body fell to the floor and Cal executed the rest of his plan. He put on rubber gloves and prepared to wash her body. He wanted no sign of his DNA anywhere. While she was still in the shower, he doused her in bleach, then wrapped her body in the plastic tarp that he had prepared for this purpose. He tied the tarp with rope, then carried the body up the stairs to the garage, ready to be loaded into his truck late that night. He went back downstairs to Tess.

"Where's Gaby?" Tess asked as soon as he unlocked the door and came into the room. "What have you done with her, you sick psycho bastard?"

"Gaby's decided to leave us, so you'll be here by yourself for a while until I can find someone else to keep you company."

Tess began to cry. Poor Gaby. But then maybe she should pity herself and not Gaby. Gaby was free. Now, she'd be here alone with him. The sole object of his sick obsession. She wailed at the thought of it. He grew tired of it and left her alone. After he was gone, the tears stopped, only to return when she thought of sweet, guileless Gaby. He would never do that to her. She would fight him with any breath that remained in her. She had to escape. That was imperative now. If he had so easily killed Gaby, he could do the same to her if he tired of her.

Chapter 12

What the hell? She had been roused by sounds of pounding, trying to understand what she was hearing. As she realized it was coming from outside, she got out of bed to look out her window. That's when she saw where the noise had been coming from. Cal Morgan's. As she saw and heard him pound a fence post into the stubborn, almost frozen ground, she wondered what this was all about. Was he that much of a jerk that he had to keep everyone out? She was no threat to him or his privacy. The closest she got to his house was in her car, passing by his house on her way out to the main road.

He'd never get that fence in before the big storm that was predicted to hit in 48 hours. She could see him struggling to pound in the posts that would support the fence. At this rate, he'd only have a quarter of the fence done before winter would force him to stop. Seemed like a waste of energy to her. Why didn't he wait until Spring when the ground would thaw and the sun would keep him warm? Now he was out there in blistering cold and wind, freezing his ass off. Well, it was his ass, and she could care less about it.

She'd kept her contact with Jared to a minimum this past week, but did plan to go with him to Smokey's tonight. She thought about him a great deal, knowing he was into his first week of cold cases. Hopefully, he'd share some of that with her, although she knew it would only be in generalities.

She had started on her second manuscript, but had not yet been inspired to start on her own book. The day got away from her and after a light dinner, she dressed for Smokey's. Jared would be picking her up at 8 and she hoped the same connectiveness would still be there. In her mind, she knew what was best for her life right now, but her heart was speaking to her in another language. Not the language of love, but definitely of extreme like. They really hadn't talked about the terms of their relationship which, at the moment, were dictated by her. He probably thought he'd done something, moved too fast to suit her or offended her somehow. She'd need to be honest with him, but she hoped it would be at the end of their night, not the beginning. She wanted to have some fun. Needed to.

Jared arrived on time and a look of happiness covered his face as she opened the door. She smiled and motioned him in, but instead of the passionate kisses that had greeted her before, he chose to give her a friendly hug.

She didn't like it and that surprised her. Shit. She wasn't sure she could keep him at a distance. She enjoyed him too much. She was sure he didn't want to be her transitional man. No one liked that placeholder position.

"Hi, it's good to see you," she said, placing her hand on his cheek, a sure sign of affection that she hoped he wouldn't miss.

There was a second of surprise, then he grabbed her hand, held it and led her to the sofa in front of the fire. So much for keeping their discussion to the end of the night. She dove in.

"I think I should explain my behavior this week," she said. "I came to Montana to live a different life. Not starting over, because I never stopped living, just changing location and my circle of friends. Then you happened and I found myself wanting to include you in my days. And my nights. But everything in me says to push you away, not get too close, just enjoy it while I can. But here's my problem with that. You're a good guy and you deserve better than that. I've been selfish and I'm sorry." She stopped and waited for a reaction from him.

"Is this where I get to speak?" he asked. She nodded. "I've been living in Wildwood a lot of years and I've had a few relationships, one very long term. But they ended for a variety of reasons. Being single gives you time to gain perspective on yourself and to really understand why the relationships ended. I came to the conclusion that if you picked the wrong person, overlooked or ignored something that you knew would doom the relationship but you plowed ahead anyway, then it would fail. So, for me, finding the right person is what I've been holding out for. I'd rather be single than with the wrong woman. I found myself wanting to include you in my days and nights, too. You're unexpected, delicious, gregarious, smart as hell and never out of my thoughts. I'm a big boy, Lauren, and I know what I want. I don't know what you want, but I'm being honest here. That's the only way I can be."

"I know that. That's what I like about you." She was 45 years old and she was having an honest and open conversation with a man she had met only a couple of weeks ago, but who made whatever this was between them so easy. It had never been like this with David or anyone else for that matter. She was drawn to him, to his casual strength and introspective mind. She just didn't know what to do with him.

"You're making too much of this, you know," he said, pulling her into his arms and kissing her. "Let's just BE, ok?"

"Ok," she said, liking the man he was even more. "Are you ready to go? Maggie and Charlie are going to wonder where we are."

His vehicle hadn't lost all of its heat when she opened the door and sat in the passenger seat. He had opened her door for her, went around to his side and got in, pushing the button to start it. As they left her driveway and drove the side road to the main road, they passed Cal Morgan's place.

"He's building a fence, you know."

"What the hell? What kind of fence?" he asked.

"Looks like a privacy fence to me, but he's an idiot to try and build it now. What could have him so fired up that he feels he needs to keep people out? I could care less about what he's hiding over there," she said, annoyance in her voice.

"What makes you think he's hiding something?"

"I'm sure he's not, but he is strange. Do you know anything about him?"

"Not much. His mother was murdered by his 12-year-old adopted brother, which may have traumatized him at the time. He was around 19 when that happened."

"Shit, a 12-year-old kid killed his mother? Is he in jail now?"

"No, he turned the gun on himself after shooting her. He didn't leave a note so there really is no way of knowing why he did it. The police questioned Cal and his sisters, but got nowhere."

"No wonder he's kind of fucked up. That would be hard for anyone to handle." It got quiet, until Jared asked a question.

"Is it okay if we put Cal Morgan in the rear-view mirror for now? Besides Maggie and Charlie, I think Babs will be there tonight with her sister. Just to give you a heads-up, I dated her sister, Kiley, for about a minute. Let you be forewarned, woman," he said, a warm smile directed her way.

Kiley was surprisingly delightful and engaged to a fireman. *Seems she must have liked men in uniform,* Lauren thought. They didn't close the bar, but they were close. Jared drove her home, kissed her, then headed back to his house to change. He had gotten a call from his supervisor about a lead in one of his missing person cases, and was headed to Flathead County. He'd call her as soon as he could. And she knew he would.

Chapter 13

He'd tried to build the fence, but the wind and cold made it impossible. He was lucky to get the six posts placed and a few slats attached. He would never finish it before winter brought even more miserable conditions. It was dangerous to be out in the extreme cold, so his efforts would wait for Spring. He just had to make sure Lauren Sedgeway kept to herself and didn't venture in his direction.

He was moving Gaby tonight. Her body was in his garage, still wrapped in the tarp. At almost midnight, he loaded her into the back of the pickup with little effort, locked the truck lid and opened the garage door. There were no lights on at Lauren's. *Good, no one will see me leave at this hour*, he thought, so he left the garage, closed the door and moved down the road to the main highway.

It was almost 100 miles to the location where, years ago, he had dumped Beth's body. Now, Gaby would join her and his search for her replacement could begin. Montana was desolated in some areas and it was easy to hide a body. Forest service roads at this time of year would be mostly closed, but he knew where he was going. His truck was heavy duty and he could get to just about anywhere in it.

He was about 60 miles from his turnoff when a car in the opposite lane and with only one headlight, lost control on a curve and headed in his direction. It didn't hit him head on, but sideswiped his driver's side quarter panel, spinning his truck into a tree. The other vehicle sped away, leaving him dazed and banged up. He sat for a moment in the cab, trying to clear his head, when the thought of Gaby in the back of the pickup exploded into his brain. His truck was damaged, probably too damaged to drive. He had felt a tire shudder and assumed it was flat. He would need a tow and MHP would probably be on site soon. It was late and the road was empty, but he couldn't risk Gaby's body being discovered. He leaped out of the truck, only to discover that he'd twisted his knee, and fell to the ground. He got up again, putting most of his weight on the other leg and opened the lid. Gaby was towards the front of the bed, having been jostled in the accident. He jumped up, went to her, and lifted her into his arms. He dropped to the ground and headed to the woods. He knew he could only go so far on his bad knee, so he was constantly looking for a place to conceal her where she most likely would not be found. He was only about 10 minutes off the road when he heard the sounds of a siren and could see blue lights about a mile up the road.

He had to find a place for Gaby, and now. He found a small ravine, placed her in it and covered her with branches. He couldn't worry about leaving DNA behind now. He should have removed the tarp, but keeping her in it meant the body would be harder for animals to scavenge. Besides, he'd be back here to move her to her final destination as soon as he borrowed a truck. The siren had stopped, so he retraced his steps, heading back the way he had entered the woods. He walked to the edge of the road near a stand of trees where he saw a Montana Highway Patrol officer at his truck, relaying information to his dispatcher over his shoulder microphone. When Cal emerged from the woods and started walking towards him, he recognized his cousin, Charlie Banks.

Charlie saw him and a sense of relief rolled over him. He walked towards him, noticing Cal's limp as the two approached each other. "Jesus, Cal, I saw your truck here and you had me pretty worried. What happened here?"

"Some asshole crossed over the line and sideswiped my truck. I ended up here," he said, pointing to the tree now embracing his vehicle.

"Are you hurt? We had a report from a guy who drove by here and called in the accident. Said he didn't see the accident but figured somebody had to be hurt."

"My knee is pretty banged up, but I don't need an ambulance or anything. Probably just a tow truck."

"What were you doing in the woods, Cal?"

"Taking a leak. The accident scared the piss out of me." He laughed and Charlie smiled.

Just then, another officer showed up and Charlie began his investigation. He walked the perimeter of the truck, then turned to ask Cal a question.

"Cal, any idea of the color of the vehicle that hit you?"

"I'm pretty sure it was red, maybe orange," Cal said. "But I couldn't see who was driving, it happened so fast." Charlie took a sample of the paint that had been left behind on Cal's quarter panel.

"What were you doing so far from home?" Charlie asked.

"I had a date in Missoula and was driving home from there."

"Pretty far to go for a date. You gone through all the bachelorettes in Wildwood, Cal?"

"Something like that. She stood me up. Hey, can you get me a tow?" he said, quickly changing the subject.

"Yeah, already called for one. You must be pretty cold. Why don't you go sit in my vehicle and warm up? Are you sure you don't want a paramedic to look at you?"

"Not necessary. I'm sure I'll be fine. I'll get to the doctor tomorrow for an x-ray, maybe a CT scan."

He sat in the car but watched every move the two officers made as they were putting together the facts for the police report. Charlie and the other officer looked into the bed of his truck, then closed the lid, which Cal had left open when he pulled Gaby from the back. He continued to watch as Charlie wandered over to him.

"Was there anything in the back of your truck, Cal? Your lid was up and we didn't see anything but a couple of road flares. You didn't lose anything when it hit, did you?"

"No, it was pretty much empty. Lid must have popped open when I hit the tree."

Cal saw more headlights approaching and was relieved to see the tow had arrived. The driver approached the officers who must have informed him that they weren't finished with the scene yet, so he shrugged and went back to his still-running vehicle. Cal was shivering but not from the cold. Gaby was back there in the woods, within a few hundred feet of the road. All it would take for her to be discovered would be for one of the officers to follow his trail to see where it ended.

Charlie and the other officer were deep in conversation, comparing notes and occasionally would look his way. *What could they be talking about?* He thought he'd been pretty calm under the circumstances and had a believable answer for everything they asked. Charlie broke away from the conversation and once again approached Cal.

"Cal, it's just a formality, but I'd like you to take a breathalyzer test. You okay with that?"

"Yes, but I haven't been drinking. I don't do that and drive."

Charlie administered the test and it was negative for alcohol.

"Okay, Cal. We're releasing the vehicle to the tow company. We're pretty much done here, but if I have any more questions, I'll get in touch with you. You get that knee looked at, ok?"

Cal nodded, then gingerly hauled himself up into the tow driver's cab. He leaned out the window, then said, "Say hi to Maggie for me."

He'd ride the 40 miles back to Wildwood with the driver, then get a lift home. Tomorrow, he'd have to borrow a truck and drive back to the spot where he had placed Gaby. She needed to be moved before some deer hunter found her.

Chapter 14

Turns out, the lead had nothing to do with any of his cases. Though Jared hadn't wanted to leave her that night, he had walked away from Lauren with a better idea of where they stood. They were in a good place. She had called him this morning, and the conversation was warm, almost affectionate. Maggie had called her to invite them both to dinner tonight and she wanted to run it by him.

"I'm here till 5 so it will have to be a late dinner, around 7 or so. Do you think Maggie will be okay with that time?"

"I already told her it would have to be later. Why don't I go early to help out and you just meet us when you can?" she said.

"That works." He paused for a moment and then said, "I miss you."

She chuckled, then assumed a more serious tone. "I miss you, too. I'll see you tonight."

He arrived at Maggie and Charlie's at 7:15. Charlie let him in and pointed in the direction of the kitchen. He immediately walked to Lauren and leaned in to give her a quick kiss. She had her hands full with cutting up vegetables for the salad, so she offered no resistance. Her smile told him he'd done just the right thing.

"Can I help with anything?" his question directed at Maggie.

"No, Lauren and I are almost done. Why don't you keep Charlie company in the family room? You can talk about things that happened in man-land today. Dinner's about 15 minutes away."

Killer Looks

Charlie was sitting in a recliner, an empty glass of scotch in his hand. He'd been scrolling through personal emails on his tablet when Jared sat on the sofa opposite him. Charlie offered him a drink after closing his tablet and getting up from the chair.

"I'll have a beer, if you've got one," he said as Charlie headed to the kitchen, returning with 2 beers.

"Man, it's just not the same without you on the roads with me. Do you feel you made the right decision?" Charlie asked, taking a long pull on the bottle.

"It's what I've wanted to do for a long time, you know that. It's slow going and following up on cases that have been cold for years hasn't been easy. But I'm only just starting to dig in, so I'm trying to be realistic about what I can accomplish and when. How about you, anything interesting happening?"

"No, just the usual. Belquist got promoted to Assistant Chief so my new boss is Alex Corden. Maybe you heard about that. Matthews and his wife had a baby girl last week. He's one proud papa. Oh yeah, I know you don't have much use for him, but my cousin Cal was in an accident early this morning out by mile marker 235."

"235? What was he doing way out there?"

"That's what I asked him. Said he was supposed to have a date, but she stood him up."

"Shit, who would stand *him* up? What time was the accident?"

"Happened around 3am. My shift was almost over, but I got the call. Didn't know it was him until I saw his truck against a tree. Hit and run. Banged up his knee pretty bad but he didn't want me to call the paramedics."

Jared's detective brain kicked into high gear. "I know he's your cousin, but that guy's a strange one. Who goes on a date that late? Especially so far from where he lives."

"Yeah, I thought it was strange, too. But that's Cal. He was out in the woods taking a leak when I got there. That was another strange thing. I was there for almost 3 minutes before he came out of the woods. I recognized his truck right away but he wasn't in it so I started searching for him. Then when I saw him stepping onto the road and he told me what he had been doing, something seemed a little off. I don't know about you, but if I had to take a leak, I'd go just far enough into the woods not to be seen by passing vehicles. Especially if I was injured like he was. His tracks led a few feet into the woods, maybe further."

"Didn't you follow them?"

"Why would I? The guy was in an accident and taking a leak. Maybe he got a little disoriented and went further than he needed to."

"Maybe," said Jared, his instincts on high alert. If Cal hadn't spooked Lauren so much, then stupidly tried to put up a privacy fence in this weather, he might not have given it a second thought. But this accident didn't make a lot of sense and Cal's reason for being on the road so late was implausible. There was something in Jared's detective brain that told him to keep a closer eye on Cal Morgan.

Chapter 15

He'd had no time for Tess today. He had to get some sleep, then borrow a truck to remove Gaby's body from the ravine. Every minute she lay there was one-minute closer to animals finding her or a hunter stumbling across her body while in search of a different kill.

Panic ruled his actions today. He'd called his buddy, Art, and was able to borrow his truck while his was getting repaired. Art's truck didn't have a lid on it so Cal would have to cover the body with anything he could find in his garage. He searched until he found an old boat cover he could use. That might look suspicious, so he also threw in a couple of boxes and some cinder blocks to keep them secure. It was already dark and the trip would take at least an hour. It would have been better if he'd left later since the traffic would be almost nonexistent after 10 pm, but he needed to get there. The snow had started a few minutes after he had gotten on the road and now he was in a full-scale white-out. He was going no faster than 20 miles an hour, his windshield wipers barely keeping up with the heavy snow. He didn't see many cars, since most people with any sense were staying off the roads. That just might work to his advantage.

Gaby was at mile marker 235. He had just passed 200. He was getting more anxious with every mile that passed, ever so slowly. His palms were sweaty and he was pounding the steering wheel.

"Come on, come on," he said as he squirmed in the seat of the truck.

Killer Looks

You've gone and done it now, haven't you? Always fucking up. Do you think Charlie believed you when you said you were on a date? How lame. What woman goes on a date at midnight? They're going to catch you, you know. Ever since that Sedgeway woman moved in you've been acting strangely. People have noticed it. It's only a matter of time before they find the secret you've been keeping.

"Not now, mother, not fucking now!" Cal said.

He drove on in the blinding snow until he got to mile marker 235. It looked so different from last night, especially in the freshly fallen snow. His footprints were gone and he was confused about just where the accident had happened. The tree, he'd have to find the tree. That would give him his bearings. It took him more than 15 minutes walking up and down the highway examining each tree. He brushed off the snow, looking for the gouge his truck had left. Finally, he found it and moved the truck closer to that location. He had entered the woods just to the right of it. He was sure he'd entered the woods there, and he trudged through the knee-high drifts, hoping he was headed in the right direction. Damn it, nothing looked familiar. He found a ravine, sure it was the right one, but Gaby was not there. He walked for two hours, leaving crisscross footprints in the ever-deepening snow. He failed to find her. He was cold and disoriented, and knew he couldn't stay out here any longer. He followed his footsteps in many directions until finally, and with dumb luck, he found the road. What was he going to do, now? Then a sudden realization hit him. If he couldn't find her, then probably no one else could either. He found a much-needed degree of calm and climbed back into his truck. He'd put her out of his mind.

The drive back home was uneventful. The snow had finally let up, the plows were out and he made it home, anticipating some time with Tess. Hell, he hadn't even seen her today, much less brought her food and water. Shit. He'd been so concerned about Gaby that Tess's needs never crossed his mind.

He pulled into his garage, emptied Art's truck bed and went into the house. He'd have to feed Tess first. He made what was easy. He carried a cup of soup, a half sandwich and a glass of water on a tray, then walked down the basement stairs. He placed the food and water on a table by the door, then unlocked it. Tess was sleeping, but when he turned on the light, she immediately got to her feet and stomped to the cage door. He opened it and he returned to the table by the door, bringing in the soup and sandwich. She ate, but never took her eyes off him. When she was done, he took the tray and returned to unlock her chain. He fastened it to his belt, then brought her into the bathroom. She carried her bucket with her. He chained her to the bolt in the floor, then left to take the tray upstairs. He came back down, carrying a clean gown and watched as she took her shower. The erection he expected didn't happen. He closed his eyes, fantasizing about past sexual encounters, trying to will an erection. Except his fantasies weren't with her. *She* was there. His mother.

Anger flared in him and he bellowed. Tess froze, staring at a side of Cal she had never seen before. He was always calm, focused and rarely spoke. Something was wrong. He usually had an erection by now, but she could see there was none. Did that mean there would be no games tonight? Or would it be a black night?

She quickly ended her shower, toweled off and drew on her gown. As he led her back to the cage, she expected him to point to the lingerie rack by the bed. He simply reattached her chain, locked her door and left. She was terrified. If she no longer excited him, her fate would be the same as Gaby's.

Chapter 16

Tess knew that she had to escape. Her cage was the first impediment keeping her confined. Next was the chain around her ankle. Finally, the locked door to the playroom. She had studied her surroundings very carefully. Her hands had tested every inch of her cage. In some places, the link was doubled, soldered together. Part of Cal's makeshift prison cell.

Over the 10 years of her confinement, she had sometimes picked away at the solder between 2 links at a point on the cage behind her bed, hoping to separate the two. Now it was her mission. She constantly worked at it, and since Cal never spent any time in the cages, he didn't see her progress. She was now able to pull one of the links towards her and she began to bend it back and forth, back and forth, hoping to snap it free from its neighboring link. It was a 4-inch piece of metal, but it could be used as a weapon. If Cal got close enough to her, she could jab it into his jugular and kill him. It would take time to break that piece, and time was running out.

She was glad she had worked on building her strength because without it, she never could have bent the one link away from the other. But it was almost there. Only a few more bending motions and… it was free. She carefully examined the piece, looking for a sharp edge that could penetrate flesh. There was only a blunt edge and even with all her strength, was not sure she could inflict the kind of injury necessary to kill Cal or at the very least, incapacitate him so that she could escape. She would try to sharpen the edge on the concrete cinderblocks behind her bed that made up the imposing and impenetrable wall. Soundproofing material was on all the walls and the ceiling, but she was able to pull aside a piece behind her bed in order to gain access to the cement wall.

She'd work hard to sharpen that edge. To make it a kill weapon. Once she'd stabbed him, she'd grab the key, unchain herself from the bolt in her cage, and unlock the door to escape. She had no idea where she was, somewhere in Wildwood, Montana, wherever that was, but she knew she could run for help.

She looked again at the metal piece in her hand, her salvation, she hoped. She had been too late to save Gaby, but that wasn't her fault. She'd asked Gaby to do the same thing to her cage. Gaby had made the same attempt for a while, but once she stopped eating, she was too weak to continue. She had given up. Tess would never give up. She was not going to be killed and dumped somewhere. She was strong, determined and her adrenaline was in overdrive. She'd have to have just the right set of circumstances to use her weapon. But right now, she had to get it ready.

Where to keep it so that Cal had no possibility of finding it was a dilemma for her. Then she knew. She'd slip it behind the soundproofing panel she had pulled away.

She had to keep tabs on him in order to know when she could work. Because the room was soundproofed, she didn't know he was in the house until the door to the playroom was unlocked. When he left the house, he always took his truck. Though she couldn't hear it well, a low rumble would tell her what she needed to know. That was the only time she knew for sure that Cal was gone. Then she'd get to work, sharpening her piece of metal. It was slow going, since the cinder block was porous and not as dense as a cement floor would be. But the floor was covered with carpeting that had been glued down and impossible to pry loose. She had no access to the cement floor underneath it. The cinder block was her only option. When she heard the low rumble again, she knew Cal was back, and she would quickly hide her work.

The metal piece was not ready. She had worked for days on it, and was now seeing some progress. Cal had been sporadic in his visits, although he did feed her each day and allow a shower. But he spent long hours away and she didn't know why. All she did know was that the longer he was away, the quicker her weapon would be ready.

Tess heard the truck's low rumble and quickly put away her project. She wouldn't mention to Cal about moving to Gaby's cage until the metal piece was ready. She was sure she could pull back a piece of the soundproofing panel behind Gaby's cot to hide the weapon once she made that cage her temporary home.

Cal opened the playroom door and Tess glared at him like she always did. He walked over to her cage, unlocked the door and then unlocked her leg chain from the floor bolt. Like hundreds of times before, he attached her chain to his belt, led her upstairs to the kitchen and sat her in a chair, attaching her leg chain to the bolt in the floor. He was preparing dinner and she was hungry. She was using a lot of calories doing her strength training every day, and sharpening the metal took a few more. She was sweating all day long now and Cal made a comment to her about her hygiene.

"You stink. Didn't you shower well enough this morning? Did you use the deodorant?"

She continued to glare, before speaking. "If the human body doesn't get enough calories, then it starts eating away at its own organs. That causes a chemical reaction that produces the odor you're smelling, so if you want it to stop, you'll have to give me more to eat." She had made the whole thing up, was pretty sure he'd check on it, but until he called bullshit on her, she might get more food to keep up her strength. In the future, she'd have to be extra liberal with the deodorant.

He placed more food on her plate then said, "Finish your dinner. You need a shower before the games begin tonight."

While she was in the shower, she watched him carefully. He had his eyes partially closed and he was stroking himself. She saw the beginnings of an erection, but not sure it had been caused by her. As she finished and toweled off, he handed her a clean gown then led her back to the playroom.

"I'm going to let you decide what kind of a night it is. Red, black, white?"

White seemed to put him in a calmer mood so she chose white.

"Good, I'd like you to put on that one," he said, pointing to a short lace camisole with matching panties. As she dressed in what he chose for her, her mind went to the place where it always went. She did as she was told, but never connected with him in any emotional way. He knew that and liked it that way. She didn't know what had made him the way he was, and she didn't care. If he'd had a bad childhood, tough shit. If he had mommy issues, the same. All she knew was that he was at his most vulnerable like this, and it would be at a time like this that she would act.

He wouldn't be expecting a weapon. He left nothing behind that could even be made into a weapon. Breakfast trays were paper, the plates were paper. The utensils were plastic and always accounted for. The buckets had nothing she could use and he routinely checked the cots when he brought clean sheets. The bolts were solid in the floor. No, he would be surprised when her weapon plunged into his neck, when he felt her twist it in deeper, cutting the jugular and causing him to bleed out. That was the vision she had and the more she visualized it, the more real it became.

Chapter 17

Jared had been away from Wildwood for about two weeks, working on a cold case murder. He had talked to Lauren on the phone every day, and was quick to tell her he missed her. He was in his element, getting to use his superior intelligence to uncover the leads that were necessary to solve a case. While he was away, Lauren enjoyed her first spring in Montana. The snows had finally stopped and spring buds and birds' nests filled with new families signaled the long and brutal winter was behind her. She had survived it, though. She had had Jared to fill her nights and her work and her friends when he was away,

The relationship was good, but stationary. She liked it the way it was. They were exclusive, but she felt Jared wanted more. She wasn't there yet, and wasn't sure she'd ever be.

She liked her freedom, her little cottage and the town of Wildwood. She'd made a comfortable life here and Maggie Banks was a close friend. She had shared with Maggie her feelings about Jared, about what he might want.

"Don't try to read too much into it," said Maggie. "If he wants more, he'll tell you. That's when you make a decision. Until then, just continue like nothing's changed. Enjoy what you have with him and that's it. If I can put my two cents in, he's a great guy and I see how you two are when you're together. You may just want more than you think you do."

Maybe. But she wouldn't have to think about it for now.

Killer Looks

She was in her kitchen pouring a second cup of coffee when she heard the sound of pounding coming from the direction of Cal Morgan's house. He was back to working on that stupid fence, she'd bet. She had seen him a couple of times when she'd driven along his property towards the main road. He'd actually waved a hello to her, which she found strange. Was he okay with her living here now? But if that was the case, why continue building the fence? Now that the snow was mostly gone and the days had been warm, maybe the ground was soft enough for him to continue, but she doubted it. She had a feeling he'd still struggle with its completion.

She was using less firewood now, but realized she was down to her last five pieces of wood. She grabbed her coat and headed over to Cal's property, slipping on the ice in her driveway that still remained in shaded areas. She wasn't sure how Cal would receive her but hoped he'd at least be cordial. As she came around the corner of his property she watched as he lifted a sledge hammer and struck a fence slat with brute force. The ground was still too hard and the slat splintered.

"Fuck!" he said, throwing the hammer towards his garage. She decided not to disturb his tantrum and retreated. She was almost out of his sight when he bellowed to her.

"What are you doing on my property?" So much for cordial.

"I was not looking to intrude, but I need more firewood and I couldn't get a hold of Maggie to ask her. I'm on the last of the piles that you stacked and haven't needed any till now. I'm really sorry to disturb you, I'll wait to talk to Maggie.

He looked at her a minute, then his demeanor changed. "I'll pick up a small load for you today when I head into town. This afternoon, okay?"

"Um, sure." Maybe she'd do a little small talk. "Ground still a little hard for the fence?"

"Yes." He didn't say another word, just watched as she scanned his property, trying to figure out what was so important that he felt he had to protect with a fence. It was a typical Montana back yard. A snow machine, a small fishing boat, a barrel for burning trash, a small shed that probably held a lawn mower and tools. Not a feminine touch anywhere. His house was larger than hers and seemed to have a basement, which hers did not. There were two small windows on the one side of the foundation closest to the road. Shit, if he put a fence there, it would have to sit on the road, not leaving much room for her car to get by.

"Well, thanks for bringing me the firewood, and good luck with the fence."

He turned his back to her, not acknowledging her or her comment, and continued with the construction.

"What an asshole," she thought, as she trudged back up the driveway, falling on her ass once, then brushing off her pride and making it back to the kitchen door. Once inside, she grabbed a warm cup of coffee and stood watching Cal's progress. She was surprised when he went to the road and looked into the two small windows she had noticed. What was he looking at, or for? Didn't he know what he had in his basement? His head turned to look in her direction and she ducked back from the window, not wanting him to see her. She didn't think he had.

About 4 hours later, Cal dropped off a partial face cord of wood for her and stacked it next to the remaining pile. She owed him $50, which she gladly payed him, grateful that he hadn't asked her to cook another dinner.

"Sorry about my temper, back there," he said sheepishly when he came to collect his money. "I thought the ground might be soft enough to begin again, but looks like I'll have to wait it out a little longer. I'm thinking of breeding dogs with my Phoebe and I'll need a fence to keep the pups out of trouble."

"Oh, so that's why you're building a fence. Makes sense. I got the feeling it was because I moved in." She chuckled, but her response from him was unexpected. A smirk. Like he knew something she didn't. *Okay, you can go now*, she thought to herself. She'd have to share this encounter with Jared. She wondered what he'd think of it.

Cal's explanation continued to confuse her. He didn't seem the dog breeder type and she'd never seen any pups after Phoebe delivered them the night she met Cal. She wasn't a dog person so she really hadn't given them a second thought, but maybe it was the dogs that were in the basement. That had to be it. She hoped he was treating them well. Dogs need to run free, at least that's what she'd always heard. Then she thought about the smell of that basement if those dogs were doing their business in there. Maybe the fence was a good idea. He could let the poor things out of there.

She put Cal, the puppies and the fence out of her mind then. Jared was coming home today.

Killer Looks

She'd asked him to come by once he was back in town and she was preparing dinner. Since it was relatively warm by Montana standards, she was grilling a couple of chops on her small patio, and had poured a couple of glasses of wine. She had heard him pull up and yelled to him to make his way to the patio.

As he came around the corner of her house, his smile did what it always did. Caught her by surprise then wrapped a tendril of warmth around her heart. She had missed him and their conversations, their humor, and the sex, which was unsettling in its intensity. She was 45 years old and had never felt so at peace. Jared was partially responsible for that.

He kissed her deeply and she returned the passion. Damn, she had missed him more than she wanted him to know. She was still trying to hold back, to prepare herself for life without him but she wondered if that was what she really wanted after all. In the months she'd known him, there had been nothing about him that had alarmed her. He had been steady, caring, affectionate and funny, as well as incredibly sexy. His brain was the sexiest thing about him and they spent hours deep into intelligent conversation, something no other man could claim to have ever done with her. He matched her, thought for thought, opinion for opinion. They didn't agree on everything, but talked through their differences easily, with no intimidation or finger pointing.

As their last kiss ended, he pulled away from her, grabbed the barbeque tool from her hand and flipped the chops with a big smile. She handed him a glass of wine and they sat down on the two patio chaises she had bought in town. She placed a throw over her lap and Jared's.

"It's a little too chilly to eat out here, but I couldn't wait to fire up the grill for dinner. I love the taste of charred animal protein some times. You can only eat so much salad, am I right?"

He laughed and agreed. When the chops were done, Jared turned off the gas to the grill and carried the chops inside to the kitchen table, which had been set for dinner. Lauren locked the door to the patio, washed her hands, then brought the warm asparagus and the cold beet salad to the table.

"Wow, this looks delicious, Lauren. I've been eating fast food and in diners for the last couple of weeks, grabbing a bite when I could."

"How are you progressing with the case?"

"I've been interviewing family members of the murder victim and I think there's something there. This murder happened in the 1970's, well before DNA testing. But there was DNA collected via a semen swab. The lab tested it in the 1990's when the technology improved but used almost everything on the swab. The testing was inconclusive. I'm hoping there's enough left for the FBI to do their thing. They only need a very small, almost microscopic amount for testing."

"So, I'm assuming the victim was a woman?

"No, it was actually a small boy. He had been strangled and sexually abused and thrown into a river high up in the mountains. His body drifted down after the heavy snow melt. He was wrapped in a tarp and that helped preserve the DNA evidence. When he was found, he had spent the majority of the winter frozen in the ice so his body was still partially frozen. He looked like he was just sleeping. I questioned the family, and we both think that his half-brother might be his killer. He's already in prison and doing 20 years for distributing child pornography. His DNA is on file thanks to the justice system, so I should hear back from the FBI in a few weeks."

"How old would the killer have been when he committed the crime?"

"About 16. His half-brother was 10 when he died."

"That's so sad. How do you deal with this kind of human tragedy every day? I don't think I could do it," she said.

"I consider it a puzzle and I try to take the human emotion out of it. But still, with kids, it's hard to do that. If this kid committed the crime when he was 16, he's been living with it a lot of years. But it's about time we got some justice for the little boy."

As they ate their dinner, they changed the topic to a lighter one, discussing the jazz festival that would be held over the 3-day Memorial Day weekend. They planned on going together at least one of the days, although she liked jazz more than he did. He was a country boy.

"So, did I miss anything while I've been gone?" Jared asked while drying the few dishes she had washed. She had talked to him every day and caught him up on most things, but she did want to tell him about Cal.

"I ran out of firewood today, so I saw Cal in his backyard and decided to extend an olive branch, even though I have no reason to do that. He barked at me when I came onto his property and then changed on a dime and said he would bring me some firewood this afternoon, which he did. He also said the reason for the fence was that he was going to breed puppies."

"Breed puppies? So, he needed a fence for that?"

"I know, it seems strange although I think he's keeping puppies in his basement now. The day I met him, his dog Phoebe had puppies. I've never heard or seen them, so I think that's where they are. The poor things have been cooped up there all winter and God knows what condition they and that basement are in. I get queasy just thinking about it."

"Why do you think that's where they are?

"Because, after I came back to the house, I looked out my window and saw him looking into those two basement windows. They are right along the road that leads to the main road. They are frosted over, so I don't know what he expected to see, but that's what I saw him doing. You know, as much as I love this house, I'm not sure I would buy it if there are going to be a lot of yapping puppies in the yard. I like the serenity back here off the road."

"Does that mean you're thinking of staying a little longer?" he asked her.

"Yes." And she meant it.

They enjoyed the 3-day weekend, Lauren started on a new manuscript and Jared was gone again, this time for a month.

Chapter 18

She was ready. It had taken weeks, but she finally was able to form a sharp edge on the metal piece. Gaby had been gone 6 months so she had been here alone all that time, wondering when he would capture his next victim and bring her here. She had had little contact with him and even less conversation, but kept her sanity by focusing on her goal. No one was going to rescue her; she would have to rescue herself.

Cal still went to work every morning and she could hear his truck as it left the driveway. The days were getting longer and Cal seemed to work longer hours. He had not visited her for 2 days. She had heard his truck, removed the metal piece from its hiding place and slipped it into a side hem of her gown that she had modified to fit the weapon. It was in the hem directly under her armpit, so would not be noticeable as she walked. It was thin, shiv-like and could do some damage. As long as she didn't have to shower and change into another gown, he wouldn't find it.

He unlocked the playroom door, performed the usual routine and brought her upstairs to eat. She tried to gauge his temperament, to see what kind of a night it would be. He was more talkative than usual.

"Building a fence out back. Keeping the neighbors away."

So that's what she'd heard.

"Might even let you outside once in a while when no one's around to see you, once it's done."

She didn't know what to say so just said, "Thank you."

Killer Looks

He looked at her, said nothing more and brought her back to the playroom. She was nervous, more nervous than she'd ever been in her life. She hoped that the nerves didn't interfere with what she was going to do tonight. He started to disrobe, pointed to the pink lingerie and as she slipped off her gown and walked towards the lingerie rack, she also slipped the weapon out of her gown and into her hand. She quickly dressed in a pink bra and panties. Nowhere to hide the weapon for long, so she'd have to be quick. He was on his back looking at her and stroking himself. She needed to get him on his stomach, straddle him and plunge the weapon into his neck. Slowly, she walked to the bed, knelt on it and walked on her knees towards him. When she was where he could touch her, he reached out, but she moved back out of his reach. She smiled at him, teased him by wagging her finger in his face. She approached him again, then with all her strength, rolled him onto his stomach, taking the weapon from her hand and sticking it into the back waistband of her panties. She then began to caress his back, to plant kisses on it. He started to moan and tried to turn over, but she wouldn't let him. She was rubbing up against him now and she could tell he was almost to the edge. This was the perfect time.

She pulled the weapon out of the waistband of her panties and plunged it into Cal's neck. He screamed, grabbed his neck and the blood poured from it. As he moved toward her, she swung the weapon again, this time slicing him in the face. The weapon flew out of her hand. Cal's rage was monstrous.

"You little bitch, I'm going to kill you," he said as he stumbled after her, stunned by the attack. She grabbed the lingerie rack, pulled it from the wall and swung at him again, this time connecting with his head. He went down. She grabbed the keys to the playroom door off the table where he had laid them, unlocked the door and ran up the stairs. The kitchen door was locked but she ran to a large kitchen window and threw a chair at it, shattering it. She grabbed a coat hanging by the kitchen door, put it on and let herself out the window. She fell to the ground, twisting an ankle and raced into the yard, trying to get her bearings. Where was she? She needed to call the police but she had to get as far away from Cal as she could. If he wasn't dead, he'd risk anything to find her. She ran into the yard and spotted a house at the end of the road. There were lights on. She ran to the door, sobbing, pounding, pounding and sobbing until a terrified woman answered the door.

Chapter 19

She was dozing on her couch when she heard an ungodly noise at her front door. A woman was crying and pounding loud enough to more than get her attention. She picked up her cell phone to call 911, but had no reception. Again. The woman sounded desperate so she'd look for the landline as she talked to the woman through her door. She wasn't opening it for a lunatic.

"Hey, stop that pounding, what do you want?"

"Please, let me in. My name's Tess Baldwin. I've been held captive in the house next to yours for the last 10 years. Please, I've stabbed him but I'm not sure he's dead. Please, let me in, call the police, please."

She hurried to unlock the door and just as she opened it, she saw an injured Cal with a shotgun, his arm around Tess Baldwin's neck and the gun pointed at her. He had a towel wrapped around his neck and she could see signs of blood. She tried to close the door but he forced it open, tightening his grip on Tess's neck.

"Get the fuck out here. I'll kill her and you if you make one move."

Her heart pounded in her chest and she could see the terror in the woman's eyes. If what she said was true, Cal Morgan, for all of his appearances, was a master criminal. And she'd just become his latest victim.

"Cal, you don't want to do this. Look, your blood is all over my porch. If you do something to me or Tess, you'll be caught."

"Do you think I'm worried? I can explain away my blood on your porch. I cut myself chopping your firewood.

See, a splinter broke off and scraped my face and my neck. I came up to the porch to get a towel from you. Simple. Start walking towards my house. Tess, you show her the way."

Lauren couldn't make sense of what was happening to her. One minute she was napping and the next, following a woman she'd never seen before to the basement of Cal's house. Inside the house, she balked every step of the way, until in a fit of anger, he pushed her and she tumbled down the stairs. She wasn't hurt, just shaken up. She lay at the bottom of the stairs, expecting it to be the home of numerous puppies, but it was eerily quiet. In one corner of the room was a pink cage. Opposite it was a purple one. This must have been where the woman had been held captive. What did she say? For 10 years? How could that be? Cal pushed Tess into the purple cage, attached an ankle chain to a bolt in the floor then came across with a right hook that knocked her out cold. Keeping the gun on Lauren, he pushed her into the pink cage, attached the chain to her ankle, bolted it and left her there.

"I tried to get you to leave, but you wouldn't listen to me. All I wanted was to be left alone with my girls, but you've fucked that up. Tess tried to fucking kill me! She's going to have to pay for that. Now I have to make sure all trace of you is gone." He left.

Did he think he could get away with holding her captive? Who would believe she would just leave town without saying anything to anyone? Jared certainly wouldn't believe it. Would he?

Tess started to stir and began to moan softly. Lauren called out to her.

"Tess, are you okay?"

She started to sob uncontrollably. "I almost got away, after 10 fucking years, I almost got away! Now he'll never let me out of his sight." Her sobs continued.

"Tess, someone will come looking for me. My boyfriend won't give up until he finds me."

"They'll never find you. We'll both die here like Beth and Gaby did."

"Gaby? Gaby Parmenter?"

Tess was incredulous. "How do you know Gaby?" she asked.

"Well, I don't really know her, but my boyfriend's been investigating her disappearance. He mentioned her name to me. How long was Gaby here? How did she die?"

"She was here 8 years. He took her away about 6 months ago and I never saw her again. I'm sure he killed her. Just like he killed Beth. Beth got pregnant and he found out. He took her away and she never came back. He gives us birth control pills now."

"What else does he do, Tess?" asked Lauren.

Tess pointed to the bed and the lingerie strewn on the floor and Lauren didn't have to guess. She knew.

She'd read about men who hold women captive, and she'd also read about why they were able to hold the women for so long before being discovered. Most people, even when they see something unusual, don't want to get involved. Things like this are not happening in their neighborhood, just in someone else's. She was not going to be one of these statistics. She would fight him with everything she had in her.

"Tess, listen to me. We are going to get out of here. We need to work together, figure out a way to overpower him. I need you to tell me exactly what your days with him are like. What's the routine?"

Tess began to tell her about the cages, the buckets, the shower room and the nights. Nights spent in that bed wearing the lingerie he dictated. Tess told Lauren how she had tried to resist him at first, refusing to succumb to his sexual needs. But he would not tolerate that. He'd grab her out of the cage, throw her on the bed and sexually assault her. She was no active participant. This happened for weeks until he finally had had enough. That's when he stopped feeding her and bringing her to the bed.

He would come for Beth each night and Tess would cover her ears, not wanting to hear sounds of the brutality Beth endured. Beth was pregnant by then, and did what he asked in order to protect her baby.

After two weeks without food, Tess was weak, barely able to move from her cot. She didn't want to die of starvation. And she couldn't try to escape if she wasn't strong. She began to think. She was no stranger to theatrics. Hadn't she used them every day in her profession?

"You want to eat again?" he had said one night, sneering at her from the bed. "Then you'll join me willingly tonight. See how much Beth enjoys it?"

She looked at Beth, then, seeing her dead eyes and broken spirit. She was going through the motions, but surviving. Tess decided that she would do the same.

As she finished her narrative, Tess was sobbing, ashamed of what she had become. Lauren could feel her pain, and offered her comforting words.

"Tess, I can understand how you might feel about yourself, but Cal's the monster here, not you. You did what you had to do to survive and nobody, absolutely nobody could fault you for that. I don't know how you did it, but you can't give up now. You and I need to work together to get out of here. I'm hoping my boyfriend starts looking for me soon, but if he doesn't, we've got to get out of here on our own."

Tess looked at her, a glimmer of hope in her eyes. She admired this strong woman who had desperately tried to stand up to Cal, to prevent herself from being taken. But strength was no match for a bullet and she had relented. Maybe, with this woman as an ally, they could escape.

Chapter 20

As soon as he left the women in the cages, he got busy at Lauren's. First, he emptied her refrigerator and brought what was salvageable to his house. Next, he moved her car to his garage, where he would keep it until he could move it, unnoticed. Over the course of hours, he took her clothes and personal items to the barrel in his backyard and burned them. The fire was raging until early the next morning as he finally burned the last of it. He got every trace of her out of the house, cleaned up the blood on her front porch as well as working into early morning cleaning the house as he knew Lauren would, before she left for good. Finally, he repaired his broken kitchen window. He was sure he had thought of everything,

All that was left was for her to write that letter to Martin. And she would write it. Otherwise, he'd kill Tess in front of her.

He returned to the basement. Tess was still sobbing in the corner of the cage. He touched his neck wound, reminding him of what she had done to him. He would have to kill her now. He would use her first, then dispose of her after he was done with her. He came to Lauren's cage, unlocked it and attached her ankle chain to his belt. He then led her upstairs to the kitchen table, where paper and a pen where waiting for her.

"Write a letter to Martin. Here's what I want it to say."

She looked at what he had written on the paper. She would never say these things to him in this way. If Jared knew her as well as she thought he did, he would know she hadn't written it. Used those words.

"And if I refuse?"

"Tess dies."

So, she began.

Jared,

I am leaving Wildwood for good. I've decided that Montana is not for me. We've had fun together, but it was never going anywhere.

Lauren

"One more thing," he said handing her his landline. "Call your boss and quit."

When she reached Hildy, she tried to maintain a calm demeanor but it was difficult. Her heart was racing and she knew Cal would hurt Tess if she refused to do as he asked. Hildy was full of questions, disappointed, then angry that she would quit in the middle of a project.

"It's not professional, Lauren. I don't feel that I can give you a good recommendation if anyone comes looking for one. I just don't understand."

"There's nothing to understand. I'm sick of my job. I want to be like my favorite heroine, Scarlett O'Hara. You know how she always said, *Fiddle-Dee-Dee and I'll think about it tomorrow?* That's me. Anyway, I'm done. Have a nice life, Hildy girl."

Then she hung up, not giving Hildy a chance to ask her about the Scarlett O'Hara reference. Scarlett O'Hara was not Lauren's favorite heroine. In fact, she and Hildy had had a rather heated exchange about the believability of the heroine as she had been written. Lauren had thought that Scarlett was weak, still needing a man after all she had been through. And never, ever had she called her boss Hildy girl. She hoped that the conversation would stick with her. If Jared interviewed her, and she mentioned that the conversation was odd, he might realize something was wrong. That is, if he was even going to look for her.

Cal was satisfied that both the letter and the call to her boss would give him the protection he needed. Everyone would think she had moved on, including the cop. He assumed Jared's pride would keep him from running after her. But even if Jared did start looking for her and came to his house to question Cal about Lauren, he wouldn't have anything to tell him. He hadn't seen her or seen her leave. Everyone knew he kept to himself.

He left the house, got into his truck and drove 50 miles east of Wildwood, where he dropped Lauren's letter into a post office mailbox. He had used latex gloves when handling anything that might leave a trace of his DNA. That included the paper, envelope and stamp. The letter should reach Jared in a couple of days. When Jared saw the postmark, he would think she was heading east. But there would be no way to trace her after that. He'd reach a dead end.

You moron, you think he's going to stop looking for her? Haven't you seen how they are when they're together? What love looks like? He'll never stop looking for her and you're the first person he'll question. You were the one who made her uncomfortable when she first moved here. You will be a suspect. You did this to yourself. What are you going to do now, Calvin?

"Mother, shut the fuck up! You bitch, what do you know about love? You never loved me or my sisters. The only person you loved was yourself. You did this to me. Made me the way I am. But don't worry. I've got this, no thanks to you. Leave me alone!"

His mother's voice faded and he focused on getting back to the house. He would wait until 2 this morning when he knew the streets would be empty and would drive Lauren's car to a place he had stumbled on while hunting elk. It was a small bluff, off FS road 14, with no protective guardrails. He could simply push the car over the bluff and it would disappear into the massive forest below. There was only a slight chance it would ever be discovered, especially because no roads or hiking trails ventured into that dense vegetation. These woods were old and compacted tight. The canopy of the trees hid anything below it. It's where Lauren's vehicle would soon be. He'd hitch his way back to Wildwood, something he'd done many times before. It was only about 5 miles and he could walk it if he had to.

Chapter 21

It had been a busy week and Jared had made progress on at least three of his cold cases. He'd made it a point of calling Lauren each night, before he went to bed. He looked forward to these calls and he was sure she did, too. She would catch him up on what was going on in Wildwood and he'd discuss his cases with her. She was a good sounding board for him and their analytical skills were matched. He had talked to her last night and she'd sounded tired, but good. She was halfway through her manuscript and was making real progress. It was a good book and she thought it might be a best seller.

He was still out of town for another 2 weeks, but they'd made plans to host a barbeque for the 4th of July. It was supposed to be a sunny weekend and they'd already had 10 people RSVP to the event. Jared had introduced her to some of his friends and they spent a lot of time with Maggie and Charlie and their friends. He was pleased but not surprised at how well she fit in.

It was already 9 pm, but he didn't think it was too late to call her. He dialed her landline, but listened as it rang, voicemail not picking up. That was strange. Then he called her cell phone, but that went straight to voicemail. Maybe she went out to dinner with Maggie and some of Maggie's friends last minute. She hadn't told him of any plans she'd had for that night, but things happen at the last minute all the time. He decided to wait till the morning to call her. He was exhausted. He'd review some case files and head to bed. Ten minutes later he was asleep.

He was up at 6, showered and went to the diner next door to his motel for breakfast. The food wasn't great but the coffee was surprisingly robust and flavorful. He was on his third cup when he decided to call Lauren. The cell went straight to voicemail. Not a surprise. But when he called her landline and she didn't pick up, he was confused, then concerned. Had she been out late and then left early in the morning? Could be, but unusual.

He glanced at his watch and realized he was late for an interview related to a working case, so he paid his bill, walked to his car, started the engine and made his way to Elmhurst Way, and the home of Gaby Parmenter's parents. He'd call Lauren tonight.

The Parmenter's house was in a settled neighborhood of Missoula. Stately trees and curved streets made it one of the most sought-after neighborhoods by professionals making mid six figures and up. Gaby's father was a plastic surgeon and her mother, a research doctor at a major pharmaceutical company. Gaby had come from money.

Both her father and her mother had agreed to meet him at 7 am at their home and he was at least 10 minutes late. Not the best way to start an interview.

As he parked the car and walked up the front walk, he took in the expansive mansion and grounds. He couldn't imagine growing up here.

Louise Parmenter answered the door and Jared introduced himself and presented his detective's badge. She was a small woman, and had obviously taken advantage of her husband's profession. Her face was unlined, but severe in its visage.

Her husband was waiting for them in the living room and he rose to introduce himself to Jared. Jared thanked them for meeting with him and he began.

"I've just been assigned your daughter's cold case and I'm hoping to find out what happened to her. I've talked to a few of her college acquaintances but certainly wanted to meet with both of you for more insight. What can you tell me about Gaby?"

Louise Parmenter, a look of anguish on her face, sighed and said, "Gaby is our only child, you know. We were devastated when she vanished. She never gave us any indication that she was troubled, looking for a way out of her life or anything like that."

"How was she doing at school? Did she like it? Were her grades good? How about a boyfriend?" Jared asked.

Paul Parmenter responded. "She seemed to be doing well in school. She made Dean's List the semester before she disappeared. She didn't have a boyfriend that we ever met, but when we talked to her college friends, they suspected she was dating someone. They said she seemed to be obsessed by this person. None of her friends ever met him, but they got the feeling that he was either older, or some sort of criminal. Otherwise, they felt she would have introduced him. A month before she disappeared, she was here at the house with her car packed and heading back to campus. We didn't hear much from her after she arrived, and it was only 3 weeks into the semester when she disappeared. We talked to her a couple of times before her disappearance and everything seemed normal. It was such a shock, and now it's been eight years. My wife and I have resigned ourselves to the fact that she's probably dead, but, of course, we want to know what happened to her. If you can help in any way with that, we'd be grateful."

"That's my intent. What you've told me is similar to other facts I've collected from the friends and acquaintances I've interviewed. It seems that she was involved with a man and perhaps he had something to do with her disappearance. After all this time, we're going to need some new evidence to move the case along, I'm afraid. We've exhausted everything else."

The Parmenters thanked him for continuing to work the case and insisted he call them if he needed them in any way. He left their house, driving through the neighborhood that he could never afford. Instantly, his mind went to Lauren. *What would it be like to share a house with her? A life?* he wondered. *Don't get ahead of yourself, Martin.*

His cellphone rang. He hit the button on his steering wheel to answer it thinking it might be Lauren. It was his supervisor, giving him another cold case. This one, closer to home.

Beth Reeves disappeared 15 years ago from a small town about 20 miles from Wildwood. The case had just been handed off to his team, well, to him, from the sheriff's office in the town of Yancy. They were moving offices and the Reeves case had been misfiled and unworked for years. The file would be on his desk when he got back to the office. He'd review it, begin his research and start to make a list of interviews he'd conduct. Standard procedure. He'd be confronted with hundreds, maybe thousands of facts and would have to sift through them, looking for relevance. Those with none would be discarded. But those that remained would start to weave a story. There would be people, places and things in this story and one unique combination of the three would give him the final solution to Beth's disappearance. He'd just have to work hard to find it.

The afternoon flew by as he read through the Reeves file. There was one lone picture of Beth, a high school graduation picture, which had been the latest photo the family had had to give to the sheriff's department. There had been some preliminary work done, which would help him, but there were many questions that had never been asked at the time, and that was going to impede his progress. He examined the picture, trying to get a feeling about her from a two-dimensional medium. She was attractive, with long brunette hair and a slightly crooked smile. He wondered if she'd ever been self-conscious about that. Such a small thing, but girls that age are often taunted by their peers about every imperfection. Would it leave her vulnerable, unsure of herself, looking for attention? Could she be the victim of a predator?

His mind raced, thoughts bombarded by thoughts as he tried to find the path to the most logical scenario leading to her disappearance. It eluded him for now.

It was already 8 pm by the time he left his desk to go back to the motel. He'd grabbed a sandwich on the way and ate it in the car. His room seemed smaller every day, and he would be glad to start working his cases from Wildwood in two weeks. No more cheap motels. But it had been necessary for him to spend his initial weeks here, going over the files, meeting with the officers who had initially worked the cases. The ones that were still around anyway.

By the time he'd gotten settled, it was 8:45 and he called Lauren's landline. It just rang and rang. Something he hadn't felt before, a sudden lurch in his stomach, caused him to sit straight up in bed, pull his legs over so that his feet touched the floor and he rested his elbow on his knee, his hand still holding the phone. He dialed again. Still no answer. Was she ignoring his call? No, it wasn't like her to play that stupid-ass game. If she didn't want to see him again, she'd just tell him. He was sure of that if nothing else. Could she have gone out a second night in a row? Maybe, but she had to know he would be trying to call her.

He put in a call to Maggie and Charlie. Charlie answered.

"Charlie, it's Jared. Is Maggie there?"

"Nah, she's out with a few of her girlfriends tonight. She's been putting in a lot of time since this is the season people buy property in Wildwood. She's been schlepping people all over. Sold a bunch of houses though, so there is that."

A surge of relief flooded Jared's heart. Lauren was with Maggie. That had to be it. But the question needed to be asked. "Charlie, did Lauren go with Maggie tonight?"

"Lauren?" said Charlie. "I don't think so, it was just a bunch of friends from Maggie's office. Why?"

"I don't want to panic, but I haven't been able to reach Lauren for a couple of days. You haven't seen her around, have you?"

"No, but I've been working extra hours, too, since Maggie's gone so much. We haven't socialized with anyone recently."

"Charlie, I don't want to ask this, but could you do a welfare check on Lauren? It's not like her not to answer her landline or her cell phone."

"Did you guys have a little tiff that she might be cooling off from? Maybe she's just punishing you. You know how women are," Charlie said.

"Maybe that's how most women are, but not Lauren. She's direct and doesn't play games. And things couldn't be better between us. I'm heading back to Wildwood tomorrow, but I'm asking you to please do this for me, or send someone else."

"Hold on a minute, Jared, Maggie just walked in."

Jared heard muted conversation in the background and then Maggie took the phone from Charlie.

"Jared, I haven't seen Lauren for almost a week, but I tried calling her, too, with no answer. I just figured she was really busy with her manuscript and was screening her calls. But for her not to talk to you concerns me. Charlie and I will drive over there right now. I've still got my key in case there's trouble. Stay by your phone. We'll call you back."

Chapter 22

Maggie gripped Charlie's arm as they took the 15-minute drive to Lauren's. It was the dead of summer and the sun was almost an hour away from setting, even though it was well after 9 pm. The fourth of July would be here soon and she and Charlie had been looking forward to Lauren and Jared's party. Everyone they had invited had responded in the positive, at least that's what Lauren had told her the last time they talked. What was it, a week ago? Had she really not spoken to Lauren since then?

Dusk had descended, and as Charlie pulled into the side road leading to Lauren's house, he noticed there were no lights illuminated, not even her porch light which was always left on. The house seemed eerily quiet. He didn't have a good feeling about this, cop's instincts, but he didn't want to alarm Maggie.

"Let me have the key and I'll go in and check on her. If there is something wrong, you let me handle it, okay?"

"Do you think something's wrong?" Maggie said, panic rising. "Oh my God, Charlie!"

"Just let me get in there. You stay here, but keep your phone handy. I'm going to check the garage first to see if her car's in there. Maybe she left for a few days' vacation or a business trip."

"Maybe, but I think she would have told Jared or me. Especially since I'm helping her with party details until Jared gets here."

She sat in the car and watched as Charlie made his way to the garage. He looked through the 3 small windows in the garage door, but her car was not there. He turned to Maggie and shook his head no. She immediately jumped out of the car and ran towards him.

"Well, hon, it looks like she's out of town for a few days. That explains why it's so quiet around here," Charlie said, breathing a sigh of relief.

"Charlie Banks, I don't believe that for one minute. I'm using my key and checking the house myself. You coming?" she asked, not waiting for his answer.

The instant she unlocked the door, the smell of bleach was overwhelming. Not many people used bleach to clean anymore, preferring instead to use more eco-friendly products. Obviously, Lauren wasn't one of them. Maggie reached in and turned on the kitchen light, illuminating half of the small house. The kitchen was immaculate, not a thing out of place. She walked to the living room and stopped in front of the fireplace. She bent down to feel if any residual heat was coming from the hearth. It was stone cold. Unusual, since she and Charlie had had to use their fireplace this past week when the nighttime temperatures had been unseasonably cold. Lauren should have had to as well. The cottage had no central heating and the fireplace was its only source of heat. A month's worth of firewood was stacked outside her kitchen, undisturbed. The hearth was totally devoid of ash and scrubbed clean, almost as if a fire had never been lit there.

Maggie moved to Lauren's study, surprised to see that the desk contained only a small lamp. There was no sign of any of Lauren's work materials. No computer, no manuscripts, nothing. *Maybe she took them with her,* Maggie thought, still trying to maintain some sense of calm. She was losing the battle. When she went into Lauren's bedroom, reality hit her and hit her hard. The room was empty of anything that belonged to Lauren. The closet, the dresser drawers, the attached bathroom. It was as if she had never been there.

Maggie collapsed on the bed with a look of confusion on her face. "Charlie, she's gone. I don't get it. She seemed so happy here. Happy with Jared. Shit, I've got to call him."

Jared's cellphone had never left his hand. He wanted it with him when Maggie called. About an hour after he first talked to her, it was Maggie.

"Jared, she's gone. All of her stuff is gone. There's no sign of her."

"That's bullshit, she wouldn't leave without telling me. That's not Lauren."

"I feel the same way, but she is gone. I'm surprised she wouldn't have told me she was leaving, since I'm responsible for renting the cottage again. But it looks like she hasn't been here for a few days. It's been cold at night but her fireplace was never used. Her refrigerator is empty and she cleaned the place from top to bottom with bleach."

"Bleach?" he said. "Nobody uses bleach anymore unless they have something to hide. Something's wrong. I just feel it. Maggie, is Charlie there with you? Can I talk to him?"

"Sure," she said, handing the phone to Charlie.

"Charlie, something's not right about this. Lauren and I were happy, planning that party. We were both looking forward to my being around more, once I was based back there in Wildwood. Please start an investigation."

"Jared, Lauren's a grown woman and if she decides to take off, it's no crime. I've got limited resources here and unless we find some evidence that points to foul play, I just can't do it."

"Fuck, Charlie, do we have to find her body first? I'm not going to sit here and do nothing. I'm going to call her boss in the morning. Maybe she knows where she is. Then I'm heading back to Wildwood. I want to take a look at that house. Begin my own investigation. Do one thing for me, okay? Off the record? Can you at least check with Cal Morgan? Maybe he saw her leave. Can you do that one thing?"

"It's late, Jared and I don't see any lights at Cal's either. I'll come by tomorrow morning to question him about Lauren. Meet me at the office when you get in town and we'll go over everything."

"Thanks Charlie, see you tomorrow."

Chapter 23

As soon as Cal saw the headlights turn onto his side road, he killed his lights. A quick look out his window and he saw it was his cousin, Charlie and his wife, Maggie. They must have finally realized they hadn't heard from Lauren. Or maybe Jared had asked them to check up on her. He wasn't ready to talk to anyone about Lauren. He knew they would come, the questions about her. But he didn't know anything, hadn't seen anything. That's what he'd tell anyone who asked. He'd get rid of them, and they'd move on. But if he was as good as he thought he was, they'd never find her. He'd already disposed of her car without detection. In his mind, he had no use for her. She reminded him too much of his mother. And Tess was dead to him. She had destroyed what they had by trying to kill him. He would have to dispose of them both, but it would have to wait. There was too much attention focused on Lauren's disappearance right now.

He was angry. Angry that his games were temporarily halted and angry that Lauren's disappearance would now bring outsiders. Lauren wasn't supposed to be involved in this. If it wasn't for Tess, for her stupid attempt to escape, he would already be looking for his next girl and not dealing with the Lauren dilemma. Now, finding the next girl was delayed.

He watched as Charlie and Maggie entered the house, saw the lights go on as they went from room to room, and saw them go out again when they realized she was gone. They would be on his doorstep tomorrow, he was sure. He could manage Charlie alright, had all his life, but Jared Martin was an unknown. He didn't know him well, but Jared had an intensity about him, a way of looking right through you. He'd seen that side of him that night in the bar when he encountered Lauren with him. Shit, he didn't need his kind of trouble.

The next morning, he descended the stairs to the basement and the cages. Lauren had been with him for almost a week and she'd been a pain in the ass the whole time. Where Tess and Gaby had been compliant, Lauren was defiant. She ridiculed him every time she saw him, must have sensed his weakness and played on it. She showered and used the bathroom, but wouldn't move until he left her alone. He didn't want to look at her anyway. She and Tess were always whispering, conspiring, he thought. Lauren told him every day that Jared was coming for her, that she would take any chance to escape. That he would make a mistake and Jared would find him and put him in prison, or worse.

He started to doubt himself. Just a little at first, but then started to second guess his ability to deceive Jared if the questioning proved intense. Jared would be relentless if he had feelings for Lauren and his many nights spent at her cottage reinforced the idea that he did. How had this all gone wrong?

I'll tell you. You're a nothing, a loser, you can't do anything right. You thought you were smarter than anyone else. That your looks would get you anything you wanted. Well, you see what those looks have gotten you now. You'll pay, boy. They'll find out about you. And I can't wait until they do.

His mother was relentless in her derision of him. Even in death, she was with him. She was in his head most of the time now, constantly interfering with his thoughts, forcing him to concentrate as he prepared for the questions he knew would come.

He left Lauren and Tess and climbed the stairs to the kitchen, eager to get away from them. As he approached the top of the stairs, he heard knocking. He quickly locked and bolted the door to the basement behind him, composed himself and slowly walked to the door and opened it, seeing Charlie standing there.

"Hey, what are you doing here so early? What's up?" Cal said, a look of surprise on his face.

"Have you seen your neighbor, Lauren, lately?"

"No, now that the trees are all filled in, I can't even see her house from here. That's kind of a strange question. What's going on?"

"Lauren has moved out of the cottage a little suddenly and there are some folks worried about her. They think it's not like her and they're afraid something's happened to her. Did you see her leave?"

"No, but then I wouldn't expect to. I haven't been here much so if she loaded up her car and took off, it might have been at a time I wasn't here. Like I said, I don't have a clear view anymore. I didn't even know she was gone. She was always a little standoffish anyway."

"What do you mean, standoffish?" Charlie asked.

Oh, you're fucked now. You said too much. How are you going to explain that comment?

"Nothing, really. I just meant she kept to herself. Didn't see her much, except when I brought her firewood.

She cooked me dinner once to thank me for getting her firewood for her. Other than that, we'd just wave hello."

"Have you seen anything unusual? Any trespassers on the property?"

"No, nothing like that."

"Jared Martin will probably be by to see you sometime today. He and Lauren were dating and she left without telling him. He thinks something's happened to her."

"I'll be glad to talk to him, but I don't know how I can help. Send him over, I'll be here most of the day. Still finishing my fence."

"Thanks, Cal. If you think of anything, no matter how small, call me, okay? Maggie's worried, too."

"Will do."

He slowly closed the kitchen door, then locked it. One down, one to go. He'd felt it had gone well with Charlie and he recovered nicely from his momentary gaffe. But Jared would be another story. His questions would not be routine. He'd try to trip him up. But he wouldn't fall for that. He'd say very little. Nothing even remotely incriminating. He was in control.

Chapter 24

Jared's first call the next morning was to his supervisor. He explained the situation with Lauren and asked for time to look for her. He knew he was pushing his luck. He'd only been on the job a few months, but he'd quit if he had to. He didn't have to. His supervisor gave him a week, but cautioned him to work with local authorities. He agreed.

On his way to Wildwood, he waited until he had a cell signal then put in a call to Charlie. He was anxious to hear what Cal had told him when he questioned him. Charlie picked up immediately.

"I know what you're going to ask," said Charlie. "Cal hasn't seen her and didn't even know she was gone. I told him you'd be by his place this morning to question him and he was fine with that."

"How could he not have noticed something? Hell, he lives next to her."

"He said he hasn't been around much and since the woods separating their houses is dense this time of year, he can't even see her house from his."

"Isn't that convenient? Charlie, something is wrong. I can feel it. Lauren would never leave without saying anything to me. We had something. We both felt it. I've been thinking all night about possible scenarios. Logic tells me that she could have just left. Or she's been involved in some kind of accident. She's traveling for work. Or she's been abducted or killed. If she just left, we should be able to trace credit cards and bank statements. If she's been involved in an accident, we get MHP and adjoining states' law enforcement to issue a BOLO on her vehicle. I'm calling her boss after I get off the phone with you to see if she's traveling for work. That leaves kidnapping and murder. That's the last thing I want to be investigating, but it could get down to that."

"We still have another 24-hour waiting period until we can issue a missing person's report," Charlie said. "I know you don't want to hear this again, but she is a grown woman, not some underage kid. She could have a very logical reason for leaving the way she did. Check your mail when you get back here. See if she left you a note."

"I'll swing by my house on the way into the station. I should be in Wildwood in another 20 minutes. See you soon."

He ended the call. He used the internet feature on his phone to get the number of the publishing house that Lauren worked for in New York City. It took him a couple of tries, but he finally was put through to Hildy Steinmetz, Lauren's boss.

"Ms. Steinmetz, this is detective Jared Martin from the Flathead County Office of Detectives in Montana. I'd like to ask you a few questions about Lauren Sedgeway, if that's ok with you."

Her cold response surprised him. Lauren had always said Hildy was her champion, always praising and encouraging her.

"Lauren no longer works for me," she said, no hint of warmth in her voice at all. Jared was stunned.

"Ms. Steinmetz, we have reason to believe that something has happened to Lauren. When was the last time you talked to her?"

"What do you mean, something's happened to her? Like an accident?" Her tone immediately changed.

"Perhaps, but I'm just trying to get as much information as I can about her last movements. When was the last time you talked to her?"

"About a week or so ago. Out of the blue, she called me and quit. Over the phone, with no discussion whatsoever. I told her I couldn't give her a recommendation under the circumstances but she didn't seem to care."

"Was there anything unusual about the conversation besides that? Did she say what she'd be doing next?" Jared asked.

"I got the feeling she wasn't going to do anything next. She made some obscure reference to Scarlett O'Hara, which I found unusual, since she was not a fan. But it confused me when she said Scarlett O'Hara was her favorite character. I know she hated the character and we had a knockdown, drag out fight over that years ago. Then she called me Hildy-girl, a name she'd never used before. It was all so strange."

Jared's heart dropped. This was not good. Her actions *were* strange. He knew she loved her job and it was a main focus of her life. And Lauren had great respect for Hildy Steinmetz based on the way Hildy had mentored her in her career. He couldn't see her calling her boss, Hildy-girl. He was certain now that Lauren was in trouble, dropping clues so he could find her.

He'd been away from his house for almost a month, and his neighbor, Brianna was collecting his mail for him. She had a key to the house and was leaving his mail on the

117

kitchen counter. He entered the kitchen through his garage and saw the stack of mail sitting there. She'd separated the magazines and newspapers from the first-class mail and that pile had a rubber band wrapped around it. He had nitrile gloves in a drawer, grabbed a pair and, trembling, grasped the pile, removed the band and started to quickly leaf through the individual pieces. It was there, a letter from Lauren. He opened the plain envelope, unfolded the unremarkable white piece of paper and stared at the simple message. He read it once, then again and then a third time. It was impersonal. The reason she gave for leaving might have made sense if he believed what he was reading.

Jared,

I am leaving Wildwood for good. I've decided that Montana is not for me. We've had fun together, but it was never going anywhere.

Lauren

He could understand if she hadn't liked Montana, although the impression she had given him was just the opposite. She had told him more than a few times that she loved it here. He could even understand if she had unilaterally decided that their relationship wasn't going to work out, but to not discuss it in person or even over the phone was so unlike her. The one thing he couldn't get past was her call to Hildy. Quitting her job was unnecessary. That one thing told him the letter was bullshit.

He pulled a plastic bag with a sealable edge out of a kitchen drawer, dropped the letter inside, sealed the bag and ran to his car. It was a longshot, checking it for prints. The envelope would have the prints of anyone who had touched it, including Brianna, but the letter should only have Lauren's. If there were other prints, which he doubted, that might lead him to a person of interest. But he had to start somewhere, even if it led to a dead end.

Charlie was off duty, but had come in to the station to meet Jared. Jared was his best friend and the way he had reacted to Lauren's departure spoke volumes. His buddy was in love.

Jared looked like he hadn't slept in days, as the door to the station opened and Jared blustered through. His eyes immediately found Charlie and as he walked towards him, Charlie motioned him to the conference room.

"Buddy, you look like shit," Charlie said.

"I know, I've been up all night trying to figure this thing out. This was waiting for me at the house," said Jared as he handed the letter, still inside its protective evidence bag, to Charlie. Charlie read it quickly and handed it back to Jared.

"Ouch, sorry buddy, that's pretty harsh."

"Charlie, it's not real."

"What do you mean? Looks real enough to me. Seems a little extreme, I got to admit."

"I talked to her boss, Hildy Steinmetz. Lauren quit her job. Right out of the blue. I can understand it we were over between us, if she got tired of Montana. But there's no reason for her to quit her job. She loves her work, *needs* her work. She said some cryptic things to Hildy that didn't make sense. They were unlike her. I think someone's forcing her hand for some reason. I don't have a good feeling about this Charlie. I think Lauren is in danger. I've got to find her."

"Okay, I see your point. Let me get Belquist in here, get a game plan. We're going to need resources. And don't worry, we've got this."

Charlie, Jared and Belquist spent the next two hours documenting the facts as they knew them, then formulating a strategy as they began the investigation.

A BOLO would be issued for her vehicle across a 5-state region, then expanded nationwide if they didn't get a hit from their first attempt. They'd need a warrant to check her cell records, credit cards and bank statements, but that would take time. Her ex-husband would be notified to see if he'd heard from her or knew of any places she would go to get away from people. If her house was a crime scene, it would have to be secured and tested. And Jared would interview Cal Morgan, the one person Lauren had said made her uncomfortable.

Charlie would take the lead on the case since the case was in Wildwood's jurisdiction, but Jared would be conducting a simultaneous investigation, coordinating with the Wildwood Police Department and MHP.

Jared needed to talk to Cal, to see Lauren's house and the condition it was in. Maybe there was a clue left behind in the house. The smell of bleach that Maggie had mentioned was someone's attempt to wipe something away. Blood? DNA? He'd need to get a forensic team out there to dust for prints, check for blood. But in the meantime, his immediate action was to talk to Cal.

Cal was outside in his yard working on his fence when Jared drove up. He could see Lauren's house at the end of the road and a pain tore through his heart. Looking towards Cal's back yard Jared could see that a dog was chained to a stake by the side of the house and immediately began barking as soon as Jared stepped out of his vehicle. Jared surveyed the yard, looking for anything unusual. All he saw were Cal's fencing materials, assorted tools and a metal barrel containing still smoldering trash. Cal appeared to be almost done with the fence and was in the process of adding a gate. He had built the fence partially on the road, just like Lauren had said he might, and anyone living in either house on the road would have a rough time maneuvering around that fence in winter.

"Morning Cal," Jared said as he headed to where Cal was standing.

"Morning. Charlie said you might be stopping by today. Got some questions for me?"

"Yes. Can you tell me the last time you saw Lauren?"

"Well, she came by about a month ago to ask me to get some firewood. That's the last time I actually talked to her. I did see her drive by a couple of times while I've been building my fence, but I'd say it's been about two weeks since I've actually seen her. I've had a couple of construction jobs that have kept me pretty busy so I haven't been here much. Like I told Charlie, I can't even see her house from here now.

"Charlie said you thought she was standoffish. What did you mean by that?"

"Oh, just that she kept pretty much to herself. Probably working hard would be my guess."

"Lauren hired a moving truck to deliver her personal belongings when she moved here. Maggie says there's nothing personal of Lauren's left in the house. Did you see a moving truck anywhere near here over the last few weeks? She had over 50 boxes and she couldn't have loaded them in her SUV. They never would have fit. I'm checking all of the moving companies locally. Someone had to have moved her."

Jared watched for a reaction from Cal, and for a fleeting second, thought he saw a flicker of emotion from that last statement.

"Remember something, Cal?"

"No, just thinking back. No moving truck that I can recall. Would have noticed that, though, if I'd been here."

"I'm checking the house next. We've got a forensic crew coming out here today to check for any evidence. The house seems too clean and the smell of bleach is a dead giveaway that something might have happened there. Someone was trying to clean up something. But fortunately for us, you can never fully cover up DNA evidence, even with bleach. If there's any DNA there, we'll find it."

"You might find some of mine. DNA, I mean. I chopped some wood for Lauren when I delivered that last load. Some of the pieces were too big so I was splitting them. One of the pieces splintered and cut me here and here." He pointed to a neck and cheek wound that, to Jared, looked fresher than a month-old wound should look.

"Lauren saw it happen and brought me a towel. I dripped some blood on her porch. It might still be there or she might have cleaned it up. I'm not sure."

"That wound looks pretty fresh. This happened a month ago?"

Cal panicked. "Maybe a little less. But you know how things are when you work construction. Wounds open up all the time and sometimes take longer to heal."

"These wounds opened up on you? What, a couple of times?" Jared asked.

"Think so, but I don't pay much attention."

"What about DNA in the house, Cal?"

"I have been in the house a couple of times, so yeah you might find it there, too."

Cal was starting to gloat. He had answered every one of Jared's questions with a plausible answer. This was going better than expected. There's no way Jared could suspect him. He was just a neighbor who kept to himself and had infrequent contact with Lauren. He had no motivation to cause any harm to Lauren.

"What's the deal with the fence, Cal?" Jared asked and began walking the inside perimeter. "Doesn't seem like something you'd do. Blocking the view."

"Just looking for some privacy, that's all."

"Just privacy, huh? Figured you got plenty of that with only one neighbor," Jared said, looking in the direction of the cottage. "And you're right, you can't see much of the cottage from here."

Jared continued walking the perimeter and he could sense Cal was showing some discomfort with his questions. As he approached the road side of the fence, pointing to the two windows on that side of the house, Cal hurried to stand between Jared and the windows.

"You've got the fence pretty close to the road. Gonna be a bitch to get around it this winter. Why didn't you stop the fence here, instead of covering those windows?" Jared asked, indicating the side wall of the house.

"I had enough slats left over, so I figured I'd just use them up and totally enclose the house," Cal said, a shrug accompanying his explanation. "Are there any other questions I can answer for you? I'm anxious to get this gate done."

Jared studied Cal, certain he saw something in his eyes, knowledge he was withholding. Cal had never mentioned anything about building the fence because he was going to breed dogs. That bothered Jared. He'd give him a chance to add that piece of information before he moved on.

Changing the subject, Jared pointed to Phoebe and asked, "How long you had her, Cal?"

Surprised by the question, Cal said, "She wandered on to my property about 5 years ago. I advertised for her owner, but no one claimed her. I've had her ever since."

"Seems like a pretty good guard animal. Ever think of breeding her? Might make some extra money if she produces good pups."

"No, don't want to get caught up in all that. I've got plenty to keep me busy."

Jared had his answer. Either Cal forgot what he had told Lauren or he was lying. Jared believed he was lying. His mind raced. If Cal was involved in Lauren's disappearance, the question was, why? Just because she moved too close to him? That didn't make sense. And where the fuck was she?

Chapter 25

Lauren was certain Jared was looking for her. At least that was the hope she would continue to cling to. But she would not sit by and wait for a rescue. She had to do something.

Her mind raced as she thought about solutions. Tess's would have worked if only she had caused enough damage. Although Cal had lost a lot of blood, he was recovering and ever vigilant. Unfortunately, Cal had retrieved the weapon after Tess's failed attempt to end his life. He could see where it had originated and now scrupulously inspected both cages every day.

Lauren knew that her presence unnerved him and saw Cal struggling with what to do with her. Jared would suspect Cal, she was sure. But she was also sure that Cal couldn't do anything but keep her in the cage. There were too many eyes on him now.

She hoped that Jared had talked to Hildy, that she had told him about Lauren's strange behavior. Jared knew how important her career was to her, so quitting her job, coupled with the note, would raise serious concerns about her safety. He would be ferocious in his pursuit of her and Cal would be one of the first persons he questioned.

But she also knew that Jared would need probable cause to get a search warrant for Cal's property. As far as she could tell, there was none. Yes, Cal was strange, reclusive and socially awkward, but that didn't mean he was a criminal. No, it was up to her and Tess to get themselves out of this.

"Tess, are you okay?" Lauren asked.

"Okay? I don't think I'll ever be okay again. Cal is going to kill me. I can see it in his eyes."

"Tess, don't think that way. He can't do anything to you. Cal would have been one of the first persons that the police talked to, so he's got to be very careful that he doesn't do anything to arouse suspicion. He needs to keep a low profile. It may sound crazy, but I think that gives us an advantage. He's going to be worried, distracted. I've interfered with his lifestyle and he's lost control. I'm going to keep pushing his buttons."

"Have you thought of a way out of this?" Tess asked.

"Maybe. There are two of us and one of him. The one time we're both together with him is when he takes us upstairs for dinner. He hasn't thought to change that routine. Before he does, we need to act. I'm not in as good physical shape as you are, so you're going to have to do most of the heavy stuff. I'll take care of the rest."

"I'm scared Lauren. I don't know if I can risk doing anything to make him angry."

"Tess, this is our only chance. The police can't come on to his property to look for us so it's up to us to get ourselves out of this. I'm a fighter and you need to be, too. You're stronger than you think you are. Just look how you've survived 10 years in captivity. It takes a very strong person to do that."

Tess was silent, but Lauren saw the look of determination on her face that she had hoped Tess would summon. She had Tess's buy-in.

"We have to mentally prepare for this, since this might be our only chance. We've each got about a 4-foot length of chain to work with. I've looked in the kitchen for something we could use as a weapon. Something close enough for me to grab as soon as we walk up the stairs. He's got some deer antlers sitting on a shelf by the door. I'm not sure how heavy they are, but I might be able to use them. As soon as you see me grab them, drop to the floor and start wrapping your chain around Cal's ankles. I'll move back as far as my chain will allow me to and then you start circling him. If we catch him off guard, he'll be slow to react and we need to get him off balance. I'll be hitting him with the antlers so he'll have his hands up defending himself. Once your chain is around his ankles, try to pull him to the ground. I'll hit him, kick him, anything to keep him down. He's strong and might try to pull on our chains, so his hands need to be occupied fending off my attack. Do what you can to help me. We need to knock him out and we only need a minute or two to escape. I'll grab his key, unlock our chains and chain him to the bolt in the kitchen. That's the plan and I hope it will work."

"Lauren, it's too risky. What if he pulls on my chain as soon as I'm on the floor and I can't get the chain around him?"

"He might do that, but remember, I'll be hitting him with the antlers. He'll need his hands to defend his face and eyes. You'll get a second chance. But we need him on the ground. He's strong enough to grab the antlers right out of my hands so we might only have seconds. The sooner he's down, the better. We're only getting one shot at escape. If we fuck this up, he'll probably kill us. Are you ready for this?"

127

"Yes, when do you want to do this?"

"Tonight," said Lauren.

Tess looked at her, nodded her head and began to mentally prepare. Lauren hoped the younger woman was as strong mentally as she appeared to be physically. Cal would be hard to overpower, but they had to try. Lauren knew that the antlers were a poor weapon and Cal could easily pull them from her grasp. But she would throw herself at him, fighting him with all her strength, while Tess tried to bring him down. The rest would play itself out.

Chapter 26

Cal had downloaded a police scanner app on his phone the day after he had talked to Jared. He needed to know what was happening in the search for Lauren. If he could keep one step ahead of the effort to find her, he could outwit Jared. He listened for hours, but there was no mention of her. All the calls he heard were for burglaries in progress and fire alarms. He could relax, for now. But he still felt it was too soon to dispose of the women.

They've got the whole police force looking for her. Do you think you can outwit them all? You should have gotten rid of both of them the day the bitch tried to kill you. Now look what you have to deal with. Think, think. You'll never get away with it!

His mother was wrong. He had the upper hand. He could kill them both, load them in his truck and close the lid, all with the garage door down. Open the door, then drive away. He didn't think anyone would follow him. But even if they did, he'd be able to lose them. He knew this area better than they did.

Chapter 27

On his way back to the station, Jared got a call. A body had been discovered off Highway 93. Hikers had stumbled across a female wrapped in a tarp and surprisingly well-preserved. She had been in a ravine, still partially filled with snow. Because of his ongoing cold case investigations, his supervisor thought this might be one of his missing persons. His heart stopped. Could it be Lauren?

He immediately put in a call to Charlie, who answered on the third ring.

"I just got a call about a female body. What do you know?" Jared asked.

"Some hikers found the body and from what they said, it wasn't well hidden. Once some of the snow melted, the body was close to the surface of the ravine. Just a few dead branches covering her."

"Have you got an ID on the body yet?"

"Not yet. The body is still at the site. You may want to hit the crime scene before they move her to the Flathead County Morgue. I know what you're thinking, but it's not Lauren. Looks to be a woman in her 20's. At least that's the report I got from the officers on the scene. We tried to keep this quiet, but the scanners have led a lot of people to the scene. We're having a hell of a time keeping people away."

"Where are the hikers who found the body?"

"Still on scene. As soon as I heard about this, I knew you'd want to interview them. I asked your supervisor to call you, then I made sure they stayed put until you got there."

"I'm on 93 now. Where's the site?"

"Just head up 93. It's about 40 miles from here. You'll see the responders' vehicles."

"Thanks, Charlie. Keep me posted if you have any more news. I'll leave the site after I interview the hikers, then head for the morgue. I want to be there for the autopsy and the identification. I'll be back tomorrow."

"You got any missing persons in their 20's?"

"A couple. I've got my files with me so if the body isn't too degraded I might be able to make an ID myself. Could give a family some closure."

"How did your talk with my cousin go?"

"He said pretty much the same things he told you. But something's off. He had made a particular statement to Lauren when she asked him about his fence. When I asked him the same question, he gave me a different answer. I caught him in a lie. Charlie, I'm sorry, but I'm going to have to pursue it. Even though he's your cousin, I think he's somehow involved in Lauren's disappearance."

"Jared, I think you're wrong about Cal. He's just a loner, a little odd, yes, but I don't think he's done anything to Lauren. Why would he? But I also know he won't be out of your crosshairs until you either eliminate him or prove he really is involved."

"I hope you understand. I love Lauren and I'm going to do anything to find her."

He loved Lauren. That was the first time he'd said it. It didn't come as a surprise, his blurting it out. He was wracked with emotion and it needed to be said. Even if he'd never said it to her. But he would. He'd just need to find her.

Chapter 28

After Jared had left, Cal finished the fence and was putting the final coat of preservative on the gate, the last area to be covered. He was tired and needed a shower, so after cleaning his brush and putting everything in the shed, he headed inside the house.

He took a quick shower, then came down to the kitchen for something to eat. He had a pot of chili on the stove for dinner, but decided to have a sandwich instead of diving into the chili. He noticed an alert on his phone and glanced at it as he was putting together his meal.

His police scanner app showed recent activity and he was curious. He activated it to listen. His mind reeled in horror as he heard the information being shared. A body had been found off highway 93. Police and ambulance on site. Victim in mid-twenties. Apparent homicide. There was more he didn't understand. Most of it was in police codes of some kind. But he knew what he had to do. It was time to run.

It's happening. They're going to know it was you. If Charlie puts all the facts in place, he'll realize what you were doing out there in the woods. And that detective. He's probably on his way here right now. Charlie probably told him all about your little accident. You were in a hurry, so you probably left DNA behind. Did you wear your gloves that night? Did your nose run out there in the cold? Maybe drip onto the body? You're fucked now. What are you going to do? What are you going to do?

"You bitch!" Cal screamed. "Shut up. Let me think!"

In an instant, Cal's life had gone from routine to out of control. He ran to the garage, grabbed some backpacks and immediately started loading food and supplies into them. In addition to gasoline for the 4-wheeler, he'd need to bring water, too, if he was going to survive in the woods. His 4-wheeler could make it into and through the woods behind the cottage, but as he got further into the forest, it would become more difficult. The progress would be slow, trying to weave his way through ever thickening stands of trees. He needed to make it to a forest service road to make the most progress. He knew every one of them around here. Two tours in Iraq had taught him how to survive, but he needed to go as deep into the woods as he could. He grabbed two rifles and his Sig Sauer 9mm along with boxes of ammunition and added them to his cache. The 9mm he tucked into the back waistband of his jeans. As he loaded everything he would take, his thoughts next turned to Tess and Lauren. He couldn't take them with him, but he didn't have time to dispose of them either. They would stay in the cages.

But another thought drifted in. An insurance policy. If he took Lauren with him, he had something to bargain with. A hostage. She would come with him. He grabbed her clothes from the closet he had stored them in and hurried down the basement stairs. Both women were startled when he burst through the door. He turned to Lauren's cage, unlocked it and threw her clothes inside. "Get dressed, you're coming with me. I'll unlock your leg chain so you can get your pants and boots on."

Lauren balked. "Are you insane? I'm not going anywhere with you."

He pulled the Sig Sauer from his waistband and pointed it at Tess. "Really? Fucking get dressed. We need to leave now!" he said, removing the chain from her ankle.

She did as she was told for fear he would harm Tess. She was sure something had happened that was causing him to run. Somehow the police were closing in on him. She thought of Jared and hoped he would not be far behind them.

As he pushed Lauren out the door, Tess started screaming and crying. "Don't leave me. I'll die here!"

Lauren tried to reassure her as Cal marched her toward the stairs. "Tess, they'll find you soon. Tell them what's happening."

Cal slammed the gun against the side of her head and she staggered. "Shut the fuck up! Why do you always have to talk? You're just like my mother! And now look what you've done. I tried to do the right thing. But you left me no choice."

He walked back into the playroom, fired one shot and closed the door. As they headed up the stairs to the kitchen he fired another shot, this time into the head of his pet dog, Phoebe.

Chapter 29

Lauren let out a bloodcurdling scream. Oh my God, what had she done? If she'd just kept her mouth shut and gone with Cal, Tess would still be alive. She had caused this and she didn't know how she would ever be able to live with what had just happened. She was in shock. Cal had put her chain around her waist instead of her ankle and it was once again attached to the belt he wore. He was pulling her up the stairs and into the garage. His open air 4-wheeler was next to his truck, packed with supplies and she realized what was happening. He was going off road, out into the woods somewhere. And she would be forced to go with him.

She had researched enough true crime to know that something was seriously wrong with Cal. He had made reference to his mother, but she'd been dead for decades. Did she have some kind of mercurial hold on him? Had she been responsible for creating this monster? His mother was his hot button and she would use that information to her advantage. Lauren was smart, had been inside the mind of serial killers through her research and would need everything she had in her to survive. She didn't know how long she would be with him, but she knew Jared was out there somewhere, looking for her.

As Cal forced her into the vehicle, he opened the garage door and backed out onto the driveway. But instead of heading out to the road, he wheeled the vehicle towards the woods behind the cottage. She could see a small path where other vehicles had once driven, leading deeper into the woods. About 100 yards in, he stopped the vehicle, secured Lauren's chain to a roll bar, grabbed his keys and left her to head back to the cottage. He grabbed some branches off a low hanging tree, and she watched as he began to swipe back and forth over the tracks leading to the woods. When he was certain no one could tell he had passed that way, he walked backwards towards the 4-wheeler, swiping away any trace of his footprints as he made his way back to where Lauren was waiting. If his pursuers followed the path any further than 100 yards, they might find tracks left by the 4-wheeler, but would they know it was Cal's? Would they think to trace it to him? There were so many unknowns.

When she looked into the back of the 4-wheeler, she could see that Cal must have been prepared for this eventuality. She could see food, water, camping gear, a gas can, warm clothing and firearms. Everything he needed to be a survivalist in the woods. Is this how she would end her life? At the mercy of a madman, her very life dependent on a fucked-up killer?

Where were they going? Did he have a plan?

"Why are you doing this, Cal? What happened?"

"Just keep your mouth shut. I don't want to hear any of your bullshit right now."

She needed to keep him talking, to find out what he was thinking. She decided to make it about her.

"Cal, I'm scared."

"Of me? That's a laugh. A bitch like you isn't scared of anything. But I have the upper hand now, don't I?"

She had acted like a bitch when he took her hostage, chained her up in that cage. She had berated him, pushed his buttons. Her only way to keep him off balance. But his comment seemed to go deeper than that.

He needed to have control. Somewhere in his life, someone had controlled him. She'd bet anything it was his mother. His murdered mother. What had Jared said? Cal's 12-year-old adopted brother had shot her and then killed himself. There's usually only one reason a child kills a parent. Abuse. What if Cal's mother was abusing him in some way? Based on what she'd seen in Cal's basement, she was sure it had been sexual abuse. She had probably picked up with Cal's brother once Cal had enlisted in the military. She almost felt a pang of sympathy for Cal, but based on the murders he had committed, those feelings quickly retreated. If what she thought was true, Cal's mother was pure evil and had left Cal severely damaged. It was the only explanation that made sense.

They had traveled for hours. It was late in the day and they'd reached a forest service road. The sun was starting to set but Cal stopped about 20 yards back from the road, well-hidden by the trees. Lauren had to pee, so Cal allowed her to walk into the woods to relieve herself. He knew and she knew that if she tried to run, he would shoot her, so any thought of running was quickly quelled. She was no survivalist, so even if she did manage to escape, she would have no chance of making it to safety. She had no idea where she was, what direction they had taken and, on foot, she wouldn't get far. When she returned to the vehicle, Cal had broken out some food and water from the cache, gotten a couple of blankets and instructed her to eat.

"We'll eat and get some sleep. Once it's dark, we'll get on the forest road to make better time. It's not patrolled much at night, but I'll see lights coming and can move back into the woods if another vehicle shows up. You just need to keep quiet if that happens," Cal warned.

"Where are we going?"

"There's an old forest ranger cabin that's been abandoned. When they cut the budget to the national parks, some of these cabins closed down. It'll be rough getting to it since the forest is encroaching on most of them. But the one I'm thinking of is high in the mountains and gives me a 360-degree view below. If anyone comes for us, I'll be able to see them long before they get there."

How would Jared find me at so remote a location? Lauren thought. She could only hope that they'd be found before they got to the cabin. But she didn't know if he was even on their trail yet. Would they use dogs? Helicopters? Could they be spotted on the run? The forest was so dense, especially from the air. She doubted anyone could see them, especially if Cal purposefully hid the vehicle from sight. He was used to the woods. Knew these woods. She had to do something to help herself. But what?

She hit on an idea. What if she left behind some kind of a sign for Jared? But what? She could carve a message on a tree every time she had the chance, but it would take too long. Cal would see her since he never let her out of his sight. Besides, other than a rock, she had no tool hard enough to do that. She could break branches along the way, but Cal would hear that. As they traveled along the overgrown trails, she was constantly pushing branches out of her way before they slapped her in the face. Without a full windshield, she'd already gotten a few small lacerations on her face. That gave her an idea. What if, when she grabbed the branches, she stripped the ends of their leaves? Each branch would snap back behind her as they traveled and Cal would never see her do it. But if she stripped every branch, enough of them might form a pattern for anyone tracking them. It was a longshot, but she'd give it a try. Her only problem was her hands. Without gloves, they'd be cut up in no time.

Maybe that could work to her advantage. She'd strip a couple of branches, then show him what pushing the branches aside was doing to her hands. She only hoped he had gloves in one of those backpacks.

Chapter 30

Ever since he'd talked to Charlie, Jared had been fighting two wars in his mind. On the one hand, he was relieved the body that had been found wasn't Lauren. But on the other hand, the body might be that of one of his missing persons who he'd gotten to know so well. It would be a rough day for the victim's family and he felt empathy for what they would be going through. But he also felt like a piece of shit, because he was glad it wasn't Lauren.

The roads were congested since it was the heart of summer vacation and the national parks drew hundreds of thousands of visitors this time of year. But he made the trip to the site in about 30 minutes. As he pulled up, he quickly surveyed the scene. Responder vehicles were parked along the side of the road. Two MHP cruisers, a forensic van, the coroner's wagon and plenty of bystanders dotted the side of the highway. He could see the yellow crime scene tape and followed its perimeter into the woods. About 50 yards in, in a heavily wooded area, he saw the coroner's tent. Inside were the remains of the young woman.

As he approached the scene, he was prepared for anything. He knew what each of his missing persons looked like, right down to tattoos, broken bones and distinguishing marks. If the body was relatively intact and it was one of his cases, he was sure he could make the identification.

The body had been found in a shallow ravine, partially covered by snow and branches. The officers had reported that little attempt had been made to hide the body, other than the few branches. The snow had kept the body hidden all winter, but once melted, it was easily seen.

Killer Looks

He entered the tent, showed his badge to the coroner and introduced himself. John Maddox had been the Flathead County Coroner for over 30 years, and was an expert in entomology and forensic anthropology. He had often been called on to identify times of death based on the degree of insect infestation in a body. He was also an expert in facial reconstruction based on possession of just a few key bones. The man was very good at what he did.

"Dr. Maddox, what can you tell me about the victim? I'm working some cold cases and this might be one of my victims."

"Detective, the victim is female, Caucasian, in her mid to late twenties. Based on ligature marks around her neck, it looks like she died of strangulation. An autopsy will tell me. Because she's been found in snow, it will be a little hard to tell how long she's been here or when she died. Based on experience, though, I don't think she's been here longer than one winter, since we should have seen more deterioration of the body if she'd been here through a summer. Because she was wrapped in a tarp, she stayed confined to this one area. I also found scarring and abrasions on one ankle, leading me to believe she was restrained in some way. We're going to go over the tarp as well as her body looking for DNA. Are you ready to see her, see if you recognize her?"

"Yes," Jared said, steeling himself for what he was about to see.

As Maddox unzipped the body bag revealing the victim's face, neck and hair, Jared leaned in to get a better look. She looked familiar, somehow, but her face didn't match any of his victims in their twenties. Disappointed, he started to rise, then something about the face jolted his memory. She looked like Gaby Parmenter, but older. Gaby had disappeared while still a teenager, so he had expected to find a teenager's body. But this *was* Gaby, aged by 10 years or so. He was sure of it. He ran to his vehicle, brought the folder containing Gaby's teenage photo and showed it to the coroner.

"I think this might be her," he said, pointing to Gaby's picture.

He handed it to Maddox and he studied it very carefully. "I'm going to say you're right, based on the bone structure of the face. I'll need DNA or dental records to confirm it."

"I'll get the dental records to you right away. Once you make the identification, I'll need to notify her family. It's not going to be easy on them especially because they think she's been dead for years. This will devastate them knowing she was killed recently."

As he watched Gaby's body being loaded into the coroner's van, his heart fell. He had found his first missing person, but she was no longer alive. Now he would need to find her killer. He knew the first question that had to be asked. Where had she been all this time?

The hikers were in the police cruiser, waiting to be interviewed by him. A young couple in their twenties, Ava and Sergio Valenzuela, were visiting the park and had spent a week hiking backwoods trails. They had gotten a little disoriented and stumbled on the body by accident. They could tell him nothing new. He thanked them, got their contact information and said he would call them if he had more questions.

Killer Looks

As he got back into his vehicle, he noticed that most of the other vehicles that had caused congestion around the scene had left. The bystanders had gotten bored and only the one MHP cruiser was still there, the officer making sure the crime scene remained secure. As he backed out, he turned to look over his shoulder and happened to see the mile marker that had been obscured by the other vehicles when he had arrived and parked. It was mile marker 235.

Chapter 31

She hoped it would work. They had been traveling on the forest service roads at night, sleeping as soon as the sun came up, way off the road. They made their way through the forest during the rest of the day, finding pathways in a circuitous manner. Sometimes she felt like they were doubling back as Cal tried to find passable pathways. But he seemed to know where he was going. Today, the woods were thick and she knew today was the day she had to put her plan into action.

He cursed as the branches slapped at the vehicle, and she reached for her first branch, pulled as many leaves off it as she could, then tried again. After a half hour of stripping leaves, her hands were raw and bleeding. She glanced back from time to time, checking her progress. She could see the pattern and her heart soared.

"I can't keep doing this," Lauren said, showing him her hands. "I've got cuts on my face and my hands."

"There's a pair of gloves in that blue backpack. Put them on and shut up."

She said "thank you" and grabbed them. As long as he didn't look back, see the pattern, she could continue to leave a trail for Jared to find.

It was getting dark again, so they stopped to eat before joining up with the next forest service road. They were climbing now, and the air was colder. She had started shivering and he had pulled a jacket and knit cap out of the back of the vehicle for her. She had a blanket on her lap. He was still wearing just his long sleeve shirt, jeans and hiking boots, seemingly oblivious to the cold.

Killer Looks

They'd been climbing for 5 days and were on the final forest service road. It was no longer maintained and was rough, overgrown plants threatening to block their way entirely. She had left her last trail about 12 miles back. She knew that leaving the trail was futile. But she had had to do something to take control. To feel like she could aid in her rescue.

Now it looked like the cabin was in sight. It wasn't much, but at least it would keep them out of the elements. They'd run into some thunderstorm activity and some rain, and it had left Lauren miserable. With only a partial front windshield and no windows, the 4-wheeler didn't offer much protection from the elements.

Cal still kept her chained to the roll bar, but she hoped that would end once they were in the cabin. She wasn't going anywhere and he knew it.

Most of their days had been spent in silence. She was afraid to talk to him, afraid anything she said would remind him of his mother. She didn't want to upset him. She doubted he had a plan once they got to the cabin. Their food wouldn't last long and he'd need to find water for them to drink. Maybe they wouldn't stay long, but instead move to a more populated area. Get lost in a crowd. Her imagination started to run away with her, picturing Cal stealing a car, throwing her in the front seat and taking off. It was silliness in the midst of this nightmare and she needed it.

As they finally approached the cabin, Cal parked the 4-wheeler behind the cabin, away from the line of sight of the road. He would cover it with branches to hide it, she supposed. The cabin was at the crest of the hill, probably around 5,000 feet in elevation. There was an outhouse off to the right, a chimney that indicated a fireplace and a small front porch. The door to the cabin was nailed shut with a couple of boards. To ward off bears, she thought. The two windows were also boarded up and the boards were weathered and the nails rusty. No one had been here for years.

She watched as Cal pulled a hammer out of the back of the vehicle and began to pull on the nails that secured the door. It took some brute strength, but he was finally able to open the door. He came over and unlocked her chain and mercifully removed it. She followed him into the cabin.

As she entered and her eyes became accustomed to the ambient light, she quickly surveyed her new home. It was dusty and smelled like old wood smoke. There was a sink, but no plumbing. Any water in the sink that might be used for washing would have to be drained into a bucket. There was a twin bed in a small bedroom. An old sofa, a couple of chairs and a small table for eating were the only other things in the cabin. This place was totally off the grid.

Chapter 32

Jared slammed on his brakes, got out of the car and slowly walked to the mile marker sign. His heart was pounding and he could hear it loudly beating in his ears. He was flushed, his stomach roiling. Mile marker 235. Where Cal had had his accident. The circumstances were strange when Charlie had told him about the details, and Jared had never forgotten about it. Cal on a date? Getting stood up? Going far into the woods just to take a leak? He had no proof, but Cal had to be involved with Gaby's disappearance. It was just too coincidental. If he had left her here, why didn't he come back and move her? He must have had her in his truck when the accident happened and he panicked and ran into the woods with her. No wonder the hiding place was found so easily. He hadn't had time to adequately hide her, especially as the cops were showing up. But to just leave her here to be found? He didn't understand it.

He walked back to his vehicle and immediately called Charlie.

When he answered, Jared took a deep breath before speaking. "Charlie, I'm out here at the crime scene."

"What did you find? Was she one of your cold cases?"

"Yes, it was Gaby Parmenter. You remember I told you she was the one who went missing from her college campus when she was 19."

"I remember. Wow, she's been out there a long time."

"No, Charlie, that's just it. She's only been here about 6 months, and she's not 19 anymore. She's in her mid to late twenties. That means she's been somewhere alive for 8-10 years. She was strangled and she's been restrained, based on scarring and abrasions around her ankle. But Charlie, she was found at mile marker 235." He paused, waiting for Charlie to make the connection.

Charlie was silent for a long time. "Where Cal had his accident. Oh my God, Jared, do you think Cal had something to do with this girl?"

"Charlie, it has to be Cal. Remember how you told me his tracks led deeper into the woods than you thought was necessary? He was dumping her out there, but couldn't hide her well enough before you showed up. That's probably not the place he was ultimately going to dump her but the accident screwed everything up. He probably went back to find her, but somehow couldn't so he just left her there. Probably figured animals would take care of her and they would have if she hadn't been wrapped in a tarp."

"But how could he have kept this girl for 8-10 years without someone knowing she was there? I've been to his house a dozen times. Where did he keep her? God dammit, this can't be happening."

"He's had all the privacy he's needed all these years. It wasn't until Lauren moved in that things changed. That's why he was building that fucking fence. Somehow, Lauren must have found out about it and he grabbed her or, God forbid, killed her. I'm on my way to Cal's now. See if you can get a search warrant for his property. If not, I'll break the fucking door down myself."

Killer Looks

"I need probable cause, not conjecture and you know it. But I'll call Judge Willis and see what I can do."

It took Jared exactly 75 minutes to get to Cal's. Charlie was already there with a search warrant. Charlie went up to Cal's porch and knocked on the door. He was met with silence. He knocked again, then listened. Still nothing. Jared raised his leg to kick in the door, at the same time that Charlie pushed with his shoulder. The jamb splintered and the door hung on one hinge.

They entered the kitchen to the sight of Cal's pet, dead with a gunshot to the head. He began yelling Lauren's name. He went through each room, firearm drawn, and cleared each one. When he got back to the kitchen, he looked for the basement door. As he broke through it, he descended the stairs, gun still drawn. When he got to the bottom of the stairs, he saw a bathroom to his left. Empty. To his right was another door, closed but not locked. As he walked into the room, he yelled to Charlie. What he saw would live in his nightmares forever. Inside were two cages, one pink and one purple. One was empty and the other held a body lying in a pool of blood, a leg chain attached to a bolt in the floor. Jared's heart fell. He raced over, tears spilling onto his cheeks, expecting to find Lauren. But it wasn't her. He felt for a pulse, found a weak one and immediately dialed 911.

He got to the hospital right behind the ambulance. He had left Charlie behind with the forensic team to process the scene. Jared couldn't wrap his brain around what he had seen. Two cages, each with a bolt in the floor. This is where Gaby had probably lived for the last 8 years of her life, chained to that bolt and the victim of a sexual

149

predator. And it's probably where he had held Lauren. The whole room was a sexual predator's fantasy complete with a bed, lingerie and sex toys. Had Lauren been a victim of that, too? He tried to put it out of his mind or he'd go crazy.

He had found the victim, Tess Baldwin, a mid-thirties female with a bullet wound to her upper chest. She had lost a lot of blood, but the paramedics had said the bullet hadn't hit any major organs or arteries. She would survive after having surgery to remove the projectile. He needed to talk to her. Find out her story and where Lauren might be.

Four hours later, she was out of surgery and eager to talk.

Jared approached her room, took a deep breath to calm his nerves and entered. He forced a smile and introduced himself.

"Hi, I'm detective Jared Martin."

Before he could say another word, the girl smiled and said, "You're Lauren's boyfriend. She said you'd come for her. I'm just sorry you're too late."

"What do you mean too late?" Jared asked, fear clutching at his heart.

"Gosh, what I meant was she's already gone with him. He took her. Then he shot me. Probably figured he'd killed me."

"Can you answer some questions for me?"

"I'll try," she said, her voice weak from the surgery.

"Do you mind if I call you Tess?"

"Of course, what do you want to know?"

"So much, but I guess I'll start with how long you've been there."

"About 10 years. There was another woman, Beth Reeves, who was already there. But she got pregnant and I think Cal killed her and her baby. Gaby came shortly after Beth disappeared."

Jared's heart froze. Beth Reeves was dead, too. And he was just about to talk to her family. Shit.

"How did Lauren get involved in all of this?"

"It was my fault. After he killed Gaby, I knew I was next. The only way I could get out was to try to kill him. So, I made a weapon from one of the cage links and one night when we were having sex, I stabbed him in the neck with it, and hit him with the lingerie rack. When he went down, I ran out of the house towards the cottage. I banged on the door, screaming, and just as Lauren opened the door, Cal grabbed me around the neck and pointed a shotgun at Lauren. Then, he forced her into the basement when he threatened to shoot me if she didn't obey him. She saved my life." Tess started to cry. He let her.

"Do you have any idea where he would have taken her?" Jared asked.

"No, I'm sorry."

Then Tess began to tell him about her life there, about the routine, the way Lauren and she were going to try to overpower Cal, but never had the chance. My God, Lauren was smart. She probably would have escaped, given more time. Then Cal would be right where he belonged. But right now, he needed to get as much information as he could from Tess and from the crime scene.

Charlie was still at the scene when he came by to tell him what he had learned from Tess. Charlie had things to tell Jared, too. The forensic team had found a cell phone in Cal's bedroom with a police scanner app. They figured that he had heard the report about the body being found and that's what triggered his quick escape. Leaving it behind meant his whereabouts couldn't be traced through it.

They had found multiple sources of DNA that would be processed as part of the crime scene. His truck was still in the garage, but another, smaller vehicle appeared to have been parked next to it, but was now missing. There were open cabinet doors in the garage and it appeared as if things had been removed in a hurry. There were empty spots on the shelves in an otherwise packed garage. Jared was trying to process everything Charlie was telling him. The most important thing now was to find Lauren, before Cal did something to her.

"This other vehicle?" Cal asked. "What is it?"

"I've got no clue. I didn't know he had another vehicle."

"Shit, this is going to slow us down. I'll run a vehicle check to see what shows up. Got anything else for me before I go back to the station? I still need to get Gaby's dental records to the Flathead County Coroner, then notify the family."

"Think there's any need to process Lauren's house now?"

"Sure, couldn't hurt, but we know Cal's got her. We just have to find her."

He was back to the station in 10 minutes. He went through the box containing all the information he had on Gaby. Her dental records had been stored there ready to be compared to a potential match. He quickly scanned them and emailed them to the coroner's office.

Then he ran a vehicle check under the name Cal Morgan, but the only result returned was his truck. He knew he had to have another vehicle. He widened his search to include just the last name, Morgan. This time, many showed up. There were a few vehicles, some mobile homes with titles and some off-road vehicles. That was unexpected. He'd almost forgotten that those needed to be licensed as well. When he looked for Cal Morgan's name, he didn't find it. He looked over the list again, hoping he'd just missed it. But as he was looking a second time, one of the names had a familiarity about it. Caroline Morgan. Wasn't that Cal's mother's name? There was a title to a 4-wheeler under the name Caroline Morgan, but the address listed was Cal's. He'd found Cal's method of escape.

Chapter 33

The bitch had been quiet. Unusually so. The mouthiness that she had exhibited when he first threw her in the cage was gone. He knew she was scared. Or else confident that the cop would somehow find her. But that wasn't going to happen.

He had planned for this eventuality, stocking his garage cabinets with everything he'd need to survive off the grid. He just hadn't planned on her being a part of this. The idea of taking her hostage had seemed like a good one at the time. Now, he wasn't so sure. He'd brought food with him, but it wouldn't last long. Another mouth to feed would dwindle his stores in no time. High up in the mountains, he could hunt for food, but preserving it would be a problem. It was still summer and even though the nights were cool, the heat of the day would spoil any meat supply. He'd need to dig a cold cellar, aiming for a depth below the frost line, so he could store food supplies. But that was hard work and it would take time. She'd need to help him.

He'd been amused by the look on her face when they first entered the cabin. Abject disgust. She had no idea what a luxury the cabin was. They could have been camping outside in the elements or holed up in some long-vacated bear den. She'd need to get used to it.

"Welcome to your new home," he said with a sneer, watching for her reaction. "You'll have one day to get acclimated, then the real work begins. There's a spring out back where I parked the four-wheeler, so start bringing in water. There's also a 25-pound bucket of rice, pinto beans, wheat flour, oats and potato flakes packets, but we'll need protein. I'll hunt for small game we can eat until I make a large kill. We'll start to build a cold cellar tomorrow to preserve it all. Until the snow comes, it's the only way to keep our food from spoiling."

"Until the snow comes? Fuck you, I won't be here that long!" Lauren hurled the words at him. They surprised him, and he fought to control his anger.

"We could be here for years and no one would find us. You'd better get used to your new life." He turned, then walked out the still open cabin door, leaving her to her new reality.

I guess you told her, didn't you? She will try to escape, you know. She's not going to stay here just because you say so. She's so much like me, isn't she?

Just as he felt exhilarated, in control, his mother's voice reverberated through his whole being.

"No, mother, *I* have the control. She's a big city girl who won't survive even if she does escape, which she won't. So, stop preaching to me. I'm not going to listen to you, no matter what you say," he shouted to her. His voice was lost among the pines. As the last word drifted into oblivion, he paused. There was one thing he couldn't deny. She *was* like his mother and he was strangely drawn to her as much as repulsed by her. That's probably why he didn't kill her. But to bring her along, slowing him down? What was he thinking?

He shook off his thoughts and started to survey his surroundings. He had been to this cabin before. Not intentionally, but had stumbled across it while hunting elk. It had been 5 years ago, long after the cabin had been deserted. He had been forced to head up the mountain when the elk moved to higher ground. Snow had descended on him with a swirling ferocity and he followed a closed forest service road, barely recognizable as one because of overgrowth, finding the cabin at the end. It had been a godsend. He was able to build a fire to keep warm and in the morning when the snow had ceased its assault, he began to assess his surroundings. He was at the top of a high ridge with a 360-degree view of the valley. Exploring, he had found the outhouse and a source of water. The forest was thick with pine trees and aspen. A rich source of firewood, so vital for survival. So remote, he could get lost here. Bring the girls if he had to.

He had left his truck far down the mountain, traveling on foot for 4 days, following the elk as they had climbed. He had crossed streams, hit many dead ends and had had to change direction innumerable times in pursuit of his prey. The one smart thing he had done was to bring a GPS device. At the top of the ridge, it functioned, giving him the coordinates he would need to find his way back to the cabin, to complete isolation.

He made one more trip back after that first encounter with the cabin. Thinking ahead, he had brought cooking utensils, warm blankets, hand tools, minor construction materials like nails, screws and fasteners, matches and plastic sheeting. He was in for the long haul if it came to that.

And now, here he was again. Back at the cabin, hostage in tow, his new life beginning. With her.

Chapter 34

It was overwhelming. Cal could be anywhere. Just because he had taken off in his four-wheeler, didn't mean he was still in the county. Hell, he could be states away by now. But the search would start locally, then spread out. He had had K-9 dogs ready to follow Lauren's and Cal's scents, but the torrential rain that had fallen for the last 48 hours assured that their trail had been lost. Montana, like Alaska, was a state you could get lost in. Ted Kaczynksi, the Unabomber, had been able to elude authorities for years, sequestered in a cabin near the small town of Lincoln, Montana, just miles from Helena. *Right in our neck of the woods*, he thought.

He was jolted out of his thoughts by Charlie, who had been with the forensic team while they processed Cal's house and property. Lauren's fingerprints and DNA were found in the basement and kitchen and at the very least, they could arrest Cal for first-degree attempted murder of Tess and first-degree kidnapping of Lauren. They'd need to build a case in the deaths of Gaby and Beth Reeves to charge him with murder. But first, they'd need to find him.

Charlie had found Jared in the conference room, Jared's temporary work space. "Sorry about Lauren, Jared. I know this is rough. We've called in the FBI for help on this one and they should be here tomorrow. Maggie is beside herself with worry. She had gotten pretty close to Lauren, especially because you were gone so much. Shit, I don't know what else to say, buddy."

"I know. Thanks." He paused, trying to hold it together. "I've got to find her," he said as his voice broke.

Tears welled in his eyes but he wouldn't cry. Not now anyway. Head down, he was looking closely at the case book he'd started, filling in the information that they already knew. Paperwork kept him busy, but he should be out there looking for her. But he was not going to waste his energy running in circles. He needed to use his brain. Get inside the mind of a killer. Could he think like him? Understand him? Anticipate his moves? Not without help, he decided.

"Charlie, how well do you know Cal? I need some insight into his personality."

"Not well at all. My dad and Cal's mother were cousins, so Cal was really my second cousin. I wasn't around him much growing up. It was a big family scandal when Caroline was killed by Cal's adopted brother. His sisters would be the ones to talk to, though. They grew up with him, saw the relationship between Cal and Caroline. I can get them here in a couple of days."

"Call them. The FBI will probably take over this case, but I'm going to insist I'm in on as much interrogation and information gathering as I can be. Charlie, I was going to ask her to marry me. I just didn't get the chance. My one fear is that she'll lose hope. She knows I'm looking for her, I can feel it. But I'm not some white knight on a horse that can ride up and rescue her tomorrow. It could take months for us to get a good lead. I don't want to think about what Cal can do to her in a few months."

"Don't let your mind go there. Tess told you he didn't touch Lauren and she'd fight like hell to keep him away from her. Just think about that, ok?" He tentatively patted Jared's back on his way out the door.

Jared smiled weakly and continued processing his notes, waving a goodbye to Charlie as he left to go home to Maggie. Jared didn't want to be the guy that everyone felt sorry for, but he could already see the sympathetic looks on the faces of his former co-workers as they filed past him once they had heard the news. He would stay focused on finding Lauren for the time he had left here. He would be returning to his cold cases, leaving the day to day investigation to Charlie's team and the FBI. And it would kill him. But he needed this great job and a promising future for Lauren to come back to.

The following day, the lead investigator for the FBI, Agent Glenn Cedar, found Jared in the conference room and introduced himself. He had been recently transferred from the Detroit Field Office to Salt Lake City and would be spearheading the investigation. Charlie had filled him in on Jared's place in the investigation and he wasted no time in giving assurances to him.

"Jared, I can empathize with what you're dealing with, although something like this has never personally happened to me. I promise you, we will use every resource to find Ms. Sedgeway and work tirelessly to bring Cal Morgan to justice. But understand, this is my investigation. I will keep you in the loop, but I caution you not to play the hero. If you get a lead, tell me. If I do, you'll be the first to know. Once we have a chance to apprehend him, I'll want you on the team and on the hunt. But we can't jeopardize Ms. Sedgeway's life in any way, so we'll proceed cautiously and by the book."

"That's fair. But I have a condition. I want to be in on every interrogation, starting with Cal Morgan's sisters."

Cedar smiled. "Charlie said you'd say that. He also told me about your exemplary investigative skills. Why would I turn that down? Agreed," he said. "Let's start asking the hard questions."

Cal's sisters were not what Jared expected. While Cal was very good looking, his sisters were plain, skittish and unmarried. Louanne was 60, and the younger of the two, Jeanette, was 58. They decided to start with Jeanette, since she was closest in age to Cal.

Jeanette was waiting for Jared and Cedar in the interrogation room. As they introduced themselves, Jared let Cedar take the lead, while he observed Cal's youngest sister.

"Thank you for coming in today," Cedar began. "I know this can't be easy for you."

"I'm not sure why I'm here. I really haven't been in touch with Cal in years. Neither of us has. I think my sister was the last to hear from him but that was simply ages ago. Right after our mother died."

"How did your mother die, Jeanette?" asked Cedar.

She hesitated and Jared watched her respiration rate increase. She was obviously in some distress.

"She was shot by our adopted brother."

"Why do you think he shot her, Jeanette?"

"I have no way of knowing," she responded, defensively.

"Really, your adopted brother shot your mother and you and your sister have never thought about it? Never wondered what could provoke a child, and believe me, your brother was a child, to take the life of his own mother? That's bullshit and everyone in this room knows it! Now, I'm going to ask you again, and think about your answer very carefully. Your brother Cal has probably killed two women already, has shot another and kidnapped yet another. If you're withholding anything that could lead us to him, or help us understand his motivation, you could be considered an accessory. Now I know you don't want that. So, I'm asking you one last time, why did your brother shoot your mother?"

Jeanette broke down, began to sob and put her hands over her face. Cedar gave her a moment, then asked her again. And again. Finally, Jeanette was able to form the words they hoped were coming.

"She made him have sex with her."

Jared was startled by her answer. He had assumed the kid had been abused. But the black and blue, broken bones kind of abuse. Not sexual abuse. The kid finally has a nice home after living in the foster care system and this is what happens to him? It made him sick. The boy probably went along with it because he didn't want to go back into the system, but it was finally too much for him. The anger that must have been there for him to do that. And then to end his own life. What sickened him more was that these sisters knew something like this was happening and they did nothing to stop it. Never reported their suspicions. There was a place in hell for them.

"How do you know that?" Jared asked.

"I don't really know, but she made Cal have sex with her starting when he was 12. So, we thought she must have been doing the same with Adam. Cal called me one night in hysterics. All he was able to say before our mother took the phone away from him was that he had done something very wrong. With our mother. In her bed. I never heard from him again after that. I assumed it had stopped."

"Jesus Christ, why didn't you report it. Have him taken out of that home?" Jared demanded.

"I talked to Louanne about it."

"And did Louanne report it?"

"We figured it wouldn't do any good. Our mother was a judge and very well respected. We were young and didn't think anyone would believe us. Cal would never have told anyone else, even if he was asked. He had been verbally abused his whole life by her. Once we were gone, she took advantage of him…in that way. We felt bad, but what could we do?"

Disgusted, Jared left the room.

Louanne Morgan showed none of the emotion her sister had. She was very matter of fact about Cal's abuse and like her sister, believed it had stopped. When Adam killed their mother and then himself, in their minds it was over. There was nothing more that needed to be said. After all, Cal was a grown man and was just fine. Their mother's reputation would remain intact and they could be proud to be the daughters of Caroline Morgan, Federal Judge.

Jared and Cedar listened with disbelief to the way these women had accepted all that had happened to their brothers. They were in no way normal or well-adjusted and had probably been subjected to a different kind of abuse from their mother. No wonder they were so fucked up.

Killer Looks

Because of their inaction, Cal had developed a sexual deviance. The FBI profiler confirmed it. He had no power over his mother, so instead exerted power over other women. Captive women. His looks made it easy for him and his isolation kept his deviance hidden. Until Lauren. And now she was just the next woman in line. The next one to control.

Chapter 35

It was October, she thought. She had been here, with him, for over 4 months. She was keeping track. Where was Jared? Why hadn't he found her yet? She knew why, she decided. She was in the middle of fucking nowhere Montana.

She was using an outhouse. An outhouse, for God's sake. Hauling water, cooking over a wood fire and doing chores. Fucking chores. She and Cal had taken 3 days to build a cold cellar, but now it was stocked with fresh game, berries and wild vegetables. How had she gotten here?

At first, she fought him every step of the way. She refused to eat, refused to cook, haul water or do anything else he asked. She slept in the 4-wheeler. Then she got hungry. And thirsty. And cold. So slowly, she had started to do as he asked. He didn't know what to do with her, she could tell. She was company for him, and, reluctantly, he was for her. They barely communicated beyond his giving her orders, and they both worked endlessly on daily chores until they fell asleep exhausted each night. She on the sofa and he in the bedroom. He made the occasional foray down the mountain and on one of his trips, he had brought home a couple of chickens he had stolen from an unsuspecting distant neighbor. Now they had fresh eggs and more chickens on the way.

This life was surreal. She looked at it as a chapter in her life. It had a beginning and it would have an end. In the future, she could file it away as a story well told, but over. Then the rest of her life would resume where it had left off. Hopefully with Jared by her side.

She thought of Jared often. Could picture him working on finding her, working on his cold cases. He couldn't give up his life for her, she knew. His life would continue on, and she would drift in and out of it. He'd follow clues, mostly dead ends, but then get caught up in the mundane. Grocery shopping, laundry, the occasional night out with his colleagues or friends, a trip to the hardware store. His life was the same while hers held nothing that was the same as before.

Cal was out hunting again. Looking for wild boar this time. If she had to eat one more elk steak, she'd go mad. How did the pioneers do it? Eating the same thing, day after day. What she wouldn't give for a big salad.

She had lost weight, eating mostly protein. And her body had never been so toned. Muscles on her arms and legs were more defined and she accomplished most menial tasks with ease. She found herself wishing for creature comforts, but the thoughts quickly came and went. They didn't fit in her life anymore.

The sound of twigs snapping alerted her to Cal's return. He carried a small boar draped around his neck and a big smile greeted her.

"Talk about bringing home the bacon…" Lauren squealed.

Cal stopped in his tracks, then burst into laughter. It was the first time he had shown any emotion since they'd been here, and it surprised her. Caused a ripple in her stomach. She almost felt glad to see him. How had she stopped hating him?

She knew. Her current frame of reference had nothing to do with what had happened in the past. Here, he was the provider, company for her, thinking of her needs as well as his own. He was keeping her alive, protected against the elements and any outside danger. She was spending every day and every night with him. Yet, she knew little about him. She didn't want to know about what he had done. But she was curious about why.

Cal brought the boar to the cleaning table he had built from an old outhouse door and slabs of stone. He had already gutted it to protect the meat against spoilage, but it would need to be dressed. As he dropped it on the makeshift table, he handed the knife he always carried on his hip to her.

"You're going to need to learn how to do this."

She gazed at the knife in her hand and thought about plunging it into Cal's heart. He saw the look on her face, but did nothing. Somehow, he knew she wouldn't do it, not even to escape. She was smart enough to know that she couldn't survive out here without him. She didn't know where he hid the key to the 4-wheeler or the direction she should take to find home. She couldn't carry all that she needed to survive on her own. And it was getting cold, with occasional snow dusting the mountains, then melting again. Soon, it would be staying. They were working hard to gather enough food to maintain them over the winter. God, would she still be here this winter?

As he explained where she needed to cut, her initial cuts were tentative. With each subsequent cut, her hand was steadier and surer. The blood was still warm and covered her hands with a sticky almost sensual layer of moisture. It unnerved her. It was hard work and as she cut, he prepped and packaged each piece. The organs would be

166

eaten tonight and he would salt the belly for bacon. The rest would go into the cold cellar which by now was keeping the meat frozen. When it was done, she had an immense feeling of satisfaction. Of a job well done. He had provided that for her. While he cleaned the table, she went inside to clean herself. A small package was on the kitchen table and her curiosity couldn't be contained. When she opened it, she found watercress, wild onions and wild garlic. She burst into tears. He had brought her a salad.

Sobbing, she turned to see him standing in the doorway. Wiping away her tears she could say nothing.

"That wasn't exactly the reaction I expected," he said, open embarrassment on his face. "I just figured you might like some greens for a change."

She finally found her voice and thanked him, realizing his animosity towards her had retreated. What were they becoming? Tolerant of each other? Was that all? She couldn't think further than that.

As they ate dinner that night, Cal was pre-occupied. Was he having the same thoughts? He couldn't believe that they would go on like this forever, could he? Jared would find her, the hostage, and she would be exchanged for Cal's freedom. He'd get away, of course, but they'd eventually find him, wouldn't they?

He broke the silence. "Saw wood smoke a little closer than I'd like. Gonna keep an eye on it. If I see signs of anyone moving this way, we'll need to be on the move. Just letting you know."

He finished his meal in silence and left the table for the bedroom without saying good night. A million thoughts rushed through her brain. Where would they go? How would they get there? Would Jared have an easier time finding her if they left the isolation of the mountain? Why hadn't anyone noticed their woodfire smoke this far up the mountain and gotten curious? She wouldn't sleep very well tonight.

Chapter 36

What the hell was happening? He had never done anything thoughtful for a woman before. At least not without an agenda. She had become submissive, working alongside him. She hadn't lost her feistiness but it didn't dominate her personality any longer. She was tolerable. More than tolerable.

He had found the watercress in a small lagoon, the last before the water froze. The onions and garlic grew there along the banks and he dropped them in his sack without giving any of them a second thought. She had made such a big deal of it, and her reaction had touched him. That was a problem. He didn't have affection for her, he knew that, but they had something. An acceptance of each other and common goals? That was more like it. She was attractive, but he still was physically repulsed by her resemblance to his mother. So, they would never have that kind of relationship. No, she was… well, it didn't matter.

What did matter to him now was the smoke he had seen while boar hunting. He knew the hunting season was underway, but not many hunters came this far up the mountain. There were hunting cabins up and down the mountain and this time of year there was a lot of activity. The last thing he needed was an unwelcome visitor stumbling upon them. If he was recognized, or she was, he couldn't let them alert the authorities. He wanted no more killings, but would not hesitate if threatened. He kept his guns loaded and always carried a pistol on his hip. He didn't want to be defenseless and vulnerable. The smoke was still a long way away, but cabins that had been vacant were now being used. The hunting season was short and the weather was about to turn nasty, so he hoped they would remain undetected. Once the snow hit, only the most ardent of hunters would venture out or approach this elevation.

When he awoke the next morning, his thoughts of the previous night were gone. His job today, and for the next few days, was gathering firewood. It was dangerous now, using his chainsaw. If he was heard cutting down trees in a protected Federal forest, someone would report it. He hoped he was high enough up the mountain to escape detection. But he couldn't wait until hunting season was over. He needed to lay in a winter sized pile of wood now, before snow and subzero temperatures made it impossible to be outside for any length of time.

Lauren would be moving the rest of the existing wood pile to the front porch while he found and cut down as many dead trees as he could find close to the property. Then he'd need her to help him move the wood from the forest to the wood pile. There was an old wooden pallet in the shed and he'd improvised some runners with an old pair of cross country skis that had been left behind. One was damaged, but should work for his purposes. Runners would make it easier to move the pallet, but he'd need to be careful not to overload it. He didn't want to risk further damage to either ski.

He ate a bowl of the oatmeal that Lauren had left on the fireiron in the fireplace. She was getting good at using the fire for cooking. She hardly burned anything now. When he stepped onto the porch, he saw that she had already moved a third of the pile to its place there. She'd be done in no time and he would come back for lunch and take her with him to start hauling back to the cabin what he was going to cut down that morning. He attached a strong rope to first one side of the pallet and then looped it over to the other, where he secured it. That left enough slack for him to slip inside the loop and place it around his chest. Instead of trying to pull the pallet with his hands, he could drag it behind him, using the strength of his legs and torso to move the pallet. It wasn't pretty, but it worked. She'd drive the 4-wheeler as far into the woods as possible and wait for him to drag the pallet to her. Then they'd both load the wood into the vehicle and she'd drive back to the cabin and unload it, while he'd go back for another load. If it went as smoothly as he hoped it would, they'd have enough wood for the winter with just 4 days work.

He left her there, at the woodpile, and headed to a stand of trees about a quarter mile from the cabin. There was just enough space for the 28-inch pallet to fit between the trees, although he knew he wouldn't always be this lucky. Further from the cabin, the trees were closer together and access would be more difficult. The chainsaw did its work and he had felled 4 good sized aspens, stripped them of their branches and cut them into a manageable size in only four hours. He tested his first load, found that he had to remove more than he wanted to from the pallet and made his way through the forest, expecting to meet Lauren with the vehicle. When he broke through the tree line, she wasn't there. He dropped his load and ran, panic fueling his adrenaline. In 5 minutes, he was at the cabin. The wheeler was where he'd left it. The woodpile was smaller than before, but she had only moved a little more than half to the porch. She should have been done by now. What the fuck?

He called her name and heard her in the cabin. She was lying on the sofa, moaning and holding a wet cloth on her hand. When he lifted the cloth, he saw telltale signs of what had happened. Two red dots, swelling and growing pain were a sign of a black widow spider bite. She probably had disturbed one in the woodpile and it had bit her. She probably hadn't even felt it. Man, she was in for a couple of really bad days. Black widow spiders were not common in Montana but they could be found in almost any state. Lauren was going to have cramping, fever, abdominal pain and nausea before she was back on her feet again. His first aid kit contained some pain reliever and alcohol to keep her fever down, but he couldn't do anything for her nausea and cramping. Shit, he'd have to take care of her and that was going to fuck up the firewood schedule. He'd needed her to help him.

She was sweating now, and he retrieved the first aid kit. He got a glass of water and an ibuprofen for the fever and pain.

"Lauren," he said, waiting for her to open her eyes. She opened them but found it hard to focus.

"You've been bitten by a black widow spider. You need to take this to help stop the fever and pain," he said as he handed her the pill.

She reached for it, struggling to raise her head high enough to swallow. He held the water glass to her lips and she drank, popped the pill in her mouth and drank again. She dropped back to the sofa and resumed her moaning. She would be delirious before long. While she slept and recovered, he'd need to keep a cold compress on her hand to reduce the swelling, try to keep her hydrated and give her pain meds, although sparingly. He only had 5 more pills.

He was afraid to leave her alone, but he needed to get the wood stacked. Well, at least he could finish moving the remains of the old woodpile to the porch. He found the nest of spiders and quickly removed and destroyed it. There'd be more where they came from so they'd have to be vigilant. It took him 2 hours to move and stack the wood on the porch, then he went to check on her.

She was burning up and doubled over with pain. He felt bad for her but it was too soon to give her another pill. He stoked the fire, then removed her clothes down to her underwear. He'd give her an alcohol rub, to see if that brought her fever down. She did not resist when he touched her and the rub seemed to give her some relief. He covered her with a thin blanket and let her sleep. She was too weak to eat but did take water when he offered it to her. He put a pot by the sofa in case she needed to relieve herself, but in the morning, found it empty. She had been sweating and was dehydrated. He gave her two more alcohol rubs over the next 24 hours and her fever finally broke. She was still suffering from abdominal pain, but the ibuprofen was keeping it under control. The next 24 hours should see a lessening of her symptoms and she would probably need to use the pot and start to eat and drink. He went to bed that night not sure what he'd find in the morning.

She was sitting up on the sofa when he left his bedroom. She still had the blanket draped around her and she had dressed. She had gotten up for a glass of water and was just finishing it when he appeared.

"What happened to me?" she said.

"I guess you weren't lucid when I told you. You got bitten by a black widow spider. Found the nest in the woodpile. It's gone now."

"I didn't know what was happening to me. But I started feeling really sick and had to come and lie down on the sofa. That's about all I remember. Except you taking care of me. Thank you for that."

"I didn't do much. Just gave you water, pain pills and a few alcohol rubs. You were in rough shape and I did what I could."

"How long have I been lying here?"

"About 48 hours or so. Took that long for the poison to start to leave your body. You need to drink lots of water and, um, hit the outhouse to get it all out."

"And the wood?"

"Well, it's all still out there. I couldn't leave you alone in that condition."

She looked at him then, apparently stunned by his response. She was probably thinking he had some small part of humanity still remaining. Maybe he did. Maybe she brought it out in him.

Chapter 37

Jared was frustrated. Five long months and no sign of Lauren or Cal. They had not found her car or Cal's four-wheeler. Neither of them were using their credit cards or accessing bank accounts and it was as if they'd vanished off the face of the earth. He still had a strong feeling that she was alive, but his hopes of finding her were waning. The FBI task force had been dismantled but Charlie's team was still focused on the investigation. Lauren's case would soon be considered a cold one and he would be the only one working on it. He and Charlie were meeting in an hour to discuss the latest theories.

He was waiting in the conference room when Charlie got to the station. His white board was set up and he was astounded at the number of leads they had followed up on with no results. There were more things crossed out than remained on the board. Charlie was the only one who understood Jared's frustration and pain. And he was the only one who didn't avoid Jared when that frustration and pain exploded.

"How you doing?" Charlie asked as he walked in the room, knowing the answer to the question even before he asked it.

"About as good as you'd expect. Just like every other day since this happened."

"Maggie sends her love."

"Thanks."

"I'm going to say something that you're not going to want to hear, but I think it needs to be said. I don't think Lauren is still alive. You know Cal's track record. He's killed or attempted to kill every woman he's been involved with. If she were still alive, we would have found some trace of her. You know the statistics. If someone stops using social media, doesn't access bank accounts or credit cards, chances are they've been killed. Neither of them has rented a car, bought a train or plane ticket, or crossed a border as far as we can tell. Cal has survivalist training and he could be anywhere in this world. He wouldn't need Lauren."

Charlie was not saying things that he hadn't already said to himself. He just hadn't agreed to any of it so far.

"I know what you're saying. Don't think I'm not thinking the same things. But am I the guy who'll give up on her? If she is still alive, she's waiting for me to find her."

"And if she's not alive, how far will you take this? When is enough going to be enough?" Charlie asked.

"I know, I know. Look, I want to take this back to the basics. I've been pulled in so many directions between Lauren's case and the cold cases I'm working on that I've lost sight of an investigative principle. The intellectual foundation for an investigative methodology. I haven't been using my brain for this, just my love for her and emotional thinking. Do you think we can get Agent Cedar here for another look at what we have? If anyone knows about current investigative methodology, it's the FBI."

Two days later, Agent Glenn Cedar arrived at the station and made his way to the conference room. Charlie, Chief Belquist, Charlie's boss, Alex Corden and Jared were waiting for him. Over the last two days, Jared had erased the white board, leaving only the facts as they knew them. It was time to drill down on those facts.

Jared began. "Thanks for making this trip a priority. I know it's not your case anymore, but you did say I could contact you anytime."

"I did," said Cedar. "I wanted to get out of Salt Lake City for a few days anyway. Taking a couple of vacation days."

"Shit, you didn't have to do that." Jared said.

"Got me here, didn't it?" Cedar smiled, making Jared feel like less of an asshole. "I think you're right about the methodology. I don't think we thought about this enough. Reduced every fact down to its basic elements. Let's start over and see where it leads us. Charlie, why don't you man the whiteboard and we'll pick each fact apart. Write down everything we say, as quick as you can."

"Got it," said Charlie.

"Jared, why don't you begin?"

"Ok, let's start with Cal. Here's what we know so far. Beginning with his childhood. According to his sisters, pieces of work by the way, he was verbally and then sexually abused by his powerful mother. The verbal abuse started while he was still a toddler and the sexual abuse around 12. The sisters showed me pictures of the family when Cal was around that age and he was mature for his age. Sexually mature, I think, although he wouldn't have known what to do with that sexuality. He didn't learn it from his friends like other kids his age; he got first-hand experience from his mother. A sick, perverted mother who controlled every aspect of his life. His sisters left him to his mother for years, knowing what she was doing to him and did nothing about it. I wish we could prosecute them but the statute of limitations doesn't allow it."

"What about the sisters? Were they able to give you any indication of where he might have gone? Some family vacation home, a place he'd always dreamed of going?" asked Cedar.

"Funny you should say that," said Charlie. "When I asked them if he had ever said where he might want to go if he had the chance, his response was very telling. He said to them, *Anywhere but here.*

"There were silent screams for help from Cal and no one could or wanted to hear them. You'd think his teachers would have noticed something was wrong with him. Victims of sexual abuse are often very promiscuous," said Cedar.

"We didn't get that from the teachers we talked to. It was just the opposite. Cal was quiet in class. Never had a girlfriend as far as they knew. He didn't lack for female attention, though, based on his looks. But he ignored them all. Kept to himself. A pattern of behavior he carried into adulthood," said Jared.

"What about the brother that killed his mother?" asked Cedar.

"He was adopted after Cal left for the military. He didn't know him, never even met him. He came back for the funerals because it was expected of him. Didn't say a word to his sisters. Just took the inheritance, served two tours and came back to settle here.

"Part of the FBI's investigation was looking into his service record. It was exemplary. We talked to his CO about Cal's time in Afghanistan. He was a fearless fighting machine, probably diverting pent-up anger intended for his mother to aggression towards the opposition forces. His kill record was the highest in his division, if you're interested in slightly disturbing statistics," said Cedar. "He learned survivalist skills over there, so he's well equipped to go underground."

"Do me a favor," said Jared. "See if there were any unsolved female murders either on the base or in the neighboring villages. See how far back his negative interaction with women goes. Look for strangulations. That's how he kills."

"Will do," said Cedar. "I also want to review with you what the forensic psychiatrist's evaluation showed. Based on the facts we gave him, here's what he said. Cal's domineering mother physically controlled him and his behavior up until the time he left her house. From that point on, her influence dictated his future behavior. His promiscuity lay dormant until her death, but once she was gone, his sexuality reached a peak. In a weird way, he couldn't perform with anyone else but his mother. When she died, his appetites were boundless. His rage against his mother was transferred to the women he kidnapped. He had sex with them, but it was always his mother that he saw. Taking the women and holding them captive was a natural progression of his behavior. He was in control, he was the dominant one. He could have sex on his terms, not on the woman's terms. When he tired of one girl, he killed her and got another. Every girl he killed was like having his mother die all over again and releasing him from her control. Here's the kicker. In cases like this, the subject will sometime start to hear voices, telling him what to do. In

Cal's case, his mother might still be talking to him in a negative way, almost like he was still a small child. His anger is still there and he will explode."

"Shit, I could almost feel sorry for him," said Jared.

"Sure, if you look past the rape, kidnapping and murder, my cousin's a great guy," said Charlie, sarcastically. "Cal had choices and he made the wrong ones. People do survive incest and he could have gotten help. He might never have lived a normal life, because he is damaged, but therapy could have prevented the awful things he did."

The room was silent as everyone processed Charlie's astute observation.

"Charlie, what else can you tell us about Cal?" Jared asked.

Charlie thought for a minute. "He was a real outdoorsman. Loved to work with his hands. Hunting, fishing, that sort of thing. He had a freezer full of game."

"That would tie into his survivalist training experience," said Cedar. "Let's circle back around to that in a minute. If there's nothing else about Cal, let's move on to Lauren. Jared, you're the best one to answer questions about her."

"Lauren was…is… smart. Fearless. A truly independent woman. But she has a soft side, too. I questioned her ex-husband about their marriage and he said they just drifted apart. He had an affair which was the reason they ended it. She came to Montana because she had fallen in love with the area while on vacation a few years ago. She was a book editor and could live anywhere so she ended up here. That was lucky for me," he said with sadness in his voice.

"Let's talk about why Cal would have taken Lauren instead of killing her. Jared, you might not want to hear this, but there could be an element of sex in his actions," said Cedar. "He was used to having women he could control, have sex with when it suited him."

"I talked to Tess about that," said Jared. "Once he kidnapped Lauren, the sex stopped. Lauren constantly berated him while she was being held captive. Taunted him about the fact that I was looking for her and he would be punished. In some weird way, she might remind him of his mother. He's attracted to her but repelled by her at the same time. I think he took her as a bargaining chip. If we close in on him, he'd use her as a hostage, hoping to get his freedom."

"I think you might be right about that. But I also think he panicked when we found Gaby Parmenter's body. He had food and supplies ready for an escape, but taking Lauren was probably a last-minute decision," said Charlie.

"So, let's try to get inside Cal's mind. What would be the hardest thing for him to do with Lauren in tow?" asked Cedar.

"Get very far. Unless he had some other vehicle stashed somewhere, all he had was the 4-wheeler for his escape. He couldn't carry much in it. Food, some tools, warm clothing, extra gas, maybe a chain saw," said Charlie.

"If that's the case, then let's assume he didn't go very far. His 4-wheeler holds about 12 gallons of gas. The mpg on that vehicle is somewhere in the 30-mile range. That gives him only 360 miles to work with. So, we draw a

360-mile circle around our location and start figuring out where he could have gone," said Jared.

"Jesus, that's pretty rugged terrain. We've searched a lot of that area already with no luck," said Charlie. "Now that the weather's turned cold, searching on foot will be brutal. The canopy is so thick that aerial searches would be mostly ineffective. We've still got 3 weeks of hunting season left, so that area is crawling with hunters."

"Why don't we use that to our advantage? I'll put up a $10,000 reward for anyone giving us information that leads to Cal's capture and arrest. Put up flyers everywhere. That way, we'll have a lot of eyes out there looking for Cal," said Jared.

"We can't let some rogue hunter try to capture Cal, though. We need a warning on the flyer that emphasizes not to approach him. He'll be armed and we don't want to endanger Lauren, if she's with him," Cedar cautioned. "Let's talk about Cal's survivalist training again. He'd need a food source, water source and some kind of shelter."

"I'll contact the BLM and get topographical maps of that whole area. It will show lakes and rivers, so we'll start in those areas. He's either built a cabin or found an abandoned one. Maybe even a seasonal hunter's cabin, but that might be dangerous. I'm guessing he'd look for one that's abandoned. Hell, he might have had one in mind. He's been hunting all over this area for years. It's a needle in a haystack, but we need to stay on this. My gut tells me he's relatively close by," said Jared.

The past five months had been hard for Jared. He did some legwork on his own, and the FBI taskforce researched Cal's military background, his electronic footprint and provided the forensic psychiatric profile. But the actual searching had been done by Charlie's team. This was Montana, covered by rugged wilderness and thousands of places where a person could hide, undetected. They had done what they could with limited resources, but the search had been directionless.

Without knowing which direction Cal had taken, they had taken the paths of least resistance. Now that they'd met and honed their focus, used an intelligent foundation for the search methodology, they were going to have to climb in elevation, hit the deep woods and cover only those places most likely to contain the elements Cal would need to survive. A lot of work had been done in 5 months. But it was mostly eliminating possibilities instead of exploring possibilities. He couldn't feel guilty about that. It was all part of the process. But now they were at the point where they had a plan based on smart thinking, probability equations and dogged determination.

Chapter 38

She recovered from the spider bite quickly and life resumed at the cabin. Still needing firewood, they had managed to make up for lost time by focusing on dead trees closer to the cabin. Cal had been hesitant at first about clearing those trees that sheltered them from not only the wind, but from prying aerial eyes. But without layers of warm winter clothes, the dropping temperatures were making it dangerous for them to be in the elements for any length of time.

Not having to go so far into the woods each time they hauled a load significantly reduced their downtime between loads and their exposure to extreme cold. She was able to get closer to the loads with the 4-wheeler since many of the trees surrounding the cabin had been culled. Because the 4-wheeler carried three times the pallet's load, she could unload the wood to the woodpile and Cal would already have another load ready by the time she got back to the site.

Two trees that bordered the outhouse were dead and in danger of causing damage to the cabin if they had to fight a strong, wintery wind. Cal said the wind would win. She was impressed, but didn't show it, by his ability to cut wedges in the trees so precisely, that the trees fell exactly where he intended. Under any other circumstance or with any other man, she would have been quick to praise him. But she couldn't let her guard down around him.

It was awkward, the time they spent together. She knew she was looking at a rapist and a murderer, but he was necessary for her survival. She had expected him to be

184

much crueler, to assault her or to torture her in any number of ways. But none of that happened. He had kept to himself, focused on the tasks that would keep them protected, warm and well fed. She wondered what would happen when they were snowed in, unable to see the sun for days. Would he change, revert to his former persona, rape her? She didn't want to think about it.

She and Cal were loading the last of the wood when she heard gunshots. Instinctively, she hoped it was Jared coming to rescue her, firing rounds to let her know he was coming.

"Hunters," Cal said, dashing her hopes. "They're getting closer, but still pretty far away. Hunting season's over in 3 days and they'll be heading back down the mountain, not up to where we are. Don't think we need to panic."

The next morning, the sun was out and the temperature had risen to 60 degrees. Lauren had spotted a filbert tree a short distance from the cabin and decided to pick as many as she could to add to their food supply. She just hoped the birds and squirrels hadn't demolished the bounty.

Cal was already up when she woke. Her first chore every morning was to make breakfast, which had become routine. While the oatmeal simmered, she fantasized about rescue or escape. She was fine with either one. Cal's footsteps on the porch brought her out of her thoughts and back to stark reality.

"There's a filbert tree over by the spring. I thought I'd see if they were ready to pick," she said as he walked through the door, carrying his rifle. She found herself using short sentences with him. Just give him the facts and move on.

"Fine, but come right back when you're done."

He appeared skittish and he saw the puzzled look on her face. "Saw some signs of hunters closer than I'd like," he said.

Her heart soared but she tried to keep a placid face. Would they find them? Rescue her? "Does that mean we'll have to leave here?"

He caressed his rifle while he looked at her. "No, I can take care of them."

Her heart sank. She had hoped the killing was over, but she reminded herself that Cal was dangerous. If the hunters somehow found them, he would shoot them before they had a chance to raise their rifles. He knew these woods, knew from which direction they were most likely to appear. And he'd be waiting for them.

She was sick of being here, couldn't imagine spending the whole winter here with him. She had been complacent and pliable because she was learning. Learning how to survive as she planned her escape.

She had been using her brain and her survival instinct to stockpile food, water and a way to keep herself warm. While Cal was hunting, she was gathering and drying moss that would be a warm insulator when she stuffed it inside the lining of her lightweight jacket. She made rice and oatmeal cakes that, when dried, would be an instant source of energy. She was careful to take only a handful of matches so Cal wouldn't miss them. And she grabbed nails. She didn't know how she would use them, but instinctively knew they would be invaluable. Finally, she wrapped everything in a small piece of plastic sheeting and concealed the bundle in a hidden opening under an outcropping near the cabin. It would be waiting for her when the opportunity came for her to run.

Cal, of course, would not expect her to run. He underestimated her desire to return to her normal life, which was his first mistake. He also assumed she was too afraid of him to even attempt an escape. But she knew it was only a matter of time before things would change. He was damaged and a man. Once they were snowbound, he would revert to his former behavior and he would assault her. She would leave today.

Chapter 39

Jared and Charlie spent days huddled over the land maps they'd obtained from the BLM. The U.S. Forest Service had also provided them with a list of the ranger outlooks in that area, both active and abandoned. When they cross-referenced them, they found 4 possibilities based on resources available and potential shelter. Each location was within the 360-mile radius parameter the team had previously set.

They met in the conference room Monday morning after working over the weekend to select, check and double check their choices.

"Hey, did you get any sleep?" Charlie asked, two cups of coffee teetering precariously in a holder while he balanced a bag of bagels. He put them down on the table without incident and handed one cup to Jared.

"I got a couple of hours," Jared said. "I'll sleep when I find Lauren." He paused, the first glimmer of hope on his face. "I think we're on the right track here. I called Glenn Cedar this morning and ran everything by him and he thought so, too. I thought we'd get a team assigned to each location. Cedar will provide boots on the ground if we need them. I want to do an aerial search of each location first. Look for signs of activity, wood smoke, anything that might indicate people have been in the area. We might run into hunters, but we'll eliminate them and move on."

"I know you're being pulled from two directions. Have you talked to your supervisor about coming back on board with us? I know you've only been able to work weekends on this, but we need you."

"Once the aerial searches have been done and we've pinpointed the most likely possibility, I'll be on that team. My supervisor has been impressed by the progress I've made on the cold cases and he understands I might need to take some time if any of these searches pan out. I'll be more than ready."

"We'll need to use the FBI on this one. We don't have the manpower to search all 4 locations at once. Plus, the threat of snow will seriously impact our ability to move very quickly. We're talking major blizzard conditions almost daily once the snow hits.

If Cal and Lauren are at one of these locations, they'll be hunkered down for the duration. Cal will feel pretty safe. That's when we might catch him by surprise," Charlie said.

"Maybe, but I wouldn't underestimate him. And he'll still have Lauren as a bargaining chip. I don't give a fuck if he gets away. I just want Lauren safe."

"I don't want to say this, but Lauren might not be the same woman you knew. There's no way of knowing what Cal has done to her. What head games he's played."

"I know. I've thought of that, but we'll deal with whatever has happened together. Nothing can make me stop loving her. Nothing."

When Jared left to follow up on a lead on one of his cold cases, Charlie arranged with Search and Rescue to do flyovers of the four pinpointed locations. The pilots knew this area after years of rescuing hikers and injured campers. And their helicopters could get closer to the ground than a small plane.

If they were going to find Cal and Lauren, they needed eyes in the sky.

Chapter 40

He and his brother, Neil, might never have seen the poster if Neil hadn't eaten fiery Mexican food and been forced to race to the nearest convenience store bathroom. While Neil took care of business, Darryl walked up and down the aisles, his impatience growing. They were already getting a late start this hunting season. And now this delay.

Grabbing a six pack, he approached the cashier, noticed the $10,000 reward for someone named Cal Morgan who had kidnapped a decidedly hot older chick, Lauren Sedgeway.

"What's the deal with this guy?" Darryl said, pointing to the poster. "Did they find him or the woman yet?"

"Nope, not as far as I know. The woman's boyfriend put up the reward, figuring hunters might run into Cal up in the mountains. He's already killed a couple of women so he's dangerous. You wouldn't want to confront him, if you value your life. He's one sick bastard."

Neil, a look of relief on his face, joined his brother at the front counter. Forgetting the poster, Darryl paid for the beer, waited while Neil hit the snack aisle and yelled to his brother when his patience ran out.

"Neil, come on man, we're burning daylight. Let's get the hell out of here."

"Ok, ok," he said as he returned with an armful of snacks, paid for them and met his brother at the fully packed truck they had parked outside the convenience store.

He and his brother looked forward to this trip every year. They went high in the mountains where most other hunters found the terrain too treacherous. But it was worth it. They didn't have to compete with other hunters for elk at that elevation and came home every year with a truck full of game, ready for the freezer. Darryl was an expert with the crossbow and they hunted for small game as they climbed, preferring to eat fresh game over an open fire rather than canned beans or jerky. They could kill and dress the meat quickly, working together, and often made extra money selling any excess meat. Fresh elk or moose could fetch $30 a pound and they'd made an easy $900 the year before.

Neil hunted with a rifle and as former military, was a crack shot. Darryl liked using the crossbow because it challenged him, requiring him to approach the prey silently and stealthily. He was often able to look into the animal's eyes as he made the kill shot.

Cal Morgan would never forget the Lazarus brothers.

Chapter 41

Lauren knew it was time to leave. She was scared but determined. After the day of picking nuts, she had taken a nap, preparing for the night that was ahead of her. Adrenaline was now keeping her awake. She decided to leave as soon as she knew Cal was asleep for the night. If she could get a four or five-hour head start on him she might be able to get just far enough to reach some sort of civilization, and a possible rescue. She also knew that if he caught up to her, she'd be dead.

She had watched as he left to go to the next ridge, the wood smoke he had seen causing concern. While he was gone, she added nuts to her food supply and decided which route she would take that night. She tried to think as Cal would think when making her selection. She knew he would expect her to take the shortest route down the mountain, figuring she wouldn't get very far without food and warm clothing. She started walking that route, which he never used, until she was 100 yards from the cabin. She then retraced her steps, walking backwards in her own tracks until she ended up where she started. It was exhausting.

Tonight, she would take the southwest direction, heading towards the area where Cal had seen the wood smoke, but cover her tracks as Cal had, using a pine bough to erase any trace of her. He would follow the tracks she had left behind, losing time as he realized he'd reached a dead end. He would take the southwest direction next and would find her tracks eventually, but hopefully, not find her.

As she listened for Cal's regular breathing and the slight snore that indicated he was finally in a deep sleep, she cautiously moved about the cabin, gathering what she could to take with her. The blanket off her makeshift bed, Cal's jacket that he had left on a chair, a small knife she tucked in her boot and the flashlight. Wait, where was the flashlight? She had seen Cal put it on the small table and now it was gone. Fuck! How was she going to make it down the mountain if she couldn't see where she was going? The full moon illumination would help, but the darkness would slow her down. She didn't have a choice. She had to leave tonight. Snow was coming, Cal had said. If she waited until the snow, she would have no chance of survival. No matter how well she had prepared, snow would kill her.

As she made her way out of the cabin, she moved to the woodpile. While Cal had been gone, she had hidden her bundle behind the pile and up against the cabin wall. Two large pieces of wood had covered it, and she quickly lifted them away, revealing her survival gear. She had made an adaptation of the bundle in preparation for her journey down the mountain. Using a piece of rope, she had fashioned a makeshift backpack out of her bundle so that she could carry it down the mountain with ease. Having to hold it would exhaust her and she wouldn't get far. She needed her hands free.

Grabbing the pine bough that she had left at the side of the cabin, she began her careful departure away from the structure, away from Cal. Shit, it was cold, she thought, as she wrapped the blanket more tightly around her. She didn't have a hat, so the blanket was the only way to cover her head, saving precious body heat. As she dragged the bough behind her, all traces of her disappeared. She was on her way.

It was slower going than she had expected. Panic came and went but determination prevailed. She thought of Jared, of a future with him and she plodded on. She heard small animal sounds that were somehow comforting. She was not alone out here. She was on high alert for the sound of the 4-wheeler, meaning Cal had discovered her escape. But as the hours dragged on, she heard nothing. As the sun started to rise, she headed for a high spot that might reveal signs of the wood smoke, and perhaps, her salvation. When she reached it, she dropped her pack and climbed to a higher vantage point. That's when she saw it. The wood smoke coming from what she figured was a hunter's cabin. Exhilarated, she knew the trek would be hard. It was still miles away.

As the sun rose, Cal awoke with a full bladder. He left his room and was headed to the outhouse when he saw that Lauren was not on the sofa. Damn, she was using it. He'd have to wait. He stoked the fire while he waited for her return, added a couple of logs and made coffee. When she hadn't returned after 10 minutes, his mother's voice grabbed his attention, causing a roiling in his stomach.

She's gone, you stupid idiot. You thought you had her under control? Guess again. She's been planning this a long time. Probably halfway to civilization by now. You know what that means. They'll be coming for you.

Rage filled him. As he realized his mother was probably right, he forced himself to temper the rage and think about his next move. He had to find her. How far could she have gotten? He instantly chastised himself for giving her so much freedom. He never expected her to try to escape. She seemed to accept their life here, never causing him any trouble. She was always where she said she was going, and always came back. How had he let himself become so complacent? He realized she had been planning this escape all along. Preparing for it. Letting him think he still controlled her. While all the time she had been playing him for a fool. That was about to end.

Suddenly, he thought of the 4-wheeler. Had she taken it? As he raced to find out, he stopped. No, he still had the key in his pocket. She was on foot. He stood on the porch, carefully calculating which direction she would take. When he made his decision, he turned to walk back inside the cabin and prepare for his journey. Food, water, and, of course, his firearms. She would not get away again.

When he was finished loading the 4-wheeler, he walked in the direction he assumed Lauren had taken, looking for footprints. He found them. This was going to be easier than he thought. It would be tough to maneuver the 4-wheeler through the dense forest and if he had to, he'd make the rest of the journey on foot. He had the advantage. Food, water, a way to make a fire, and of course, the weapons that would bring her back under his control. She had taken his jacket, leaving him at a disadvantage, but he had extra blankets with him. He wasn't sure how much of a head start she had on him, but the wheeler would close the distance gap pretty quickly. It had taken them 4 days to get to the cabin's location and she'd only been gone 3, maybe 4 hours. Civilization was days away on foot. He would find her long before she found someone to help her.

Killer Looks

He maneuvered the wheeler through the path she had taken. It was slow going but her tracks were easy to find. About 100 yards from the cabin, her footprints disappeared. What the fuck? He continued in the same direction for another half hour, hoping to see them reappear. They didn't. She had tricked him. As he doubled back to the cabin, he decided she had probably gone in a southwest direction, the only other logical choice. On foot, he walked the trail he assumed she'd taken and sure enough, her footsteps appeared about 50 yards in. She was smart, but not smart enough. He was coming for her.

Lauren knew the direction she would take to get to the hunter's cabin, but cold and hunger were wearing her down. If she was going to make it to the cabin, she needed food and water and warmth. She unwrapped her bundle and took out the oatmeal cakes and a bottle of spring water. She then grabbed the moss and started stuffing it between her clothes and her lightweight jacket. It didn't help much, but at the least, it insulated her from the wind. She gathered some dead branches and started a fire with one of the precious matches. Soon, with a full stomach and a respite from the cold, she was ready to get underway. She made sure the fire was completely out, loaded her now lighter bundle on her back and headed down the mountain.

She had walked about 3 miles when she heard a sound. Tendrils of fear grabbed at her heart, stopping her in her tracks. The 4-wheeler. No, it was coming from the sky. As she looked up, she saw a helicopter flying overhead, low, just over the tops of the trees. Instinct told her to race toward it, wave her arms, shout I'm here, I'm here, but just as quickly as it had come, it was gone. The pounding of her heart subsided, and tears began to flow. OK, so they didn't see you. But at least they were looking in the right direction. If she could find a clearing, she'd make the biggest "L" she could with branches and pine boughs. If they came back around, they would be sure to see it. But there were no clearings and she just plodded on, stopping for food and water and to empty her bladder. All of the walking was keeping her warm, but she didn't want to get overheated and start to sweat. Her body would cool, and once night came, she risked getting hypothermia. So, she moved slowly through the forest, fighting the desire to run towards rescue.

She knew Cal was behind her, already on her trail. The 4-wheeler would help him for a while, but the trail she had taken was too dense with trees for the vehicle to manage for very long. He was probably already on foot and closing in on her. She was exhausted and needed to stop for the night. She felt like she was still headed towards the hunter's cabin, but wanted a confirmation. There were no high spots in this part of the forest, just trees. She figured the only way she could get at higher vantage point was to climb one of these trees. The thought of it terrified her. What if she fell? What if she couldn't get high enough to see the hunter's cabin. She hadn't climbed a tree since she was a kid.

Oh, what the hell, she thought. She found an aspen that seemed to have some sturdy branches strong enough to hold her and she began her climb. Pine trees grew higher, but the branches were so dense that it would be impossible for her to get very far. No, the aspen would have to work. As she climbed, holding on for dear life, the forested terrain gradually receded and she could see the hunter's cabin. She had been off in her direction a few degrees and would have bypassed the cabin without seeing it if she had stayed on the same trajectory. She was glad she had double checked, even as she shakily descended the tree.

She looked for a possible location to bed down for the night. She wanted the wind at her back and decided to build a lean-to out of pine boughs between two trees. She also placed boughs on the ground to keep her off the cold forest floor as she slept. She built a fire, ate and drank, and exhausted, drifted off to sleep.

When she opened her eyes, it was already light. She had slept too long. Instinct told her that Cal was not far behind her and she needed to move. She quickly doused the fire, gathered up her bundle and headed out after relieving herself of the previous day's food and water. *Aspen leaves were a surprising substitute for TP*, she thought.

She was perhaps a half a mile away from the cabin, when she heard twigs snap behind her. Panicked, she started running, screaming as she ran, hoping the hunter was nearby. She'd only taken 20 steps when Cal suddenly appeared from behind a tree, directly in her path of escape, and pointed a gun at her. She fell to her knees, sobs wracking her body. She had come so far, survived this long, only to see her life end just a few hundred yards from possible rescue.

"I trusted you," he spat. "I kept you fed, warm and untouched. And this is how you repay me? By leaving me?"

By leaving him? What was he saying? She wasn't leaving him, she was running away from him. Trying to get back to the life she had before. With Jared. She had seriously misjudged him, his psyche. He had some twisted idea that they were a couple. She had to use that to save her life.

Chapter 42

With the flyovers scheduled for that morning, Jared struggled to concentrate on anything else. But he had interviews to conduct and files to review so he immersed himself in the two new cases that had been sent to him. Charlie would call him as soon as he got the reports from the pilots.

Working from his home office, he was surprised when his doorbell rang. A quick look out the front window of his remodeled 60's ranch, revealed Charlie standing at his door.

"I thought you'd call," Jared said as he let Charlie in.

"I know, but I think we might have found where Cal and Lauren have been staying and I wanted to give you the details in person."

"Whatcha got? Jared casually asked over his shoulder as he went to retrieve the BLM and Forest Service maps from his desk. He returned with them and laid them on the dining room table, where he could spread out. His hands were shaking and Charlie could tell he was struggling to maintain a professional demeanor.

"OK, here's where they might be," Charlie said, pointing to a site on the map about 100 miles from town. "It's pretty remote because of the treacherous terrain. It's an old Forest Service cabin that's been abandoned for years, but it looks like some trees on the property have been cut down recently and there's a wood pile by the cabin. We flew over it before when Lauren first went missing, but the tree cover didn't give us any visibility."

"We've also got this possibility," he said, pointing to a site on the map about 300 miles out, just over the border into Washington state. "This one sits right on a creek, but it has an impassible road leading to it. Shows signs of recent activity. I did a records search on it and it's owned by a woman in California. I talked to her right before I left the station and found out there's not supposed to be anyone living there. She inherited it from her grandfather years ago and has never even seen the place. Either it's squatters or it could be Cal. So, we really need to go to both places. If it's squatters at the second place, they need to be removed."

"How close can we get to each location by helicopter?" Jared asked.

"The trees are going to make it difficult for a helicopter to land unless there's a sizeable clearing nearby. I think we can put a helicopter down within 5 miles of the first cabin," he said, pointing to a location on the map. "The second one is a little trickier, because of where it's located. See these mountain ranges?" he said as he pointed to the map. "We've got some serious crosswinds and it will be difficult to maneuver a chopper close to the location. The good news is that there are forest service roads that meander all through there, so instead, we can access the cabin by truck. It'll be a 6 or 7-hour timeframe before we can get to the location, though. Some of the roads are a little sketchy, so we may end up having to bring in ATVs, too."

"What can we do to get the ball rolling on this?" asked Jared.

"Already got it covered. Depending on the weather, we'll have the chopper ready to fly to the first location by tomorrow. Still working on manpower for that one. Cedar's sending a team to assist us with the second location. If Cal and Lauren are there, Cal will be arrested for kidnapping. Guess we'll figure out the other charges once we have him in custody."

"And if it's squatters?" Jared asked.

"We'll work with local authorities to arrest the squatters if that turns out to be the case." Charlie said, pausing before forming his next thought. "I guess you've got a decision to make. Where will you be tomorrow?"

"I've already alerted my supervisor and I'd like to be on the chopper. Logic tells me that instead of distance, Cal chose to head to the high country. If Cal and Lauren are found at the second location, she'll need to be taken to a hospital to be checked out. God knows what he's done to her. I'll get there as soon as I can."

"So, I guess we have a plan, then," said Charlie.

"Yup. One way or another, we'll have some answers."

Chapter 43

He heard the scream that punctured the quiet stillness of early morning. As he tried to determine its direction, he grabbed his crossbow and ran. His brother was still not back from his overnight hunt, but he knew the scream wasn't his. It was a woman. Shit, what was a woman doing out here? Hunting? Lost? Injured?

As he ran in the direction of the scream, the noise suddenly stopped. He could hear a man's voice, not a woman's. Confused, he slowed to a walk, then to cautious steps until he could see the tableau playing out before him. A woman was kneeling on the ground in front of the man connected to the masculine voice he had heard. She was sobbing, a look of abject fear on her face, but defiance in her eyes as she raised her head to look at the man as he spoke.

"I trusted you," the man spat. "I kept you fed, warm and untouched. And this is how you repay me? By leaving me?"

What was this, a lover's spat? No, it was more than that. The man was holding a gun on the woman. This shit was getting serious and he knew he'd have to do something.

As he stepped into the scene, his crossbow raised and aimed at Cal, he spoke.

"Buddy, I don't know what's going on here, but you need to put that gun down."

Startled, Cal turned his pistol in the direction of the man's voice and fired. He missed. The man had quickly moved behind a tree, pivoted and aimed for Cal. As the man released the projectile, he watched as it hit Cal in the upper chest, just below the shoulder. Not a kill shot, but he would need medical care. He watched as Cal fell to the ground, dropped the pistol, and let out a bellow of pain. Cal's hand instinctively went to cover the wound, and he stared at his attacker in disbelief as he nonchalantly leaned over and pulled out the arrow, causing Cal to scream in pain.

"What the fuck?" Cal moaned.

"You tried to shoot **me,** you son of a bitch! I was only trying to keep you from hurting this woman," he said, his eyes locked on Lauren. "Are you alright?" he said to her, as he stooped to pick up Cal's gun.

"Only if you get me out of here. He's been keeping me in a cabin a few miles up the mountain. I was able to escape and headed toward a cabin near here. I saw wood smoke and hoped to find someone to help me. Do you have a cell phone I can use?" Lauren asked.

The man laughed. "You won't get cell service up here. Still too far from any cell towers."

"I've got to get in touch with the sheriff's office. I know they're looking for me."

His eyes squinted and a sudden realization came over him. This was the guy on the poster and that woman. He had all but forgotten about them. But not about the $10,000 reward. He would bet that they didn't know anything about the reward. A new idea hit him. If someone was willing to pay $10,000, he bet they'd pay more. A chance to make some real money and it had fallen right into his lap.

"Let's get you both back to my cabin. We need to get that wound dressed or this guy's gonna lose a lot of blood. We've got plenty of food and firewood. My brother, Neil, took the truck to hunt for small game last night, but he should be back soon. We can get you both in the truck and down the mountain tomorrow."

"Thank you so much," said Lauren, as she started to cry. "I was beginning to lose hope, Mr.," she said, unsure what to call him.

"My name's Darryl Lazarus. My brother and I come up to our cabin every year about this time to hunt. First time we've come across human targets, though." He looked at her and produced a small laugh, unnerving her. She needed to be on her guard. Something was strange about this guy. But what choice did she have but to go with him?

She helped Cal to the cabin, while Darryl kept the gun pointed at him. Cal was weak, but it looked like the bleeding had slowed. In 10 minutes, they were at the cabin, Cal was lying on a small cot and she had a pan of warm water and was cleansing the wound. The first aid kit had a couple of butterfly bandages, which she applied after covering the wound with antibacterial cream. If he needed more than that, he'd have to wait until they were back in Wildwood.

"Would you like some breakfast?" Darryl asked Lauren. "I've got coffee and biscuits."

"Yes, thank you. Could I have some of that drinking water for Cal? He might not be hungry, but he needs fluids."

"I'll get him some after we eat. Looks like he passed out anyway."

She looked over at Cal and saw that he was asleep or passed out, frowns of pain evident on his face. As much as she wanted to be away from him, she didn't want him suffering.

She heard a truck horn and she guessed Darryl's brother was back from his hunting trip. As she started to rise from her seat, Darryl barked at her. "You stay here. I'll be right back."

She sat back down, startled by his gruffness, but as he exited the cabin with crossbow in hand, she ran to the small window and peered out. Darryl was standing by the driver's window of the truck, leaning in to talk to the man she assumed was his brother. Occasionally he would look towards the cabin, laugh and then slap his crossbow.

Something was definitely wrong. She could sense she had gone from one bad situation to another. At least with Cal, she knew what she had. With these two strangers, she no longer felt safe or any closer to going home.

Chapter 44

The brother entered the cabin with Darryl. He carried a shotgun and a pistol on his hip along with a string of rabbits.

"Lauren, this is my brother Neil. He's up to speed on the situation and we both know what we have to do. Let's get that breakfast and you can tell me about this guy," he said, pointing to Cal. Cal continued to moan in pain, but he seemed to be going in and out of consciousness.

As she watched the brothers move about the cabin, a cold chill spread over her. Darryl had called her Lauren. She didn't remember giving him her name or Cal's. How would he know it? Had he seen a news report? Were there posters with her picture on it stapled to telephone poles? It freaked her out. He somehow had the upper hand, knowledge of her situation before she even told him about it.

Neil placed a cup of coffee and a biscuit in front of her, urging her to eat. Her stomach was in knots but she took a sip of the coffee. He looked her up and down, slowly, then spoke.

"So, tell us about this guy. Darryl says he was holding you at a cabin up the mountain? Must be one of those old Forest Service ones. How'd you get hooked up with him?"

She decided to tell him as little as she could get away with. "Just in the wrong place at the wrong time, I guess."

"You his sex slave or something?"

"Actually, he hasn't touched me. We've been companions of a sort. Now that he's incapacitated, and you boys are bringing me home, it doesn't matter anymore.

"Yeah, about that. Me and Darryl want that reward money."

"Reward money?" So that was it, she thought. There's a reward for her return or maybe it's for Cal's capture. "I didn't realize there was a reward."

"Seems your boyfriend wants you back so he put up a $10,000 reward. Darryl saw the poster on our way up the mountain. Didn't think twice about it until he saw you both in the woods. The way we figure it, if your boyfriend is willing to put up that much, he might just find us a little more. Darryl and I have had some money woes and you and that man over there's gonna make us flush again. Nothin' personal."

She just stared at him. Gave him a blank look, but inside, her brain was careening through several scenarios. None of them good. No matter what happened, they wouldn't let her go. She'd seen them, could identify them. They'd get their money, be on the run, leaving her and Cal dead.

"You two are going to be our guests for a little while longer," Darryl joined in. "We got a little negotiatin' to do with your boyfriend. Until we get back, sorry to say we have to tie you up. Wouldn't do us any good, you two running away from us and messin' up our payday."

Dejected, she watched as Darryl pulled a length of rope out of a utility bag on the floor, cut it in 4 shorter lengths and began to bind Cal's legs and then his hands. Cal didn't move.

"Sit in this chair," Darryl said as he moved it next to the cot. He then tied Lauren's legs and hands and reaching into his pocket, he pulled out a cell phone.

"Just a quick picture of you two and your boyfriend will know we mean business," he said to her as he took a series of photos. "Once we're down the mountain, we'll drop this burner phone at the sheriff's office with a note asking for $100,000. You're worth that, right?"

"He doesn't have that kind of money, you idiot. He's a DCI agent."

That stopped Darryl right where he stood. *Shit, a cop. That could make this plan more difficult to pull off,* he thought.

"Neil," he yelled to his brother who was outside the cabin. Neil heard his brother and quickly responded.

"What's up?" he said as he entered the cabin.

"The woman's boyfriend is a cop".

"Well, shit," Neil said as he walked to stand in front of Lauren. He bent down, his eyes level with hers. "That makes this whole thing harder, but still doable."

She watched as an evil smirk appeared on his face, then flinched as he stroked her cheek. Instinctively, she pulled away. He laughed at her.

"We might just have a little fun with you when we get back. Knock you down a peg or two. See if the boyfriend likes damaged goods," Neil said.

Bile rose in her throat, and her body reacted with a shiver of revulsion. She was in trouble.

As the brothers left the cabin to begin their trip down the mountain, Lauren struggled with her bonds. It was no use. They were too tight and her attempt to free herself resulted in huge welts on her wrists, and bleeding.

Cal was her only way out.

"Cal, wake up. Cal, wake UP!"

He stirred and attempted to open his eyes. He moaned in pain.

"Cal, these fuckers are going to kill us if we don't get out of here, now! I need you to help me get out of these ropes."

Cal raised his head and looked at her, attempting to focus and noticing his bonds.

"Listen to me. The guy who shot you knows who we are. Jared posted a $10,000 reward and he and his brother are trying to collect on it. They're on their way down the mountain to try to extort $100,000 from Jared, using us as hostages. Cal, once they get the money, we're expendable. I've seen them. Can identify them. Are you listening?" she screamed at him.

Chapter 45

How could it all have gone so wrong? They'd talked about the possibilities. Gloated over the idea of big money for a change. Once they had the money, they'd head over the border into Canada, then up to Alaska. Get lost up there.

That damned tweaker had fucked it up. Just a simple task. Get paid to drop off the burner phone and the note for the boyfriend inside the door of the police station, then get the hell out of there. But a cop recognized him, knew there was an arrest warrant for him for intent to distribute, and grabbed the kid before he could leave. When the kid didn't return right away for the rest of his payment, the brothers decided to do a quick drive-by. The kid was just standing there, outside the police station, his head down.

"Man," yelled Neil from the passenger side of the truck. "What the fuck are you doing? You were supposed to drop it and run. Get the hell out of here!"

The kid raised his head, shrugged and said "Sorry, dude."

A handful of cops, guns drawn, approached the vehicle from behind and ordered them out of the truck. Neil grabbed his shotgun, started firing out the window at the cops who ran for cover as Darryl sped away. In the rear-view mirror, Darryl could see two patrol vehicles fast approaching.

"Neil, they're on us! Get the tires, the windshields. Stop those sons of bitches!" Darryl yelled.

Killer Looks

Out of the corner of his left eye, but too late, Neil saw a motorcycle cop pull out of a side street, running parallel to the truck. As Neil fired at the patrol vehicles behind him, the MHP officer ordered him to drop the weapon. When he leveled his shotgun at the officer, the officer took aim and fired. The last thing Neil heard before his head exploded, was his brother's voice. "Damn, I think he killed you."

Darryl, with his brother's dead body lying on the seat next to him, swerved toward the motorcycle, sending it and the officer careening into a stand of trees. One of the patrol vehicles stopped to help the officer, but the other was still in pursuit. Darryl couldn't outrun him, but he could outfox him.

Up ahead, he saw the turn he'd been looking for and, downshifting, made it with ease. Immediately, two forks presented themselves and he took the one on the left. About 100 yards in, there was a collapsed pavement, covered by water. It didn't look dangerous, but it was deep and Darryl knew that a patrol car would bottom out and break an axle. In his 4-wheel drive truck, he could maneuver around it. He circumvented it and 30 seconds later, could see the patrol vehicle closing in behind him, lights and sirens engaged. It was now or never, Darryl thought, and the officer hit the water going close to 60 mph. Looking in his rear-view mirror, Darryl saw that it was as if a giant hand had grabbed the vehicle, lifted the back end and dropped it down again. It was, literally, dead in the water. The officer, stunned, his gun drawn and fully aware of the danger he was in, tried to use his radio to call for back up. A shotgun blast stopped him mid-sentence.

There was dead silence. Only the blue lights remained flashing. Darryl knew his life as he had known it was over. His brother was dead, he was responsible for the probable deaths of two cops and was facing a death sentence if he was caught.

His only bargaining chip were his two hostages. The cops would go to his trailer looking for him, but by then he'd be up the mountain and at the cabin. He didn't care about Cal, but the woman, well, she was his ticket to freedom.

Chapter 46

Jared was at the airstrip watching the search and rescue helicopter making its approach. He had spoken to Cedar earlier that morning and confirmed that his team was on the move by caravan to the second location. He was anxious to get to the first. His cell phone rang and he was surprised when he looked at the caller ID.

"Charlie, you just caught me. The helicopter is setting down now and I'm ready to leave."

"Jared," Charlie said. "There's been a new development. It's too much to go into over the phone. Head back here now. The chopper will wait."

"What are you talking about? What's more important than getting to Lauren?"

"Jared, it is about Lauren. Please, just get here."

Jared sped back to the station, his heart racing. Was Lauren dead? Injured? What was this new development? He brought his car to a screeching halt outside the station, ran inside and found Charlie.

Charlie was in the interrogation room with a strung out tweaker. When he saw the confusion on Jared's face, he motioned him to sit down, said he'd explain everything.

"Jared, this is Lyle Strand. Mr. Strand here has been our guest before, but today he showed up at the station, unaware that he had an outstanding warrant."

Jared was angry and it showed on his face. "I don't give a fuck about this piece of shit. What's going on?"

Charlie pulled a burner phone out of his pocket and slid it across the table to Jared. When he looked down at the picture on the screen, he saw Lauren, her hands and feet tied, and an obviously injured Cal, seemingly unconscious, and likewise bound.

"And there's this," Charlie said, sliding a piece of paper towards Jared.

To the boyfriend,

We have found the two people you are looking for and would like to claim the reward. We think it's a little small, so we're asking for $100,000 instead. You'll hear from us again with details.

Jared just stared at both the phone and the note, trying to process what he was seeing.

"Is this the guy who has them?" Jared said, pointing at Strand.

"No, but he delivered the phone and the note this morning. Officer Malcolm was on the desk and recognized him. Knew there was a warrant for his arrest so grabbed him before he could leave. Gave up two guys that paid him to deliver the package. He was supposed to meet up with them for his final half of the payment, and when he didn't return, they swung by the station looking for him. They must have thought he had taken the money and run. We had him stand outside, and when they pulled up, we had officers waiting."

"What the hell?" Jared said.

"There were two of them, brothers, and once they saw us approach, the one in the passenger seat started firing at us. The officers ran for cover, and we sent two patrol cars after them. A motorcycle cop took out one of the brothers, but the other one forced him off the road and he was killed. One of the patrol officers had eyes on him and followed him down a forest service road. The fucker ambushed and killed him, then took off."

"So, this killer has Lauren?"

"I'm afraid so. She's his leverage. He's probably on his way to where he has her and Cal. He'll try to use her as his ticket to freedom. But he's got nothing to lose now. He could kill again."

"Who are these brothers?" Jared asked.

"The Lazarus brothers. They've been in here a few times for drunk and disorderly. The older brother, Darryl, served about two years for breaking and entering. Low level criminals. Always down on their luck and looking for a big score. But the killing of two officers just made them a target for law enforcement across the state. We've got their pictures plastered all over the media." Charlie continued.

"They were both dressed in hunting gear, so we figure they must have somehow found Cal and Lauren up the mountain, just where we anticipated they might be. Probably out hunting and either stumbled on them or went looking for them. A clerk at the convenience store on Market street remembers seeing the brothers. One of them asked about the reward, and then they took off. These guys aren't criminal masterminds, so my guess is they somehow stumbled on them and decided to take advantage of the situation. We sent a team to their last known address, with no luck. We think the brother that was shooting at our officers might be dead or badly injured so that might slow them down. Either way, they know they're dead meat when we find them."

"Which means Lauren is even more important to them. Any idea where they were headed?" Jared asked.

"Based on the tire tracks, we've already got a team of officers on trails leading west. Cedar's men are on their way back to help in the search. The chopper will take you and me back up to the original site where we thought Cal and Lauren might be and the others will meet us there. We can then fan out in teams, and find them. We *will* find them," Charlie said, reassuringly.

"Lauren has to be scared to death already. Now that they're hunted criminals, she's going to be the only one standing between us and their freedom. Cal's expendable at this point, especially if he's injured. If he gets to Lauren and they have to run, he'll leave a dead Cal behind."

"I agree," said Charlie.

"We're wasting time. Let's do this," said Jared as he and Charlie jumped in the SUV and raced to the airfield, fierce determination on their faces.

Hang in there, baby. Just hang in there, Jared thought.

Chapter 47

Cal could hear his mother yelling his name. All he wanted to do was sleep. He fought to stay asleep but her voice, that insidious voice, wouldn't give up. He was in pain, a searing burn in his shoulder and the pain was rousing him. He heard his mother's voice again. No, not his mother, Lauren. He struggled to open his eyes and saw her next to him tied to a chair. He was on a small cot, his hands and feet tied and a bandage over his shoulder. Had she done that? What happened? Where were they?

"Cal, thank God you're awake. Listen to me. We need to get out of here. You've got to help me get out of these ropes. If you don't, we are going to die."

Cal raised his head and looked at her, trying to bring her into better focus. What the hell was she talking about?

"Cal, focus! Two brothers found us near their hunting cabin. That's where we are now. They shot at you, grazed your shoulder. You've been out of it. Jared has a reward out for me and they found out about it. They're trying to get more money from him, so they left to deliver a picture of us he took with his phone along with a ransom note. They'll be back anytime. Don't you understand? I've seen their faces. Do you think they're going to let either of us live if we can identify them? You've got to help me!"

Cal rolled over on his side and struggled to sit up. He put his legs over the side of the cot and the room started spinning. Shit, he felt like shit. He closed his eyes and put his head down, trying not to be sick.

"Cal," Lauren called to him, as she bounced her chair closer to him. "I've got a knife in my boot. If you can grab it and cut the ropes on my hands, I can do the rest."

"Knife?"

"Yes, I have a knife in my boot. Reach down and use it to cut my ropes. Hurry!"

Suddenly, a trace of adrenaline trickled through Cal's body and he finally understood all that Lauren had been saying to him. Still unsteady but determined, he managed to find the knife and transfer it to his hands. Instead of cutting Lauren's ropes, he tried to cut his own. It wasn't working.

Seeing what he was doing, Lauren got angry. "Listen to me, you son of a bitch. I dragged you here, dressed your wounds and you do this? You're too weak to manage your ropes on your own. Our only shot out of here is if you cut my ropes. Then I'll cut yours. Your biggest worry is not if I escape from you but if these guys come back and try to finish us off. Now do you understand?"

Still confused, he swore it was his mother talking and he had to obey her. He leaned over and in just a couple of minutes had cut through Lauren's bonds. She immediately grabbed the knife and sliced through the ropes around her ankles and his. Getting to her feet and stomping them to get the circulation back, she helped Cal get to his feet. He was wobbly, ashen and frozen in place.

"We need to get out of here, now. They took your guns with them so we've got nothing to protect ourselves with except my knife. But there's stuff in here we can use. Grab anything warm. Find some food, anything that you think will help us survive out here. Once they find we've gone, they'll come looking for us. It's going to snow out there soon and our tracks will be easy to follow. If we can get to where you left the 4-wheeler, we might be able to outrun them. I left my bundle not far from here and I've got some matches and water. We'll stop there first. Now, move!"

Cal grabbed a flashlight, the blanket from the cot, a long oilcloth duster and the rope they had been tied with. It was all he could find. The fire in the cabin was almost out, but there were still embers remaining. Grabbing a tin cup, Lauren carefully scooped some embers into it, took it outside, and finding a few pieces of firewood and some kindling, started a campfire near the cabin. It wasn't roaring, but in time, it should burn well. If anyone was coming to rescue them, a fire and its black smoke could give them a starting point. She would have set the cabin on fire if she wasn't worried about protecting the forest. An out of control burn could hinder their rescue rather than help it. No, better to start the campfire instead.

Cal met her at the door to the cabin. He had donned the duster, since she was wearing his jacket. The blanket was around his shoulders.

"My bundle is this way," she said, taking a trail into the woods. He followed her and they soon found it by the tree where she had left it.

"We are in a fight for our lives. That guy, Darryl, didn't think twice about shooting at you. We've got to work together to hide from them."

He thought for a moment, got his bearings and pointed to a trail.

"I came from that way. I left the 4-wheeler about 4 miles back. I do have some supplies there that will get us through the next few days," he told her.

"Ok, then what? You know this area. Where do we go after we pick up your supplies? Back to your cabin?"

"No, that's too obvious. We need to leave the area. We'll take the four-wheeler down the mountain until I can find a truck to steal. I'll switch plates with another vehicle so that it gives us time to get away."

"Sounds like a dream, but no thanks. I was thinking we head down the mountain toward civilization and you let me go."

"No, you're coming with me," Cal said.

"I'm only going to slow you down. I don't care where you go from here, but you need to get me back to Jared. If there's no reward money, the brothers will have to stop looking for us."

"Fuck the brothers, I need you as my bargaining chip if the Feds find me. So, suck it up and start walking," Cal said to her, giving her a shove.

Lauren would look back on that night as the one where she almost died. Cal was still weak and the walk left him exhausted. He had to lean heavily on her for support. About an hour after they had left the Lazarus cabin, the weather changed. A cold, bitter rain brought their trek to the 4-wheeler to a halt. As Lauren was forced to build a lean-to out of spruce boughs, she didn't think she could get any colder. She was shivering constantly now, her clothes beginning to soak through. Cal was useless, too weak to even build a fire. With her knife, she was cutting boughs, desperately searching for dry wood under the thickest trees

Killer Looks

where the rain hadn't yet penetrated. She was able to build a small fire, but the lean-to was pathetic. As the rain turned to snow, she knew she needed warmth. Cal was inside the lean-to on a bed of boughs, still in his waterproof duster and the blanket around him.

"I've done the best I can do with the fire. Everything is just so wet. We need to get warm or we'll never survive the night. I'll stoke it with the rest of the dry wood, but it won't be enough. We need to use our body heat to keep us warm," she said.

He looked at her, knowing she was right. He unbuttoned his duster, motioning her to lie down next to him. He wrapped his arms around her as she spooned against him, then covered them both with first the blanket, then the waterproof duster. It was the best they could do for the night. If they survived, it would be because of her efforts and their body heat.

Chapter 48

They were already on his trail, he was sure, but he had a head start on them. And he knew where he was going. They had probably wasted time going to his trailer to look for him and his brother, and he hoped nobody had seen his truck heading up the mountain. The sooner he got to his hostages, the safer he would be.

He looked over at his dead brother lying propped up against the passenger door in the front seat of the truck. Something like grief played at his emotions, but he put it out of his mind. He was in trouble because of Neil. He's the one who started firing and forced him to take out that motorcycle cop and the sheriff's deputy. Now he was fucked. All he wanted was to get the reward and get the hell out of this town.

He'd take Neil to the cabin, where the cold would keep him from decaying much, and once he had left his brother behind, somebody would bury him. A decent burial was probably more than his brother deserved, but if it made somebody feel good doing it, he'd be okay with it.

It was almost dark now and he was forced to drive with his lights off. But, he knew these roads and was at the cabin without incident. As he pulled up to the cabin, a campfire was in full burn. Thick, black smoke was swirling up into the air, a beacon for air search if there ever was one. He barreled out of the truck and into the cabin. His hostages were gone. He bellowed with rage, his chance at freedom obliterated. He quickly used a shovel and water to extinguish the fire, still shaking with anger.

Killer Looks

They couldn't be far. And the man was injured. He could find them. He knew these woods. Could track pretty well, too. He could take the truck for about a mile then he'd have to go on foot, but he had camping gear and supplies in the truck, and could make it in the elements. Checking the cabin, he saw what they had taken. It wasn't much. He was sure they were headed back to the man's cabin, where he had resources and could fend off any intruders. He had to leave now, before he was surrounded.

A half hour later he could go no further by truck. His pack on his back, he avoided any open areas and stuck to the trees. It would be slow going but he needed to avoid capture as much as he needed to find his hostages. He had a general idea of where the man's cabin was, but no direct route to get there. It would be hit or miss, but if his tracking skills were as good as he thought they were, he'd find them.

About a mile in, the rain started. Cold, drenching rain that washed away any sign of the pair's tracks. It soon turned to snow and he decided to camp for the night. He would risk a fire, and he had a sleeping bag as well as a small tent. He doubted the pair had it as good.

When the first light broke, he quickly decamped and began his trek up the mountain, searching for tracks he was pretty sure would no longer be there. But he kept climbing anyway. About two hours into his climb, he heard a noise overhead and looked up to see a helicopter on the same trajectory as he had been. They were either looking for him or the pair. He had to find them first. He headed for a ridge that would give him a visual vantage point, careful to keep a low profile. He could see the chopper circling a

location and figured they had found the cabin. He knew
that Cal and Lauren couldn't be there yet. They were on
their way but couldn't have covered that much trail in such
a short amount of time. No, they were somewhere ahead of
him, between here and the cabin. And they were his.

Chapter 49

Her shivering had stopped and they were warm. He had slept surprising well, having been fatigued by the arduous walk down the mountain. His shoulder still burned but he felt his strength returning. The pain was much less. It had stopped raining and the temperature had risen into the 40's, an overcast sky above them. The rain would come again, or worse, the temperature would drop and it could snow. They had to get moving.

As he shifted his weight away from her, she awoke. Eyes still closed, she smiled, then stretched. A frown replaced the smile as she opened her eyes, seeing Cal's face next to hers.

"Let's go. We're sitting ducks out here. Take care of your business then we head down the mountain. I'll douse the embers and get us something to eat."

Rather than objecting, she did what she had to do, made it back to their campsite and met him at the 4-wheeler. She looked at him as she sat and took an oatmeal cake from him. He was getting stronger, she could tell.

"You'd better let me drive. You don't look well at all," she said.

"I'm fine. Besides, you don't know where we're going," Cal responded.

"And you do? That asshole is right behind us. And he's armed. We can't outrun him for long. Let's think about this. We need to find another place to hide, not let him catch us out here in the open. We're still miles away from civilization. I know you want to head down the mountain to steal a truck, but that's miles and days away. We'll have to either leave the 4-wheeler behind when the area gets impassible or go it on foot. You'll never make it and you know it," she said.

He hated to admit it, but she was right. Although he was better, exertion would not be his friend. He wouldn't get very far, and they needed to use surprise to their advantage. They couldn't face a gun or a crossbow and win. They had heard the men's truck far behind them last night, so they knew the men had made it back to the cabin. When they saw that Cal and Lauren were gone, they wouldn't wait till morning to go look for them. They'd jump in their vehicle following their tracks in the snow, but before long they would have had to ditch the truck and pursue them on foot.

"We're not that far from the brothers' cabin. They won't be expecting us to head back there. They'll be following our trail so if we circle back, we can prepare an ambush for them," Cal said.

"What kind of ambush?" Lauren asked.

"Build traps with the supplies we do have. I figure we have about a 3-hour advantage, maybe a little more. But let's use 3 hours just to be on the safe side. I've got the arrows you took from the cabin," said Cal.

"And I've got nails with me," said Lauren. "So, what do we do with them?"

"We used to come across homemade traps all the time in Afghanistan. Not very sophisticated, but deadly."

"You mean a booby trap of some kind?"

"Yes, but I'll have to adapt it to what we have to work with. I've got an idea for a log projectile. That should be the quickest and easiest to make, but we have to time it just right. I'll have to use you for bait."

"Why can't you be the bait?" she said, angrily.

"Because I have to set the trap and it takes more strength than you have to do it."

She didn't have a comeback.

As they made their way back to the cabin, Cal began to explain in detail how the trap would work. Using the rope that they took from the cabin, they would suspend a large 2-foot log from a thick tree branch, creating a swinging weapon. There should be an unsplit log near the woodpile that could work. Cal would hammer nails into the side that would project from the front of the log. He would also attach the arrows to the sides of the log to do more damage. Lauren would be the bait that would lead them to the exact spot where the log would impact both of the brothers when released by Cal. They'd only get one shot at it so the timing had to be precise. Cal would release the guide rope and the weight of the log would do the rest. Even if the weapon missed, it would distract the brothers and make them vulnerable to a physical attack by Cal. If they could get their hands on one weapon, they had a chance.

As soon as the cabin was in sight, they carefully approached it. Cal checked the door, but it was locked. Knowing they were safe for the time being, Cal got to work. He was still weak but adrenaline gave him the strength to execute their plan. He found a strong tree that he could climb and remain in, unseen. A large branch of the tree that hung over the trail to the cabin was the ideal one from which to suspend the log. Lauren got busy tying

229

lengths of rope together to not only wrap around the log but to create a pulley that could lift the log to the ideal height. Cal would attach a guide rope to the log and once released, the log would swing in a pendulous arc. Cal attached the arrows to the log and had to use a rock to pound the nails that protruded through the front. Now, they would need to test it.

Cal climbed the tree while Lauren used the pulley to lift the log. He pulled the log back towards him using the guideline, then let it go. Using a long branch temporarily attached to the bottom of the log, they followed the trail it made on the ground and found the sweet spot. Lauren marked it with a pile of dead leaves, removed the branch from the log, and together they hoisted the log into the tree again, waiting for the brothers to find them. Lauren tied her hands loosely together then attached a rope to her ankle. She looped the rope around a nearby tree. The length of the rope allowed her to move within a few inches of the pile of leaves. She would pretend Cal had left her there to die in the cold. As the brothers approached her, she would move behind the pile of leaves and hopefully they would walk in a direct line to where she was standing and Cal would set the log in motion, aimed toward its intended victims.

From his vantage point in the tree, Cal could see a man approaching. One man. Where was the other one? He couldn't be in the cabin, could he? They never went inside, finding the door locked. No, the man would have heard the pounding if he was anywhere near them. Cal silently caught Lauren's attention and signaled the man's approach. He held up one finger, then two as he shook his head no. Then he held up the one finger again, nodding yes as he did. He hoped she'd understood there was only one man and to stay vigilant in case the second showed up.

As the man broke through the tree line, Lauren saw that it was Darryl, shotgun in his hand and a crossbow slung over his shoulder.

"Well, what do we have here? Where's lover boy?" Darryl said as he stood watching her. He didn't approach her, but surveyed the area.

"He, he left me here to die", she said as she cried crocodile tears.

"We don't need him anyway, do we? You and me, we've got some catchin' up to do," he said with a sneer.

"What about your brother?"

"What about my brother? He's in the cabin. Dead as that tree over there," he said pointing to his right. Lauren panicked. Two feet higher and he would have spotted Cal.

"What happened to him?" she sniffled.

"He went and got himself killed, but I took out two cops before I made it back here."

Lauren's heart sank. Was Jared one of the cops he killed?

"Imagine my surprise when you were gone. But you were pretty easy to track. Not sure why you came back here, though. Of all places."

"We thought we might be able to steal your truck if you had come looking for us on foot. That's why we doubled back. But it wasn't here and Cal got angry. Really angry. So, he tied me up and left me here. He's halfway down the mountain by now. Please, please untie me. I'm so cold."

"And I know just the thing to warm you up," he said, leering at her.

She was terrified. The longer she stood there without him approaching, the more chance there was that he'd uncover their plot. Finally, he stepped forward and inched his way toward the pile of leaves. What was Cal waiting for? Why didn't he let the log go? Suddenly, she heard a loud yell and watched as the log came toward Darryl while at the same time, Cal fell to the ground. Cal was stunned and as he stood to push Darryl into the path of the log, he lost his footing. The log sideswiped Darryl in the arm, cutting through his jacket and drawing blood, but continued on to finish the arc. They had never thought about where the log went once it finished the arc. They had assumed it would lodge itself in the body of its victim and come to a stop. But that didn't happen. As Cal raced to tackle Darryl, who was clutching his bleeding arm, the log began its backward arc. Cal kicked the shotgun to Lauren, who by now had freed her hands and was struggling to grab it. As Cal turned to make sure she had it, the backward arc of the log began and, with horror, Lauren saw its inevitable destination. This time it didn't miss. A surprised look covered the victim's face before he hit the ground. The man was dead.

Chapter 50

The chopper had put down about five miles from the point on the map that pinpointed Cal's possible location. While the rest of the team unloaded the packs they'd carry, Jared and Charlie tried to get a visual sightline that would be their reference during the climb up the mountain. Even if the trail was circuitous, the points of reference would keep them moving in the right direction.

"That series of 3 peaks is what we need to keep in view. The trails up here are almost nonexistent so we'll be making our way at the mercy of the terrain," Charlie said.

"How long do you think it will take us to get there?" Jared asked.

"We're looking at tomorrow, Jared. That's if we get lucky and the weather holds. If a snowstorm hits, we'll have to hunker down until it passes. Can't risk getting lost in a whiteout."

Just then, Charlie's walkie talkie squawked and he quickly responded. "Raglan, what have you got, over?"

"We just found the Lazarus cabin. We've got a couple of male bodies up here. One inside the cabin and one a few feet from it."

"Looks like the one in the cabin died of gunshot wounds and the other, well, he was ambushed by a booby trap. ID on the body in the cabin is Neil Lazarus. The other body was badly burned so we're not sure of his identity. Could be Cal Morgan or Darryl Lazarus. Coroner should be able to tell us".

233

"Another thing, though, Charlie. I've got a team following a blood trail leading into the woods. Could be the Sedgeway woman or one of the men, over."

"Ok, we'll stay put until you have more info. But get back to me as soon as you know anything, over."

"I guess you heard that," Charlie said as he turned to Jared.

"I don't feel good about any of this, Charlie. A burned body? No sign of Lauren? A fucking blood trail? Where is she?"

"Look, we'll know something soon. We haven't found Lauren's body so she's very likely still alive. And the blood trail means nothing until they follow it to the end. You've got to keep positive about this. You owe that to Lauren," Charlie said.

"God, what must she be thinking?" Jared asked.

"She's thinking that you're doing everything you can to find her. Hold on to that."

Chapter 51

She stood there shaking while he burned the body. Burned the body. How could she believe what she was seeing? He said it would slow down the investigation, give them time to get away. Get away? All she wanted to do was sleep, hoping to wake from the nightmare locked in her psyche. But she knew that wouldn't happen. This was real. Incomprehensible. Life-altering. She looked at the impaled body one last time, forced by him to do it, and watched as the face became unrecognizable in the flames.

Before the burning, she had had a slim chance to end it all. But the shotgun was snatched from her before she had time to react. To fire a round. The tears started and an overwhelming feeling of despair clouded her mind, obscuring the vision of the horrific event.

Then she just went away. In that one instant, in the time it took for one blink, her mind faded into oblivion.

She heard a voice, a distant one, but pushed it away. Something was happening to her body, but her mind was no longer connected to it. She'd feel the occasional cold, thirst and hunger, but could do nothing to mitigate them. *This must be what it feels like to die*, her mind thought.

Chapter 52

It had taken months of investigation and hard work by law enforcement agencies on the state, local and national levels, but only a few hours for Lauren's eventual rescue once they determined her possible location. Using the site of the Lazarus cabin as a base, searchers had been working their way along a blood trail that led away from the cabin. Only a mile from it, they had found the body of Darryl Lazarus who had been injured by the ambush and had bled out. Lauren Sedgeway had been found in a comatose state next to him. It took time to get her down the mountain, but she was alive and Jared was grateful. When news of her rescue reached him, he raced up the mountain and met the rescue team as they approached a clearing large enough for the chopper to land. Relief flooded his face, but her appearance decimated him. The shell of a woman stared unseeingly at him. He would never forgive himself for not finding her sooner. As the team loaded her on the chopper and headed to the hospital, Jared followed.

He sat next to Lauren's hospital bed, holding her hand while he waited for the doctor. Upon her arrival at the hospital, Dr. Andrew Malan had examined Lauren and had found her to be dehydrated, frostbitten on one toe and unresponsive to outside stimulus. She would recover physically, but the real Lauren was locked away, unable to communicate.

"Jared, I knew you'd be here," said Dr. Malan as he entered Lauren's room.

"I wouldn't be anywhere else," Jared said. "Doctor, what can you tell me? When is Lauren going to wake up? What's happened to her?"

"We probably won't know the extent of what's happened to her until she can begin to communicate with us. She's experienced considerable trauma and has retreated inside herself to heal."

"But she's a strong woman, doctor. Fearless. She has to know I'm waiting for her and will take care of her," Jared said.

"If she's as strong as you say she is, she has to do this on her own. The mind is a wonderful gift. Lauren needs to process what's happened to her, put everything in perspective and pick a new path she can follow. Just look at her. Though she's here with us, she's really not here. Her body is, of course, and she's physically getting better every day, but based on what you've told me about some of the things she's experienced, she's not ready to join us yet."

"How long will it take?" Jared asked.

The doctor smiled but Jared knew he didn't have the answer.

"There are a couple of things you need to be prepared for. The relationship you had with her is gone. She will not be the same. Depending on what she's lived through and seen, she may look at the world differently. She may withdraw. Want little contact with anyone, especially men. You may have to build a new relationship with her, if she'll even agree to try. I'm sorry to be so brutal, but she's not going to wake up like in the movies and live happily ever after with her prince charming. Her PTSD won't let her until she gets it under control. She'll need a lot of therapy just to adapt to the world she's being thrown back into. You need to understand that. She'll need time to get a recognizable Lauren back."

"How can I help? I feel so responsible."

"You can start by not letting her see that from you. The only ones responsible for her condition are the ones who caused the trauma, not you. She'll work through what was done to her, or she won't. There's no way to tell. Some people can talk through everything, others lock it all away like it never happened. The danger in that scenario is that it tends to sneak into the present a memory at a time and causes confusion and sometimes repressed terror. We can only hope that Lauren will recover in her own time and learn to live with what's happened to her. Just be there for her when she's ready to begin."

Chapter 53

The cottage was waiting for her when she left the hospital. Maggie had been her rock, buying her a new wardrobe, a vehicle and replacing most of the personal things Cal had destroyed. Her job with Hildy was there if she wanted it, but it was too soon. It was too soon for Jared, too.

He had been at the rehab facility as she went through therapy, but she found it difficult to communicate with him. He had high expectations that she just couldn't fill. So, she had asked him to give her time. The hurt on his face was palpable, but she couldn't even think about anyone but herself.

She was ecstatic when she learned that Cal hadn't killed Tessa. Tessa had been a big part of her recovery as together they shared what they had both been through at Cal's hands.

Charlie had given her some of the facts as they knew them, but needed her to add what had happened to her. She told him what she remembered, but the trauma of seeing Cal killed by their boobytrap and then burned by Darryl was excruciating. She had lost herself then, and Darryl had had to pull her along as he tried to escape. Finally, he gave up on her and worked his way down the mountain without her. He died there, the loss of too much blood finally killing him. She wandered in a daze, and when she found his body on the trail, sat down next to him. That's where the rescuers found her.

She would continue with therapy, but right now, all she wanted to do was go home. When Maggie arrived to pick her up, she quickly gathered her few personal things, put them in a plastic bag provided by the facility and stepped outside to breathe the fresh Montana air. In spite of everything that had happened to her, she had been happy in Wildwood and hoped to rebuild her life here. The friendship offered by Maggie and Charlie was crucial to her recovery and she wanted to spend as much time as she could with them. Maggie was just fine with that. Charlie was torn, considering how Jared was handling all this. His friend was grieving for the lost relationship, the Lauren he had fallen in love with and the future he had hoped to have with her.

"Maggie, thanks so much for driving me home. It looks like I never left here!" said Lauren as she surveyed the interior of the house.

A fire was blazing in the fireplace and she could smell fresh coffee. It was her safe place and she would continue her healing here.

"Lauren, I know I've told you this before, but you will get better."

"I know," said Lauren. "I am still trying to process my relationship with Cal. Nobody understands it, and frankly, neither do I, but I just can't hate him. I think I had feelings for him in some strange way. In spite of everything he did to everyone else, he took care of me, protected me and ultimately died trying to save me. I can't forget that. As long as these feelings are still there, I can't let Jared back into my life. It wouldn't be fair to him. Doctor Gilley is still hoping for a 'breakthrough' so that I can look at Cal from a proper perspective. That's what I'm working toward."

"Do you still have feelings for Jared?" Maggie asked.

"Maggie, I don't know. Maybe. But I've put him so far out of my mind that I'm just not sure. I could be his friend, but I know that's not what he wants. But I also don't want him waiting for me, especially if I never come to grips with the whole Cal thing."

"Just don't write him off yet, ok? He loves you."

"He loves the woman I was, not who I am now. There's a big difference. I feel bad about what he's going through, I really do. I just can't help him right now. Maybe in time."

"Can you get to therapy tomorrow by yourself?" Maggie asked, changing the subject. Her therapist, Dr. Gilley, had released her from the mental health facility but still wanted to see her 5 days a week as an outpatient.

"Of course. I didn't forget how to drive. Although I will miss David's Land Rover. I guess a Jeep is a little more practical. Did they ever find my car, by the way?"

'No, I'm sorry, they didn't. It's somewhere out in the wilds of Montana, probably a home for a family of chipmunks by now."

Lauren laughed loudly, the first time she had done so since she was rescued. It felt good to laugh. To feel normal. Was that what she was now, normal? No, not yet, but soon, she hoped.

Maggie had stocked the refrigerator for her and Lauren was delighted to find the ingredients for lemon chicken. As she cooked the dish for herself, her mind wandered back to the first time she had cooked that for Jared. They had made love that night and it had been good.

Make that very good. But was it just the memory of the sex or was it feelings for Jared? She didn't know, and it infuriated her. Why couldn't she get Cal out of her mind and let Jared back in? She would ask her therapist that question tomorrow.

Her therapist was running 15 minutes late the following day, so she had time to stop at the convenience store for a cup of coffee on her way to her session. As she left the store, an old poster, the one Jared had hung all over town, stopped her in her tracks. It was the first time she had seen it, and a flood of emotions bombarded her. She had known about the reward Jared had offered for her safe return, but to see the simple cardboard poster that had brought the Lazarus brothers into her world was too much for her. Cal's face was there. And hers. Memories flooded back. Tears began to flow and she couldn't move. She was transported back to the cabin, to witnessing Cal's death. To the feelings for him she couldn't process. Blackness descended and she welcomed it.

Her eyes didn't want to open, but someone was calling her name. Was it Cal? No, he was dead. Maggie? Maybe. With considerable effort, she forced her eyes to focus. Dr. Gilley? Was she in her office? No, this wasn't her office. There was too much noise. So much noise.

"Lauren, you're at Mountain General Hospital. Do you remember what happened to you?" asked Angela Gilley.

"Dr. Gilley? I was coming to see you. I stopped to get a cup of coffee but that's all I remember."

"You've had some sort of episode and you were brought here by ambulance. You're okay physically, but they found my card in your purse and called me. I'd like to see if we can help you to remember what triggered this. You said you went to get some coffee. Where was this?"

"The convenience store on Market. I went in, got my coffee and headed out the door."

"Did you see anyone you knew?"

"No, I don't think so." Suddenly, her brow furrowed and she said, "Cal. I saw Cal."

"You saw Cal?"

"Not Cal, but his picture. On the poster. The reward poster."

"And what happened when you saw it?"

'So much. Memories of our time at his cabin. At the Lazarus cabin. His death. It was too much for me and I guess my brain just shut down."

She looked at the doctor then, tears in her eyes. "Am I ever going to be able to function again without this stuff happening?"

"Lauren, you've been through so much; much more than you can process all at once. That's why therapy is so important for you. I think this needed to happen. It's one more thing that will get you closer to recovery. Make sure you make it to my office tomorrow and we'll continue to explore this. They're letting you out of here in a few minutes and I'd be glad to drive you home."

"If you can just drop me at the convenience store I'll get my car. I can make it home from there. I'll see if my friend, Maggie, can keep me company tonight."

"Wouldn't be a bad idea."

Chapter 54

Lauren sat in the reception area of Dr. Gilley's office, fear and unease crackling through her nerve endings. It had been months of therapy and she still had difficulty placing Cal in his proper place in her reality. There was something in the recesses of her mind that impeded her progress and Dr. Gilley was suggesting hypnosis therapy. Her colleague, Dr. David Luccesi, was a psychiatrist with unparalleled success, aiding trauma victims in their recovery of suppressed memories. Though anxious to begin this new treatment, she was uncertain if she could handle the possible results.

Right on time, Dr. Gilley greeted her with a smile and led her to her office where her colleague was waiting. Her first impression of Dr. Luccesi surprised her. She expected him to be a grizzled, gray haired septuagenarian but was pleasantly surprised to find him refreshingly youthful in appearance. Though in his mid-forties, he was trim, fit and decidedly attractive. A quick glance at his empty ring finger implied he was single. She wasn't sure why that mattered, but was delighted with the thought. *Don't go falling in love with your therapist*, she cautioned herself.

"Lauren, I'm very pleased to meet you. Dr. Gilley has shared your experiences with me and I'm hoping that together we can move the healing process forward," Luccesi said, taking her hand in his.

"It's nice to meet you. I am a little skeptical that that can be accomplished but I want to get back to a sense of normalcy. My feelings about Cal don't make sense, considering all I know about him. But if your methods can help me, I'm ready to begin," Lauren said.

"Dr. Gilley will be observing and we will record this session, if it's okay with you," Luccesi said.

"Sure."

Using approved medical techniques, Dr. Luccesi made Lauren comfortable and soon she was in an impressionable state, ready for the probing questions of her doctor.

"Lauren, I want you to think about the time when you first encountered Cal. When you first moved to Wildwood," said the doctor. "What was your first impression?"

"He was very attractive and I guess he flustered me a little."

"What happened then?"

"I followed him to my house and he started a fire for me."

"Anything unusual happen?" the doctor asked.

"No, he left to take care of his dog. She was having puppies," she said.

"What about your next encounter?"

"I guess it was when he dropped off another load of firewood for me. He surprised me by asking me to make him dinner."

"Was it a date? Did you feel attracted to him then?"

"No, it wasn't a date and I guess I was attracted to him but not seriously. Just appreciated a good-looking man."

"Did anything happen at dinner?"

Her brow furrowed as she was remembering, then she said, "Yes, he started to make me uncomfortable. I got the feeling he was upset that I moved next door to him. I ended the dinner rather quickly."

"Did you see him again after that and did those same feelings continue?"

"Yes, then I found out why. He killed those girls. He killed those girls!" she said with anguish in her voice.

"Okay, okay, we'll leave that for now. Tell me about leaving with him," Luccesi said.

"He made me go with him. Then he shot Tess and his dog. I hated him then."

"Okay, let's talk about your time at the cabin. What was that like?"

"We worked hard. Finding food, chopping and hauling wood. Always doing chores."

"What else do you remember happening to you at the cabin?" asked Luccesi.

"I was bit by a black widow spider. Cal saved my life."

"Is that when your feelings about him changed? Because he saved your life and looked after you? Kept you fed and sheltered?"

"I don't know. I'm so confused. I remember hearing him talking to me while I was delirious. He stayed by me instead of finishing the things we needed to do before the cold weather set in. He told me about his mother. About the things she used to do with him. I know he said I reminded him of her. But he was strangely attracted to me. I think that's why he didn't hurt me the way he hurt those other women. I was so grateful to him for that. I knew the

246

horrible things he had done, but he hadn't done them to ME. He was my only human contact for months, until the Lazarus brothers came along. When I ran away and he found me, he asked how I could leave him after all the things he had done for me. In his mind, not mine, we were in a relationship. In a way, I felt bad about that. Felt sorry for him." Lauren paused, unable to go on as tears welled in her eyes. The doctor waited until she had calmed down.

"Tell me about Cal's death, Lauren."

A look of horror crossed her face as she detailed what she had seen. Cal impaled on the log. Darryl Lazarus pouring whiskey on him and setting him on fire, making her watch.

Dr. Luccesi broke in. "Lauren, Cal was a murderer and a rapist. He didn't deserve to die the way he did, but he was a damaged man. His mother did that to him. Not you. You couldn't save him from the things he did or from himself. What latent feelings you have for him would never be there if you hadn't been victimized yourself. You made a connection with him out of fear, loneliness and need. What you're feeling now are misplaced emotions and once you can put them in their proper place, you can move on. Are you ready to move on, Lauren?"

He ended their session with that question. When she was ready to continue, they would have a new starting point.

Chapter 55

Hypnosis therapy was what ultimately brought a sense of peace to Lauren. Working with Dr. Luccesi, she was able to put her relationship with Cal into perspective. She worked through a myriad of feelings, finding breakthrough moments on her own, with direction from Luccesi. She was starting to heal. Although she wasn't diagnosed with Stockholm Syndrome, many of the symptoms she exhibited were similar. Unlike those victims who often sympathized with their captors, she found nothing at all acceptable about his actions. She did not sympathize with him other than for what his mother had done to him. But he had choices and he made the wrong ones. She had no sympathy for that. She was grateful to him for saving her life, but everything else he had done was not forgiven. She could now put him out of her life and her thoughts.

It had been six months since her last session with Dr. Luccesi, although she was still seeing Dr. Gilley occasionally. Hildy had her back at work and she was busy with a new manuscript, this time her own. She was writing a book about her ordeal. It would be cathartic for her and as she relived each part of the story that would be included, she could step back and be objective. She could convey the emotion of the story without any of the possible negative effects on her own mental health. She felt strong, in control and healed.

Hildy had requested a meeting in New York with the publisher and she was eager to get on a plane, to escape the wilds of Montana for a while. She'd be back, back to her home, but for now she could indulge in a life away from Wildwood, even if just for a few days.

The airport was busy, but as she waited to board her plane, she saw a familiar face. Dr. Luccesi. Seeing him triggered memories of her ordeal, but they were quickly dispatched to the hidden place where they now belonged. He had helped her find that place and for that, she was eternally grateful. She would not approach him, even if that were the friendly thing to do. She had a patient/doctor relationship with him and that would be where it stayed.

As she turned back to her tablet and the book she was reading, a shadow crossed in front of her, then crossed back. When she looked up, David Luccesi was smiling at her, a look of pleasure on his face.

"My God, Lauren, how are you? You look wonderful!" he said.

"Thanks to you and Angela, I'm doing better than I ever thought I would."

"I almost didn't recognize you," Luccesi said.

"I guess a new hairstyle and a new wardrobe have something to do with that. I needed to make some changes and these were the easiest. I'm on my way to New York to meet with my publisher. I'm writing a book about my experience, which has been easier than I thought. My publisher says it will be a best seller, but I won't care if no one reads it. I'm doing this for me."

"That's a very healthy attitude, and I'm proud of the progress you've made. I'm going to New York myself but on a later plane. I'm speaking at a symposium on the upper east side, but I'd love to get together with you. Will you have any free time while you're there?" he asked.

"Do you think that's a good idea? I was your patient, after all."

"You *were* my patient, but we don't have a professional relationship now. Besides, I'm just interested in how you're doing. If it makes you uncomfortable, I understand."

His smile faded a bit and he turned to walk away.

She called out to him. "I'm staying at the Intercontinental on 55th. Call me and I'll see what I can do." His smile returned and she waved him goodbye.

Her room at the hotel was small but luxurious. After days of meetings she was ready for a relaxing evening. David had called the night before and they planned on meeting in the bar at the Plaza, but just for drinks.

As she dressed, her reflection in the mirror surprised her. She had transformed her body while with Cal and maintained her lithe frame with frequent runs in the Montana countryside. A little black dress coupled with a Chanel jacket and stilettos completed her outfit. She was ready.

New York had always been a town she loved. It was frenetic, romantic and non-stop. But you could get lost in the city, be anonymous and create a persona just for the night. What persona would be spending time with David tonight? What could she possible talk about that he didn't already know? But it had been a long time since she'd been on the arm of an attractive man, and she was looking forward to it.

She arrived before him and watched him as he glanced around the room and spotting her, hurried to her side. Female patrons followed him with their eyes and she realized why. He was a strikingly handsome man. Dressed in black slacks, a crisp white shirt and leather blazer, he grabbed the attention only a confident, purposeful man could. His smile was infectious and she felt herself smiling in return as he sat at the bar stool next to her. He smelled wonderfully of Polo Red, her favorite fragrance for men.

He spoke first, taking her hand and holding it.

"I'm so pleased that you could find time for me. I just wanted to tell you that the moment I saw you in the airport, I saw a different woman than I had been treating. You exuded confidence, both in the way you held yourself and in the way you interacted with other people. I must admit I watched you for some time, with almost unbelieving eyes. Angela told me you were an exemplary patient, but, Lauren, I had no idea. You're an inspiration, considering all you've been through. It looks like you can conquer anything. Do you feel that way?"

"Is that the doctor asking?" she asked.

"The doctor? I guess so. But you're not my patient anymore so let's just say it's a friend asking."

"To answer your question, I guess I feel like I can conquer a lot, but everything? Not yet. I'm still struggling with relationships and trust issues and even this evening with you would never have happened a month ago. But here I am, and it's okay."

She laughed then, an easy laugh, and found herself talking to a friend, not her doctor. He shared personal stories with her, focusing on his early childhood years and medical school. For the last four years, he had been working with police entities using hypnosis to help crime victims remember details of traumatic events. Dr. Gilley

251

had gone to med school with him and had followed his career closely. That's why she had consulted with him about Lauren's case. Given the details, he had at first declined, but because of his friendship with Angela, had freed up his schedule to help Lauren. It had been a turning point in his practice.

"So, you can see why I was so anxious to meet with you. I wanted to thank you for what working with you has done for me. And my practice. I made lots of money working with the neurotic rich who wanted to stop smoking or lose weight and I'm ashamed to say, never regretted taking their money from them. But working with you opened my eyes to the difference I could make working with crime victims. So, I'm now accepting more of those kinds of cases, not just the occasional ones. I'm still making money to help pay the bills, but this new direction is giving me much more professional satisfaction."

She had been surprised that he was so candid with her, but he must have been comfortable with revealing so much of himself. She wondered why, but put it out of her mind. Maybe it was the cocktails talking. He would probably be back to his same professional self in the morning. And she'd be on a plane back to Wildwood. Back to Jared.

Chapter 56

Jared had thrown himself into his work while Lauren was recovering, but damn, it had hurt when she wanted no part of him. He could see the sympathy in his friends' eyes so he avoided them. He became a workaholic and only went home to shower and sleep. He ate at his desk or on the road. The only time he could forget his misery was the two hours it took for his run each morning. Rain or shine, sleet or snow, he ran. He wondered what a therapist would think of that.

Once Lauren was found, Charlie wrapped up the case. His report was extensive, and Jared had read it all. He couldn't believe what Lauren had been through. Even with the factual tone of the narrative, he could see why she had been in an unresponsive condition when discovered next to Darryl Lazarus's body.

With the death of Cal Morgan, he could close the case of Gaby Parmenter and Beth Reeves. Tess had been able to give some details, but it wasn't until they found Beth's remains at mile marker 235 that the Reeves family had closure. Gaby's parents had been devastated to learn that their daughter had been alive for so long and the old wounds were re-opened when he had to break the news to them about the circumstances of her death. He doubted they'd ever recover and saw them visibly age, withdraw into themselves as he delivered the details.

He had no answer for them when they asked how Cal could have gotten away with the things he did. He was deflated then, as he left their residence, and had struggles of his own dealing with the havoc Cal had wreaked on their lives and his.

He missed Lauren terribly, but knew he couldn't rush her. She would come to him in her own time, if she came to him at all.

It was just barely light out when he dressed for his run. He decided to try a new trail, one that was a little farther from home, but a worthy workout. He had found a flyer on his front porch with details about the new trailhead opening off highway 93. Trying something new. That's what he needed. It was summer, but the mornings were cool in the mountains. So, he added a jacket he could remove as the air heated. He drove the ten miles to the trailhead and noticed only a couple of other cars already parked there. They had a head start on him so he'd probably see the runners heading down the trail as he was heading up. It wasn't an easy run and he'd slowed down as the incline became more severe. He was just coming around a jog in the path when a figure in red racing down the path suddenly realized Jared was there and struggled to go around him. It didn't work. They collided, fell and rolled, sending both perilously close to a drop off. He was dazed but had the presence of mind to hold the other body close to him, stopping their momentum and keeping them from going over. The event had taken all of 10 seconds to unfold, but the danger had been real.

He lay on his side, his arms still around the figure in red and realized very quickly that the body was female. Blonde hair peeked out from a cap and he could hear the woman trying to catch her breath. Apparently, the collision had knocked the wind out of her. She coughed, tried to sit up and fell back against him. She tried a second time and was successful.

"Was it as good for you as it was for me?" the woman asked, turning to look at him.

Her comment took him completely by surprise and he burst into laughter. He hadn't laughed in a long time and it felt really, really good. The woman was beautiful. She had creamy skin, a toned body and a deadly smile. Wrinkles were just starting to appear around her eyes, but they added character to her face. He could almost see her eyes twinkle; they were such a bright crystalline blue. Collecting himself, he asked, "Are you alright?"

"Except for my pride and a large tear in my ridiculously expensive just-worn-for-the-first-time-today lululemons, I'm fine," she said, quickly covering the tear that revealed a tiny lace thong. He came embarrassingly close to an erection and turned away from her, clambering to his feet.

"I'm Detective Jared Martin. I'm so sorry that this happened."

"Hey, don't worry about it, Detective Jared Martin. Something told me I should be out here running today, but neglected to warn me of impending doom. Did you get the memo?"

He laughed again, loving her quirky sense of humor.

"I'm Kim Wellen, by the way," she said holding out her hand, a fantastic smile lighting her face. "Are you hurt?" she asked.

"Me? No, but I seem to have lost a shoe in the collision. Help me find it?"

"Could that be it, WAYYYY down there?" she asked a minute later, pointing to an area about 50 feet straight down from where they were standing.

"Yeah, that's it," he lamented, knowing he'd pass on trying to recover it.

"Well, Mr. One Shoe, we'd better get down from here and get you home. Need any help?"

"I think I can manage. How about you? No aches, no pains? Concussion? Wouldn't want you driving if you're impaired in any way."

"Is that the Detective talking or the concerned citizen? I'd have to respond differently depending on who you are."

"Let's say I'm the Detective," he said, giving her his best cop look.

"Oh no, sir, I'm doing exceptionally well and feel in no way impaired. I will proceed with caution, come to a complete stop at every octagon-shaped sign and will not pass go and will not collect $200."

"I see. And if I was the concerned citizen? What would you say?"

"Hell yes, I'm okay. Move your ass, mister. I've got to get to work!"

They proceeded down the mountain and along the way, got to know each other. She was an administrator at the hospital in Wildwood, having just moved from Seattle a little over a month ago. The job was a joy and she was settling in. She was renting a condo near the ski area, but planned on moving closer to the hospital as soon as she could find an acceptable house. She was getting to know her way around and had socialized with a few people from the hospital. A divorcee, she had a daughter in college, a cat named Jiminy Cricket, and a love of chocolate; dark, not milk.

He shared with her his cold case work in generalities, but did not mention Cal Morgan or Lauren. She'd probably find out about his involvement in that case if she got around to listening to the gossip mills.

When they got to their cars, his, standard police issue and hers, a vintage mustang, she held out her hand, ready to shake his. "Nice to meet you, Detective Jared Martin/concerned citizen. If you can ever tear yourself away from your work, how about showing me the highlights of Wildwood sometime?"

He shook her hand, held it and taking him completely by surprise said, "How about tonight?"

She smiled, nodded in agreement, got in her car and drove away. She had never given him her address or phone number.

Chapter 57

Jared's world had just re-awakened. Kim Wellen had cannonballed her way into his life and he found himself thinking of a woman other than Lauren. He still loved the Lauren he once knew, but she was changed now and his feelings were in limbo. He hadn't wanted any other woman in his life, but Kim made him feel connected to his life today, not a life from the past.

She was in her car and driving away before he realized he didn't have either her address or phone number. She wasn't playing hard to get, but he had a sneaking suspicion that she had deliberately failed to share her contact info with him. She had to know that he'd go to the hospital looking for her and she probably liked the thought of that. Just making sure he was serious about spending more time with her. She was right.

He had read about moments like this. The life changing ones. He had gone on for months, missing Lauren, immersed in his case load, rarely deviating from the routine. But today, he took a break from that routine and literally ran into a woman he was attracted to, her appealing personality and incredible looks having an immediate impact on him. The cloud of despair he had carried on his shoulders suddenly lifted and he could breathe again. He wanted to see her again and soon.

Fortunately, he had lost his left shoe so was able to make the 10-mile trip back home without difficulty. He showered, then drove to the hospital. He didn't want to appear too eager, but he was looking forward to seeing her again and firming up their plans. Shit, he'd have to make plans. He had no idea in hell what she liked to do, other than run. Maybe he'd give her some idea once she saw him again. He didn't care what they did, as long as they did it together.

He got out of his car, and walking with a purpose, approached the hospital, went inside and made his way to the reception desk. It was manned by a volunteer he recognized. Mrs. Cornwall, his former high school English teacher, now retired. His heart sank.

"Jared Martin! How can I help you today!" said Mrs. Cornwall.

"I'm looking for Kim Wellen, the hospital administrator. Can you please give me her phone number?"

"Well, I can't do that but I can ring her for you. Will that work?"

"Sure," he said, hoping he could use a phone far enough away from her so that she wouldn't hear his conversation.

"Why don't you take that phone over there and I'll connect you?" she said, pointing to a phone in the reception area. She would be out of earshot of their conversation.

The phone rang twice, then she answered. "Kim Wellen."

"Hello, Kim? It's Jared, Jared Martin. You ran into me this morning?" He was stumbling over his words.

"*Detective* Jared Martin? Yes, I remember you. Did you forget something?"

"We have plans for this evening, but I never got your address or phone number."

"Well, that wasn't very good planning, was it?"

She broke out in laughter, hoping to assuage his discomfort. "Give me your cell number and I'll text you my contact info." He did. "I'm up for anything, so don't sweat it. Tell me where and when to meet you and I'll be there. Oops, I've got another call I have to take. You have a great day and, Jared?" she said. "In spite of my tumble and the ruination of my lululemons, this has been the best day I've had since I moved here. Thanks to you. See you tonight!" Then she hung up.

His mind was reeling. His stomach doing flip flops. Meeting Kim was like being inside a fireworks display. The chemistry was intense and he expected she felt it, too. He found himself wanting to plan something special for them, but everything he thought of he had done with Lauren. He immediately felt a pang of guilt, but quickly dismissed it. Lauren was out of his life, at least for now, and he had to get on with living.

He left the hospital, heading back to his home office, when he passed the specialty candy shop on Treadway Street. A sign in the window caught his attention. *Candy-making class tonight at 7. Register now.* Ordinarily, he would have paid no attention to the sign. But, if he had read her correctly, he took a gamble that she would love this out-of-the-box activity. He stopped, quickly registered them and texted her the time and the location. He hoped to make it a favorable first date.

As it turned out, Kim loved the class. She was spontaneous and funny as they worked together to make chocolate candy they could share. She had the whole class in stitches the entire night and people gravitated to her. She had a smear of chocolate on her cheek that Jared thought he should wipe away, but she looked so cute with it, he left it there. It was gone when she returned from the restroom and she never mentioned it. As he walked her to her car, they chatted casually. He knew then that he wanted to see her again.

"Kim, thank you so much for this great night. I've been working so hard that I'd almost forgotten how to have fun. I'd like to do this again."

"Hmmm, make more candy?"

"You know what I mean," he said. "God, are you going to make this hard on me? I'm rusty at this."

She smiled, then reached out to hug him. "I think that would be nice. Here's a cliché, but why don't I cook dinner for you? Tomorrow night?"

"Tomorrow night would be fine," he said, pleasure evident on his face.

She hugged him again, then opened her car door and slid into the driver's seat. "I'll text you my address. Does 6pm work for you?"

"Yup, I'll see you then."

The months that followed were filled with dinners, day trips, joint runs and activity-filled nights at either his house or her condo. They had quickly gotten around to sex and it had been frequent and hot. She was very attentive, barely letting him out of her sight, and he felt alive again. When he suggested she move in when her condo lease was up, she eagerly agreed.

As he was helping Kim pack, thoughts of Lauren came rushing at him. He had planned to propose to her and a stab of guilt pierced his heart. She was still in therapy and gave no indication that she wanted him back in her life. He had to move on, didn't he? Find some happiness? Kim was good for him. Very different from Lauren. He had introduced Kim to Maggie and Charlie with some trepidation. But when they had seen how happy he seemed, they welcomed her into their circle of friends. Maggie was more standoffish than Charlie, but Jared knew it was because of Lauren. She still saw Lauren on a regular basis, but shared nothing of Lauren's life with him. He'd guessed Lauren wanted it that way.

Maggie invited Jared and Kim to a get-together at their home late in the fall. Maggie hadn't had much of an opportunity to interact with Kim and wanted to spend some time with her. Jared was obviously captivated by her, but there was something about her that Maggie couldn't shake. Maybe it was because she was so different from Lauren. Where Lauren had been intelligent and classy, Kim was gregarious and at times, outrageous. But Jared seemed to enjoy that. She just wondered if, long term, Kim would be enough for Jared.

While Charlie and Jared spent a few minutes in Charlie's office discussing a case, Maggie was left alone with Kim.

"Kim, I'm glad we have some time to get to know each other a little better. You seem to be important to Jared and since he's such a good friend we wanted to know the woman who has given him a reason to keep going. He's had a pretty rough year, so it's nice to see him happy again. I'm sure he's told you about the ordeal he's been through."

A dark look appeared and then quickly retreated from Kim's face.

"He hasn't told me much. Just said a woman he was dating was kidnapped. I'm sure he's over her by now."

Maggie wasn't sure how to respond to her comment. Since Jared hadn't seen or talked to Lauren in months, she didn't know how he would react if Lauren came back into his life. She knew he had loved her deeply. Could he forget about that love so easily? She wasn't sure he could. And though it might seem like she was interfering, she had to tell him that he would need to see Lauren, talk to her, before moving on permanently with Kim.

Chapter 58

Lauren's trip to New York had been fabulous. She came back with a renewed sense of who she now was. She had worked hard to find her new normal and she had succeeded. She still had a couple of sessions with Dr. Gilley that she hoped would help her find a way to approach Jared, to see if he could accept her and find a place for her in his life. But what had happened to her could never be forgotten. She just had to learn how to put the feelings associated with her ordeal in their proper place.

She had guilty feelings about Jared. Maggie had said he was a broken man because of what she'd endured. And she had selfishly kept him out of her life while she was in therapy. She had hoped he'd understood, but could he ever forgive her treatment of him? Could he accept that the relationship they once had was gone and a new one would have to deal with her trauma? She was still skittish, had trouble sleeping, but every day she felt stronger, more in control. She thought of Jared often, reliving their first meeting, their intense conversations, the lovemaking. She missed him and needed to see him.

Two days after she returned to Wildwood, she sat in Angela Gilley's office. The session was about Jared.

"Lauren, it's taken us a while to get to this point, so tell me why you feel you're ready to see Jared."

"I've put my experience with Cal into perspective, as you know," Lauren said.

"Yes, I've been astonished at how quickly you were able to come to grips with everything that happened to you and with what you witnessed," Gilley said.

"I had something very special with Jared, but he knows the old Lauren, not the woman I am now."

"Do you feel you're that much different? That your personality changed, or your way of looking at a relationship is damaged?"

"I do feel differently. I'm angry that this happened to me and destroyed what I had with Jared. I've been able to control my anger for the most part, but once in a while it reappears. That part sucks. If I see Jared and we can attempt to recover our relationship, I'm scared that I won't know how to react to him. Will he be expecting me to be the same, even though he knows I can't possibly be the same person I once was? Will he look at me as damaged goods? I know I hurt him when I asked him to keep his distance from me, but will he understand why I did it? In the back of my mind, I thought he might try to contact me since so much time has gone by, but he never did. Now I'm scared he's moved on."

"How would you feel about that, Lauren?" asked Dr. Gilley.

"I don't know, although I suspect I would be very hurt. But I'd try to understand, I guess. After all, I couldn't expect him to wait, especially when I pushed him away."

"Knowing you might be hurt, are you still willing to approach Jared?"

"Dr. Gilley, he's a good man. I have to risk the pain, I think. I can imagine my life without him if I have to, but I'd rather he was part of my life."

"You're a strong woman, Lauren. I think you've got this. Depending on what happens, you know I'm always here for you."

"Thank you."

She drove to the cottage, to her safe place, determined to call Jared. She contemplated calling Maggie first, to see if she agreed with her decision to contact Jared, but thought better of it. She didn't want anything to break her resolve.

As she dialed his number, she thought about how easy it had been between them. They fit together. Could they recapture that?

"Detective Martin," Jared said as he answered the call.

"Jared, it's me, Lauren." There was absolute silence and her heart was pounding, a flush of red creeping up her neck to her face.

"Hello, Lauren," he finally said, obviously surprised to hear her voice.

"I'm not sure what to say to you, but I think we owe it to each other to meet. I'd like to see you if you can find some time. Explain everything to you," Lauren said.

Jared was stunned. She was the last person he expected to be calling him. She was ready to talk. My God, it had been so long, but hearing her voice had stirred old feelings. Maggie had told him he needed to talk to her before he moved on with Kim. Shit, Kim. What would she think of his meeting Lauren?

"Jared? Are you still there?"

"Yes, I'm here. Alright, Lauren, I'll meet you."

"Can you stop by the cottage after work today?

"I'll be there." Then he hung up.

Chapter 59

Jared was conflicted. When he had asked Kim to move in with him, he felt it was the right thing to do. Maggie had warned him that he should talk to Lauren before moving on with Kim, but he had ignored her. Now he knew why he should have done it. Just hearing Lauren's voice had resurrected all the old feelings. He had loved Lauren deeply, but it was different than what he was now feeling for Kim. Kim was fun to be with, beautiful and always on. She adored him and wanted to spend every minute with him. That was flattering after being rejected by Lauren. When he met her, Kim was exactly what he needed at the time. But Lauren, Lauren had his heart.

He had no idea how the conversation with Lauren would go, so he decided not to tell Kim that he was seeing her. Kim was working late anyway, and he would tell her when she got home. No sense giving her anything to be worried about.

As he drove to the cottage, he remembered the last time he had been there. The smell of bleach, all traces of Lauren gone. He had been in a panic to find her, not knowing that she had been next door in one of Cal's cages. As he turned down the side road that led to her driveway, he was jolted by the sight of Cal's property. The house and outbuildings were gone and a for sale sign was the only thing visible on the land. Cal's sisters had removed all trace of him and the depravity that had existed there. Maybe an outsider who didn't know the history of the property would buy it one day, but the sisters had better prepare for a long wait.

The cottage looked the same, and pleasant memories of his times there surfaced and stunned him with their intensity. How was he going to get through this meeting with Lauren? What was different about her? What about Kim? So many thoughts were rushing at him at once.

Lauren must have heard his car pull up, because as soon as he stepped onto the porch, she was there at the door. She looked incredible. Her hair was shorter, but perfectly styled. She was impeccably dressed as always and it was obvious she'd been spending time at the gym. Probably part of her therapy, he thought.

She smiled at him and invited him inside. He could tell she was nervous, but, hell, so was he.

"Would you like a glass of wine or maybe a cup of coffee?" Lauren asked.

"How about coffee?" Jared said.

"Coffee, it is. I'll be right back."

As Jared watched her walk into the kitchen, it was like they had never been apart. But they had. And she'd hurt him. How could she justify that and expect him to be okay with it? He could feel anger rising and fought to control it.

She returned with coffee, poured him a cup and took one for herself.

"Thank you so much for doing this. I know it can't be easy for you."

"It's not," he said, a trace of anger in his voice.

"I guess I deserve that. I'm not expecting anything from you; really, I'm not. I just want to tell you my story. Explain why I did what I did, so that you can understand why I pushed you away. And I can't begin to thank you for everything you did to find me."

She had tears in her eyes and she fought to contain them.

"Jared, I cherish the time we had together. You know I wasn't looking for a relationship, and I kept my distance from you when I thought you were getting too serious. But then, before Cal kidnapped me, I had a conversation with Maggie. I didn't know if I wanted the same things you did. Know what she said? She said you would let me know if you wanted more and I should make my decision about our relationship then. But to just enjoy being with you and see where it would lead. She thought we were great together and you were a good guy. She also said I might want more than I thought I did. She didn't get an argument from me."

"Then that freak kidnapped me and I had to fight to stay alive. I knew you would look for me and that's what kept me going. Tess and I were going to try to overpower him and escape, but then he heard about Gaby's body being found and he forced me to leave with him. When he shot Tess, I blamed myself. As he was pulling me by a chain around my ankle, I told her that you would find her and to tell you everything that happened. I didn't realize my mistake until he casually pulled the trigger. No emotion at all, like she didn't matter. I was horrified and kept reliving it, intensifying my guilt. If only I hadn't said anything, he might not have shot her, but instead just left her there. I thought she was dead."

"It took us 4 or 5 days to get to that cabin. I was cold, miserable and scared. I kept thinking you would ride up on your white horse and rescue me any minute, but it didn't happen. Instead, I worked my ass off gathering food, chopping firewood and doing anything else to keep us warm and fed. Then I got bit by a black widow spider nesting in the woodpile. I was sick and Cal took care of me. I was in so much pain and delirious. He told me then about what his mother had done to him. Every time he was under stress, he thought he could hear his mother talking to him. He even answered her. But he was always mad at her for what she did and sometimes I think he thought I was his mother.

Jared, he was the only thing between me and death. I couldn't reconcile the horrible things he had done with the caring way he treated me. But I learned from him and planned my escape. I think it shocked him when I left, and then he followed me."

"I headed toward the hunter's cabin I had seen, hoping someone there would help me. Darryl Lazarus found me just as Cal did. Cal was yelling at me, asking how I could leave him, like we were in a relationship or something. It was surreal. Cal threatened him and then Darryl shot him. He recognized us and that's when he decided to extort money from you for my return. I was pretty sure that once they got the money, I was expendable. So, Cal and I ran. He was pretty weak so we doubled back to the cabin. It was Cal's idea for the booby trap and we worked together to build it. I was the bait. Cal slipped and fell out of the tree and the log caught Darryl in the arm. I think the nails we hammered in there must have hit an artery. He started to bleed badly. The log swung back while Cal was trying to get Darryl's gun to me, and he just couldn't get out of the way in time. It killed him. There I was, Cal dead, and Darryl swigging Jack Daniels for the pain. He poured that whiskey on Cal and burned him. He made me watch. That's when I lost it. You know the rest."

"My therapist, Dr. Gilley, has helped me to see that the feelings I had for Cal were similar to feelings sufferers of Stockholm Syndrome experience. He took care of me, tried to protect me from that maniac, Darryl Lazarus, and died trying to save me. The stories he told me about his mother also came into play. But I realize those feelings were false and I've put Cal where he belongs. But while I had to work through those feelings, I couldn't fully commit to a relationship with you. It wouldn't have been fair to you. I wasn't healthy and you couldn't fix me, no matter how much you loved me. I know I risked losing you by doing that, but I loved you too much to destroy your life. Mine was already in pretty bad shape."

"But now, my life is back on track. I still go to therapy once in a while if I feel I need it, I'm back to work and I'm finally writing that book. But it doesn't have an ending yet. I guess that depends on you."

Jared had read the police report, but listening to Lauren's own words left him amazed. What an incredibly strong woman to have survived what she did! He had even more respect for her now that he'd heard everything.

Jared stared into her eyes, seeing anticipation. How could he hurt her? But he was with Kim now. As much as he cared about Lauren, and he did care, Kim had been there for him when Lauren hadn't. He understood why she did what she did, but for now, he couldn't forgive her.

"Lauren, you are an incredible woman."

"I hear a 'but'," Lauren said, sadness tingeing her voice.

"I've met someone else and I really care for her. In fact, we're living together."

"I see. Well, I guess that tells me what I need to know. Thank you for listening. I hope you're happy and she gives you everything you need. I can't say it doesn't hurt, but I will always cherish our time together, Jared."

She rose from the chair, and led him to her door. As he reached to open it, he turned to her.

"Lauren, I did love you. Hell, maybe I still do. I have to think. And I have to tell Kim. She's not you, but she has made me happy so far. I thought I could move on, but seeing you, knowing what you sacrificed for me, has me confused. Give me some time to reconcile all of this. To see where things go with Kim. I'm sorry, that's the best I can do right now."

"I understand and it's more than I expected. I will give you time, and you know where to find me. Take care of yourself, Jared."

He left her house and drove straight home. Kim was probably already there and wondering where he was. He had stayed at Lauren's longer than he had expected to. It was good to see her. To hear her voice again. Study the curve of her neck. He knew he had missed her. There was no denying that.

Kim was waiting for him, a look of concern on her face. As he walked in the door, she ran to him and threw her arms around his neck.

"I called your cell phone when you weren't here when I got home. I thought something had happened to you. I even called the hospital. Where were you?" she demanded.

"Whoa, wait a minute. I planned to tell you about it as soon as you got home. I just didn't expect you to be home first. I got a call today from Lauren."

"Your ex-girlfriend? What did she want?" Her tone had changed and she exuded sweetness.

"She has finished her therapy and wanted to tell me her story in her own words. It was heart-wrenching hearing first hand everything she had been through. I admire her for how well she's getting her life back. I told her about us. She says she's happy for me."

"I'm glad you're home. Are you hungry? I put a casserole in the oven about a half hour ago. You have just enough time to scrub-a-dub-dub before dinner."

"I'm starved. I'll be down in 10."

He kissed her and headed upstairs to shower. He had muted his cell phone while at Lauren's and decided to check his messages. He had 34 missed calls from Kim.

Chapter 60

Lauren and Maggie met for lunch the day after Lauren's conversation with Jared. Maggie was anxious to hear how it went, especially because she had no idea that Lauren planned to call him.

"Well?" asked Maggie.

"He looks just the way I remembered him. I think he was glad to see me, although he was hard to read. He told me about Kim."

"What did he say about her?" asked Maggie.

"Just that he cares for her and they're living together."

"I told him he should have told her about you before he let her move in, but of course, being a man, he didn't listen. I'm not sure how Kim's going to take this. When I talked to her, she was sure Jared was over you. Is he?"

"Honestly, Maggie I don't know. He said he was confused. That he might still love me."

"He said that?"

"Yes, but he also said he needs to see where things go with Kim. He asked me to give him time."

"And, of course, you'll do it."

"I have to. I'm sure I'll run into them sometime since this is a small town. I don't want her to think I'm trying to take Jared away from her. I'm not. He knows how I feel. He needs to know how he feels. Besides, I'm not a total recluse. David Luccesi is coming into Wildwood to consult with a new patient and he's asked me to dinner tomorrow."

"Good for you. I'm glad to see you getting back at it. Is there something going on with him? Is he a fallback if Jared stays with Kim?" asked Maggie.

"Definitely not. David is a good dinner companion and very attentive. But that's as far as it will ever go. He seems to be okay with it."

"Why don't the two of you stop by the house after dinner for a cocktail? We'd love to meet him."

"I'm sure he'd be fine with that. Besides, I want Charlie to know that Jared and I have talked. I know he was Team Jared when I pushed Jared away from me."

"If Jared can forgive you, so can Charlie. Now let's eat, I'm starving."

The dinner David had planned had ended up a disaster. He got a flat tire on his way to pick up Lauren and when they finally got to the restaurant, they were turned away due to a water main break. As they trudged through 2 inches of water to get back to David's car, Lauren burst into laughter. David soon followed.

"Do you have a backup plan?" Lauren asked.

"How about a burger from the diner?" David suggested.

"I think we're a little overdressed, but I'm game if you are," she said.

"Let's do it."

The diner was on the next block and nearly empty. As they found a table, their conversation was easy. David was a bit bombastic, but she could forgive him that. He probably hadn't eaten in many diners as down-home as this. If any.

Instead of burgers, they both ordered a cobb salad which was surprisingly good. Her fork stopped in mid-bite as the door to the diner opened and Jared, accompanied by a beautiful blonde woman, walked in. *This must be Kim*, she thought, a sharp pain knifing her chest.

At first, Jared didn't see her. She had positioned herself directly in front of David and his body blocked her from Jared's view. But as soon as he walked towards the back of the restaurant, he spotted her. Kim was deep in animated conversation with him, but as soon as he saw Lauren, he stopped mid-sentence. Confused, Kim followed his gaze to a woman seated at a table. Jared grabbed Kim's hand and led her to Lauren's table.

"Kim, I'd like you to meet Lauren Sedgeway. Lauren, this is Kim Wellen." Lauren thought she saw longing in his eyes, which didn't escape Kim's notice.

"Kim, it's so nice to meet you. This is Dr. David Luccesi," she said, trying her best to hold her smile. Kim was breathtaking. No wonder Jared was enthralled with her. She watched as Kim appraised her and she saw something in her demeanor that made her uncomfortable. She quickly looked away and returned her gaze to Jared.

"David was one of my therapists and now we've become friends. I don't think I would be where I am today if not for him," she said, smiling at David and touching his hand. She saw mild discomfort in his face and she knew she was putting him on the spot.

"Nice to meet you Dr. Luccesi," Jared said, holding his hand out to shake the doctor's. David obliged and then an uncomfortable silence made Jared want to get away.

276

"We're just here to pick up a take-out order, and I see it's ready. Nice to see you, Lauren, and nice to meet you Dr. Luccesi. You all have a great night."

Jared and Kim walked away and she watched as Kim possessively held on to Jared's arm, staking her claim to him. David watched them walk away then turned to Lauren.

"So, that's Jared. Are you okay?"

"I didn't know how much pain would be associated with seeing him with another woman, a beautiful, younger woman."

"Don't sell yourself short. You are a beautiful woman. And I can understand the pain. You still have feelings for him. I can see that."

"They're stronger than I knew. But I need to give him time to decide what he wants. If it's not me, then I'll deal with it."

They finished their dinner, although Lauren's appetite had disappeared. As they drove to Maggie's, Lauren was quiet, lost in her thoughts. Spending time with Maggie was just what she needed.

Chapter 61

On the drive home from the diner, Jared could see that Kim was quiet. He didn't want to play the game of trying to read her mind, so he decided to jump in.

"Are you okay?" he asked her.

"Okay? You stopped dead in your tracks when you saw your ex. How do you think that makes me feel? I thought you were over her."

"She was an important part of my life and I can't just forget her like that," he said, snapping his fingers. "I was ready to propose to her before her kidnapping happened." He instantly realized what a stupid comment that was to make, and Kim immediately reacted.

Icily, she said, "You're with me now. We're living together. There is no place in our lives for her."

He couldn't agree, but he wanted to be fair to Kim. Seeing Lauren again, especially in the company of another man, was eye-opening for him. There were still feelings there; strong feelings. But he couldn't forget how he had met Kim at the lowest point in his life and how she had made him feel alive again. Did he love her? Did he still love Lauren? He'd have to sort out his feelings now, and the only way to do that was to spend more time with Lauren. He knew she still loved him, but if he decided to stay with Kim, she would need to move on. Maybe with David Luccesi. The thought of that didn't sit well with him.

He'd have to be honest with Kim.

"I'm so sorry about all of this. You've been incredible."

"Is it over for us? Are you thinking of going back to her?" Kim asked.

"Honestly? I'm not sure of anything right now. I have been so happy with you, but I need to understand what I feel for Lauren. I want to be fair to both of you. If I still have feelings for Lauren, I can't fully commit to a relationship with you. But if it can't work with her, she needs to move on and you and I can build our relationship from there. To do that, I need to spend some time with Lauren. I know this is not what you want to hear, but I think you should get away for a few days until I figure this all out."

She stared at him and he saw a look on her face he had never seen before. Ever since he had known her, she had been upbeat and animated. But now she displayed a look of disappointment and hurt. And something else he couldn't read.

"If that's what you want, I'll leave while you work this out. I'll just need to let the hospital know. I'll leave tomorrow to go visit my sister in Helena for a few days. I'll be back on Friday, so that will give you a week." She waited for a reaction from him but he didn't respond, only looked at her with apologetic eyes. "We belong together," she said as she left to go upstairs to pack her bag.

Chapter 62

That bitch, Kim thought as she threw her bag into the trunk of her car. She was leaving what had been her home for the past few weeks because of that woman. Jared was hers. *Hers!* She remembered a time, years ago, when another woman, Bethany, had tried to take her college sweetheart from her. She couldn't remember his name now, but Bethany lived to regret it. *It hadn't gone that well for you, Bethany, had it?* Poor Bethany, a little shove from behind and she lay battered and broken at the foot of her favorite deserted trailhead, having fallen over 100 feet to her death. The police had investigated, but had found it to be a tragic accident. Kim had followed her, unseen, and had hidden behind an outcropping on the trail. When Bethany began her descent and then passed her, Kim simply shoved her hard enough to send her tumbling over the edge. Bethany never saw it coming. No one would have expected sweet, beautiful Kim to become a killer. But she got what she wanted. And if she had to kill to get it, she would.

Hadn't it been easy with Jared? When she first moved to Wildwood, she had seen him in town and the attraction to him was instantaneous. She knew about his relationship with Lauren, and her pulling away from him, so she started to craft a plan to meet him. She had to leave an indelible impression, proving she wasn't any ordinary woman.

She had left that flyer on his front porch and for the next 3 days, had waited for him to try the new trailhead. She had stalked him, watching his routine, and knew he went for a run every day at 6 am. He usually ran in his neighborhood, but when he got in his car headed for highway 93, she was pretty sure where he was going. She beat him there by minutes, climbed the trailhead and using a high vantage point, knew when he would be hitting the jog in the trail. That's when she made her move and deliberately ran into him. She knew her looks and her humor usually won over any man she targeted. Sad, vulnerable and lonely Jared hadn't had a chance.

But she hadn't counted on his feelings for Lauren. He was supposed to be done with her. She would leave like he asked, but she wasn't going to Helena and she wasn't going to lose Jared to Lauren. No, the odds needed to be tipped in her favor and she knew just how to do it.

Chapter 63

Lauren answered the phone in her office and listened to the sexy voice she'd know anywhere. It was Jared.

"Lauren, it's Jared."

"I know." A flood of memories of their time together cascaded through her emotions.

"It was nice seeing you last night."

"You seemed a little uncomfortable," she said, teasing him a little.

"Lauren, I'm torn up inside. Seeing you with the doctor pissed me off. That's when I knew there was still something between us. I think you felt it, too."

"I did, but you're with Kim now; shit, you're living with her."

"Kim has gone to spend a few days with her sister in Helena. I told her I needed to spend some time with you, to see if I can sort out my feelings."

"Wow, she must have hated that. I see how she clings to you."

"Actually, she was fine with it."

"Really? I wouldn't be. So, what do you want, Jared?"

"To see you. See if getting back together is what we both want."

"Alright."

"How about we start with dinner? My place tonight?" said Jared.

"What time?" she asked.

"6 works for me."

"Okay, I'll see you then."

When she drove up the street towards Jared's house, her heart was filled with anticipation. She loved him, but knew he still had feelings toward Kim. But they had a history that began before he met Kim and her hope was that the pull of that history would win out. She felt a little sorry for Kim, though. Kim had gone headlong into that relationship, not knowing how connected Jared still was to his past relationship. She couldn't imagine how hurt Kim would be if Jared decided to spend his life with her, leaving Kim behind.

She arrived at Jared's, grabbed a bottle of wine from the front seat and made her way to his front porch. Ordinarily, she would have walked right in, but tonight she rang the doorbell. She heard footsteps hurry to the door and seconds later, Jared opened it, smiled at her and led her inside.

"Please, come in." He closed the door then instinctively reached to hug her as he always had before, but stopped himself, a confused look evident on his face. To put him at ease, she touched his arm and then pulled him to her, initiating a hug that lasted a full minute.

When they broke away, both were lost in their thoughts. *It's still the same,* Lauren thought. *I can't live without her,* Jared thought. They looked into each other's eyes, drawn to the feelings that had risen between them, and kissed. Tenderly, at first. Then, with a passion that couldn't be denied.

Lauren pulled away, heart pounding, and began pacing the floor.

"I love you, Jared. My therapy has helped me through most of my issues, but that one thing is certain. I love you."

"Lauren, I was devastated when you couldn't trust me enough to be there for you while you healed. I guess I was vulnerable and lonely, and then Kim came into my life. She was good for me, then. I don't want to hurt her."

"I know that. But will it hurt her more, knowing you still have feelings for me? How could you move forward with that relationship, be fair to her?"

"I couldn't. And I won't. You are my love, and probably have been from the moment I first saw you at Smokey's. It was so easy with us. And it felt damn good. There is more intensity in my feelings for you than I have ever had elsewhere. But there is one thing I need to know from you," he said.

"What's that?"

"When we were together before, you weren't sure what you wanted long term. You seemed to be okay with the relationship as it was. You even had a conversation with Maggie about it. How do you feel now, and please, be honest with me?"

"I want to marry you. To spend the rest of my life with you. I think it took almost losing you to make me realize what I wanted. It's such a cliché, I know."

"I'll need to tell Kim when she gets back on Friday. It's not right to keep her guessing. I'm not sure how she'll take it. I just hope she understands. In the meantime, I want to spend as much time as I can with you until then."

"I have a deadline I'm working under so my days will be filled with work. But my nights are free," said Lauren.

"How free?" Jared asked, a hint of mischief in his voice.

"I have an overnight bag in my car, if that gives you the answer you were looking for."

They made dinner together, then spent hours talking, catching up and getting to know each other again. When they made love, their commitment to each other was finally sealed.

Kim watched, unseen, as Lauren made her way into Jared's house, *her house*. And when Lauren spent the night, something inside Kim snapped. It was time to put her plan into play.

Chapter 64

The next morning, Jared and Lauren started their day with a run. Unused to early morning physical activity, Lauren struggled to keep up. But she was willing to keep going and by the third run that week, she had started looking forward to it. They alternated from his house to hers and on Thursday, knowing it was the last day before Kim returned, Lauren felt brave enough to try the new trailhead Jared had been using. He had a case he needed to work on that morning, so she decided to try it on her own. She'd call him when she got home from her run and wait to hear from him after he talked to Kim.

Jared had left her house around 5:30 that morning. He needed to drive to Kalispell but would return by around 3 pm that afternoon. He wasn't looking forward to his encounter with Kim, but he'd have to suck it up and just be direct with her.

Lauren left her house around 6:30 am, driving on highway 93 to the trailhead. She didn't see the car following her or stopping just short of the trailhead, obscured by a grove of trees. As Lauren exited her car and started her climb, Kim, dressed in black, followed her and found a hidden place to ambush her. When Lauren got close, Kim would spring into action.

As Kim waited for Lauren to begin her descent, she fumed. Oh, Jared would grieve over the untimely death of Lauren, but she'd be there, ready to comfort him. She'd move back in and their relationship would grow. He would forget all about Lauren.

Killer Looks

Lauren was lost in thought as she came back down the trailhead. She was pretty proud of herself for getting to the top, even though she had had to walk part of the way. But coming down, she was able to run and it was exhilarating. As she reached the halfway point, a figure dressed in black blocked her path, forcing her to stop. It was Kim. Confusion showed on Lauren's face, but the look of menace on Kim's face made Lauren see a grim reality. She was in trouble.

Kim pulled a gun from her pocket and pointing it at Lauren, began her tirade.

"Why couldn't you just have stayed away from Jared? He's mine. You pushed him away and right into my arms. Do you think it was just an accident the way Jared and I met? No, I planned it, just like I plan to end your relationship with him. I left a flyer for him telling him about this trail so that I could arrange to run into him and now here we are. At the site of your impending demise."

"Kim, you don't want to do this. You can't shoot me."

"Shoot you? No, that's not what this is about. You're going to have a tragic accident. You're going to take a fall and I'm sorry to say, you won't make it. Then Jared will need me, and I'll be right there."

"It'll never work. No one will believe I just fell," said Lauren.

"Oh, it will work. You see, I've done this before. Bethany thought she could steal my boyfriend but she learned differently. The only difference is she never saw me before I pushed her. But you, I wanted you to see who would cause your death."

287

She sprinted towards Lauren, catching her off balance. Before she could do anything to stop her, Lauren screamed and found herself being pushed over the edge of the trail.

Just as Lauren disappeared from view, Kim heard the sound of running footsteps heading up the trail. She quickly turned in the opposite direction, looking for concealment. Once hidden, she could wait until the runners were gone and leave unnoticed.

When she no longer heard any movement below her, she began her descent. It was then that she heard the sound of an ambulance and saw two runners attempting to rescue a badly injured Lauren from the group of bushes into which she had fallen. They had made their way down the steep incline and had obviously called 911. Lauren was unmoving and if she wasn't dead now, she soon would be.

Chapter 65

Jared got to the hospital as soon as he got the call. Charlie called him to let him know that Lauren had just been admitted, and that it was bad, really bad. She had taken a fall over the edge of the trailhead on highway 93, but two runners had heard her scream and called 911. It had taken time to remove her from the treacherous terrain and doctors were worried about a head injury she had suffered.

Lauren was in surgery to remove pressure on her brain, and to repair a broken femur and pelvis. The prognosis was not good, the doctor had told him.

As Jared sat in the surgical waiting room, Kim was suddenly by his side.

"I came back a day early to get some work done here at the hospital, and I heard what happened to your friend. I'm so sorry. Is there anything I can do?" Kim asked.

Jared looked up at her, pain obvious on his face.

"No, nothing. I'm just waiting for her to get out of recovery so that I can go to her room. Kim, there are some things we need to talk about, but now is not the right time. I've got to focus on Lauren."

"Those things can wait. I understand it's very serious, and she might not make it. I'm here for you to help you make any kind of arrangements that need to be made," Kim said.

"Arrangements? What are you talking about? It will be a long recovery for her, but she will improve little by little, day by day."

"You need to face reality, Jared; be prepared for what very likely may happen. I know it will hurt, but she may not survive."

"Kim, I don't want to hear any more," Jared said, then left to find someone who could give him an update.

Lauren was finally out of surgery and recovery, but had been transferred to ICU. Jared was by her side and had been for most of the day. Charlie had called him and wanted to stop by, and Jared was anxious to know how the investigation was progressing.

Charlie showed up about an hour after their phone call.

"How is she?" Charlie asked as he walked through the door.

"She's stable, but she suffered some really serious injuries. They got the bleeding stopped in her brain and repaired her broken femur and pelvis. She's got a long road of recovery ahead of her."

"I'm sorry buddy, I really am. Maggie will be by in a little while to see her. She's devastated by this. She loves Lauren like a sister. Has she been awake yet? Able to tell you what happened?" Charlie asked.

"No, they're keeping her in a medically induced coma until the swelling in her brain goes down. It could be days before she wakes up and they don't know what the head injury has done to her cognitive abilities. I'm scared, Charlie. Scared of losing her."

"Losing her? Does that mean Kim is no longer in the picture?" Charlie asked.

"Kim doesn't know that Lauren and I reconciled. It wasn't the right time to tell her, not with all of this going on. She actually stopped by and wanted to help me make arrangements. Like Lauren was going to die. I just walked away from her. I'll have to deal with her later, I guess."

"I've got the police report with me, if you want to look at it."

"Just give me the overview. I'll look at it later."

"The two guys that found her heard a scream and hurried to investigate. At first, they couldn't find her, then decided to follow the edge of the trail and that's when they saw that she had fallen. They called 911 and worked their way down to where she was. They tied a jacket around her neck to try to keep her head stable, and that probably saved her life. The paramedics had a hell of a time getting her up from there. Took a couple of hours. The officer on the scene sent for forensics and they did some shots of the trail and where she had fallen. Footprints in the dirt looked like there might have been a struggle. He kept the trail closed until the investigation was complete. Got some prints of athletic shoes. There were at least 4 sets. We eliminated one set as belonging to Lauren and the other two to the two runners. There's one set that we've yet to identify."

"What do you mean by a struggle? Are you saying Lauren might have been attacked on that trail?"

"We're not ruling out the possibility. Witnesses saw a figure in black walking along the side of the road leading away from the trailhead. We're checking any footprints we might find alongside the road against the ones on the trail. But there is that chance that the other set of footprints could have already been there and don't belong to anyone involved in what happened to Lauren. She could have been unfamiliar with the trail and simply lost her balance and went over the edge. We'll have to wait till she wakes up to see if she can tell us anything."

"I'm going to be here as much as I can until she wakes up. But I don't want her alone while I'm not here. I can't imagine anyone wanting to hurt Lauren, but I'm hiring an off-duty officer to stay outside her door when I leave, just to be on the safe side. If someone did attack her, she may have seen them. I don't want them getting a second chance," said Jared.

"You'll need to clear it with the hospital. They like knowing who's walking their halls. Patient privacy, you know. In the meantime, we'll do a little more investigating, but not sure we'll come up with anything new. If Lauren wakes up, let me know so we can question her. Let's do this by the book, okay?"

"Yeah, okay, I'll call you. If we don't do this right, and she was attacked, I don't want to jeopardize any prosecution."

"Good to hear. I've got to get back at it, but call me if you need me. For anything. And if I were you, I'd have that conversation with Kim immediately. No sense giving her false hope. Then you can focus on Lauren with nothing hanging over your head."

Charlie was right, he would have to talk to Kim. And soon. But how was he going to tell her?

He left Lauren with Maggie, who had arrived just as Charlie was leaving. He needed to find Kim. As he walked the hallway to her office, he half expected her not to be there, but as he came to her doorway, he saw her seated at her desk, on the phone. She motioned him in and he sat in one of the leather chairs in front of her desk. He had never been in her office before and curiously, the only personal items he could see were candid pictures of him that she had somehow taken without him noticing. Her overnight bag was on the floor to his right, partially opened and revealing a muddy athletic shoe. *She must have been for a run this morning*, he thought. Before that thought could go any deeper, she was off the phone, around her desk and sitting in his lap, her arms around his neck.

"I'm so glad to be back. I'll leave early today and head back home. How about if I make dinner?" she said, lightly.

He moved to stand up and she reluctantly unwrapped her arms from around his neck, stood and watched as, hands in his pockets, he started pacing.

"Kim, there's no easy way to say this. Lauren and I have reconciled. We plan to marry as soon as possible. I never wanted to hurt you, and I hate doing this. But I got into this relationship without making sure the old one was over. It wasn't. I'll help you find an apartment or a house, whichever you decide, and I'll pack up your things for you. You can pick them up this evening."

Kim looked at him, no expression on her face at all. He expected her to cry, or throw things, but her cold resolve was unexpected.

"I'd like you to leave," she said, sitting in her chair and swiveling it so that her back was to him. He did.

Chapter 66

Kim was remarkably different when she stopped to pick up her things at Jared's later that same evening. She was beautifully dressed and made up the way she knew he admired, her usual wisecracking self in full deployment and it was as if nothing had changed between them. She had rented another condo on a month to month lease so that, she told him, she could move back in at any time. No trace of the Kim he had seen in her office remained. When the front door closed behind her, he had a feeling she wouldn't let go so easily and it could become a problem. But he had Lauren to think about now, and with Kim out on her own, he could devote as much time as he wanted to Lauren's recovery.

When Jared arrived in Lauren's room the next morning, her doctor was with her. Lauren had shown signs of coming out of the coma on her own after they had withdrawn the sedation drugs from her medical regimen. Her brain swelling was subsiding and her brain activity increasing. The doctor expected that over the next 12 to 24 hours, Lauren would regain consciousness. He couldn't guarantee that she would be able to communicate yet, but her cognitive abilities showed signs of reappearance. Jared was ecstatic.

Jared had spoken with Charlie about off duty officers and he had made arrangements with Trent Bonham, Carlos Sanchez and Wendy Collier to cover the shifts necessary when Jared couldn't be there. The officers were only too happy to help out their former colleague.

Now, all he had to do was wait for Lauren to wake up.

Killer Looks

Lauren can't wake up, Kim thought. Kim would have to see to it that she didn't. If Lauren was able to tell Jared what had happened, there was no chance she could get him back. How had the bitch even lived? Bethany hadn't. Why was Lauren so lucky? When Jared had told her it was over, she didn't blame him. He was weak. Lauren had manipulated him, she was sure. After all, hadn't *she* manipulated him into a relationship? Taken him away from Lauren?

She didn't have much time. In a matter of hours, Lauren would wake up and begin to communicate. She had to put an end to her now. But how?

A security report left on her desk revealed that Jared had hired off-duty cops to guard Lauren while he was away. The only time she could have access to Lauren was when Jared was there. She would go to him as he sat by Lauren's bedside, tell him there were no hard feelings and that she was moving on. She would say she hoped he and Lauren would be very happy. Then she would weep a little, ask him to get her a cup of tea and while he was gone, pump 4 syringefuls of air into Lauren's IV. She'd be dead of an embolism in no time.

Tomorrow morning. It would happen tomorrow morning.

Chapter 67

Lauren began to hear noises. They were indistinguishable at first, just a steady drone, then they fought to break through her consciousness. She was in a hospital, finally recognizing the sounds and smells that were all too familiar. She felt a blood pressure cuff suddenly spring to life, squeezing her arm with a minor discomfort that confirmed she was still among the living.

But what had happened? Her thoughts were skittering through her mind like tiny worker ants, moving in haphazard directions, searching for…something. What was it? Why couldn't she remember?

Open your eyes. That was what she wanted to do. Needed to do. To pull herself out of the fog that threatened to envelope her forever. She couldn't let that happen. She had to be present, for…someone.

She felt herself being spiraled into full consciousness, and finally realized what had happened to her. She had fallen. But where? Why was she only getting fragments? As she shifted in her bed, pain suddenly grabbed her and she gasped. What was wrong with her?

At that moment, the door opened and two people entered the room.

"The doctor said we can expect her to wake up at any time," a man in a nurse's uniform said to a young woman who accompanied him. "Let's check her vitals and replace her drip bag," he said as he approached the bed.

As he bent down to run a thermometer over her forehead, she opened her eyes, surprising him. He jumped, then immediately came back to her bedside.

"Lauren, I'm Andy Lawlor, your night nurse. This is Callie, your nurse's aide. Can you hear me? Are you in pain?"

Lauren struggled to answer, but found that she only made small unintelligible sounds. Andy could see the frustration and panic on her face.

"Don't worry, you've been in a serious accident, but you're going to be alright. Your brain must have told you it was time to wake up. Stay with me, Lauren. If you're in pain, just press this button twice and a pain killer will be released into your IV," he said, putting the button device in her hand and checking the morphine bag.

"I'm going to get the doctor on call to take a look at you. I'll be right back."

Wendy Collier was outside Lauren's door, working the night shift until Jared arrived later that morning. As Andy exited Lauren's room, he said, "She's awake. You might want to call somebody to let them know."

When the phone rang, Jared instinctively looked at the clock on his nightstand and saw that it was 4am. He quickly answered, hearing Wendy Collier's voice.

"The night nurse just told me that Lauren's awake. I wanted to let you know as soon as possible."

"Give me time to shower and I'll be there as quick as I can. Do you know how she is?"

"No, but I guess it's a good sign she's awake, right? Besides, they're not going to tell me anything. I'm just her bodyguard. She needs you, so move your ass."

It took him 20 minutes to shower, shave, dress and drive to the hospital. His heart was racing as he stepped off the elevator on the 3rd floor and walked the hallway to

Lauren's door. Wendy Collier met him, a huge smile illuminating her face, and she opened the door to let him in.

Lauren's eyes immediately went to the door as soon as it opened and she caught sight of Jared. There was no look of recognition on her face. Her gaze returned to the 3 people who were standing around her bed, each of them performing separate evaluations. Heartbroken, he approached the bed, desperately wanting to hold Lauren in his arms. Instead, gently leading the doctor away from Lauren, he introduced himself to the on-call doctor who was just beginning his examination.

"Detective Martin, why don't you step outside while I finish my exam and I'll meet you there after I'm done." Jared reluctantly agreed, but he was desperate for information and desperate to talk to Lauren.

A few minutes later, Dr. Mathias Gentry opened the door to Lauren's room and stepped outside. Seeing Jared seated in the chair that was once occupied by the officer, he approached him. Jared immediately leapt to his feet, anxiety causing the deep furrows in his brow.

"Physically, Lauren is in for a long recovery," Gentry said as they both walked to a private consult office. "She can remember falling, but nothing else at this time. I think the memories will come flooding back rather quickly. I looked at her MRI and now that the swelling has subsided, there appears to be no discernable damage to her cognitive abilities. I think you are probably the best person to bring those memories back. But I will caution you. She doesn't remember how or why she fell, and I know the police will want to talk to her. Just take it slowly. She's still in a great deal of pain and will be in and out of it as long as she's on pain meds. I'll make some more notes for her surgeon, and I'm sure he'll be by later today to see her. Good luck, Detective."

"I can see her now?" Jared asked.

"Of course. She's more awake now, but approach her slowly. We don't want her upset."

Jared took a deep breath, then opened the door to Lauren's room. The male nurse had tried to make her comfortable, but he could see the pain on her face. As the doctor had suggested, he approached her with caution, directing a smile towards her. He was hoping to alleviate any trepidation she might have.

"Lauren, it's Jared. How are you doing, sweetheart?"

She looked at him, confusion and then recognition causing her to smile back at him.

"Jared? What happened to me?" she said, but he could see she was struggling to keep her eyes open.

"There's plenty of time for that. I'm going to be right here and when you wake up, we'll talk, okay? Just get some sleep." Jared watched as her eyes closed and her body relaxed.

"She'll be out for an hour or so," said Andy. "I've got to check on other patients, but just ring the call button if you need anything."

"Thanks," said Jared, as Andy slipped from the room.

Jared sat, watching Lauren sleep and grateful that she had survived her ordeal. He picked up his cell phone and put in a call to Charlie.

"Hey," said Charlie as he sleepily answered his phone. "I hope there's a good reason you're calling me at 5 am."

"Lauren's awake. Well, she was awake. She's on some pretty heavy pain meds, but she knows she fell and she knows who I am. I talked to the doctor and we've got to go slowly with her. She's pretty fragile, but he thinks the memories will return and return quickly. She's asleep now, but once she's awake again, you need to be here when I start asking her questions."

"Buddy, that's great." Jared could hear Charlie telling Maggie that Lauren was awake. "I can be there in a half hour," Charlie said.

"Make it an hour; she's still asleep."

Chapter 68

Jared knew Lauren was a strong woman, but surviving her fall and the subsequent physical therapy that would be required would test her limits. The kidnapping was one thing, but to see her battered body lying almost helpless in the hospital bed was almost more than he could handle. But he would be strong for her. It was the least he could do considering what she would have to endure over the next few months.

He was surprised when he saw the door to Lauren's room open and Kim step inside. He didn't know what to think about her visit. She smiled at him as she walked to Lauren's bedside.

"How is she doing?" Kim asked.

Irritated, he said, "Fine. Kim, what are you doing here?"

"Jared, this is a small hospital and when I got here this morning, I heard Lauren had woken up. I just came by to see how you both were doing. Was she able to tell you what happened?"

"Not yet," he said.

"Jared, I just wanted you to know that being with you is a memory I will always treasure. Although it hurts, I am moving on and hope that you and Lauren are very happy together. I thought *we* could have the perfect relationship, but I see how important Lauren is to you. I only wish…" Kim started to sob and Jared resisted the impulse to comfort her.

"Kim, I'm so sorry. I don't like seeing you like this and I know it's my fault."

"I'm sorry for breaking down like this. I've got to go back to work, but I need a little time to compose myself. Would you mind getting me a cup of tea?"

Jared hesitated, unwilling to leave Lauren's side in case she woke up. The last person she'd want to see was Kim. But Kim looked so pitiful, that he acquiesced.

"I'll be right back."

As Jared left the room, Kim, who had collapsed into a chair next to Lauren's bed, quickly rose, a syringe in her hand. She reached for the IV line, used the syringe's plunger to draw air into the tube and placed the needle in the pick line, depressing the plunger as she did. She repeated the process three more times, then watched, in horror, as she saw Lauren's open eyes following her movements.

Just then, Jared entered the room carrying the tea and followed closely by Charlie. Kim quickly hid the syringe in her pocket, thanked Jared for the tea, and left the room.

Jared suddenly heard Lauren struggling and rushing to her, watched as she pulled out her IV.

"Lauren, what's wrong? Baby, you've got to keep that in if you're going to get better."

"Kim, Kim put something in my IV," she said as, exhausted, she fell back on her pillow.

"What?" Jared said as the realization hit him. Kim had planned this. She got him out of the room so she could attempt to murder her, get rid of her competition.

He flew out of the room, Charlie close behind him. As he yelled for a doctor, Charlie left to find Kim.

Jared was panicked and his cries for help were answered quickly. A team of doctors and nurses flooded into Lauren's room, working feverishly to save her life while Jared explained what Lauren had told him. A youngish resident looked at her pick line and frowned. There were visible air bubbles in it and had Lauren not seen what Kim had done, over a matter of hours she may have died from an embolism or been in a permanent vegetative state.

A technician immediately hooked Lauren up to an EKG machine to monitor her heart. She was placed on her left side and oxygen was used to increase the blood oxygen levels, hoping to shrink any air bubble that may have gotten through. Any blockage that might have been the result of an air bubble would immediately show up on the EKG and would guide the doctors' continued treatment. They would monitor her constantly. They reinserted a new IV, pumping fluids into her to increase blood volume, hoping to dissolve any existing bubble. It was a waiting game.

Chapter 69

Wakening and seeing Kim with the syringe immediately brought Lauren back to the hiking trail. She remembered. And now, she was pretty sure Kim was trying to finish the job. She had to remove the IV as quickly as possible to avoid having whatever she had injected enter her bloodstream. Jared. She had to tell Jared what Kim did. Not just here in the hospital, but on the trail. And she had to tell him about Bethany. But she was so tired. And her room was full of people. People, she supposed, who were trying to save her life. She'd have to sleep for now.

Jared was by her bedside when she woke up later that morning. His look of concern vanished the minute she smiled at him.

"Baby, you're going to be fine. There's no sign of any more air bubbles in your veins. They did find a tiny one, but once they located it, they pumped more fluids into you and it just disappeared."

"What about Kim?"

"We're still looking for her. Charlie has the entire force out there, but I'm afraid she may have planned for the eventuality that her plan would fail. She could be anywhere."

"That's a scary thought," she said.

"Yeah, but I'll keep you safe. I'm never letting you out of my sight again." He got quiet, then asked, "Are you ready to tell me what happened?"

"I think so."

"Good. Charlie's just a phone call away. He needs to be here for this."

Killer Looks

Charlie arrived 10 minutes after Jared's phone call. He carried a big bouquet of flowers, courtesy of Maggie's thoughtfulness.

"Lauren, Maggie and I are glad you're gonna be with us a little longer. I've notified the state authorities and the FBI and they have detectives and agents looking for Kim. We'll find her."

"I'm not so sure," said Lauren.

"Why would you say that, Lauren?" Charlie asked.

"She killed before and got away with it."

"What?" asked Charlie and Jared simultaneously. "Okay, let's start at the beginning. I'm recording your statement," he said as he laid a small recorder on the nightstand next to her bed.

Lauren began. "In a way, I blame myself for everything that happened."

Jared interrupted. "Lauren, that's not true."

She looked at him and said, "Jared, let me finish this, then we can talk, okay?"

Sheepishly, he agreed.

"It started with Cal and my screwed-up time with him. I pushed you away, Jared, when I shouldn't have. If I had just explained to you what had happened, we might have been able to work together in my recovery. I was trying to do what I thought was the right thing for you, you know. But I know I hurt you. You were vulnerable and that gave Kim entre into our lives. She targeted you. You probably didn't know that, but she was more than eager to tell me. She orchestrated your meeting. She's the one who left that flyer for you. She must have stalked you every day, just waiting for you to try that new trail. Then she ran into

305

you on purpose, not the way you told me you had met her. By chance. She's a beautiful woman and I can't blame you for wanting to spend time with her. Especially because you thought I didn't want you in my life. But with therapy, I realized how much I loved you. That's when we talked the first time. There was something about Kim that bothered me. In spite of her stunning outward appearance, the night I met her she seemed to hide a sinister side. Not sinister, exactly, but there was something in her eyes. She seemed fine with meeting your ex, me, but I don't think she was. Then, when you and I decided to reconcile, she didn't want to lose you, I'm sure. She followed me to that trail and ambushed me. She had a gun, but wasn't going to shoot me. She was going to push me into the ravine below the trail. When I said she wouldn't get away with it, she said she'd gotten away with it before. She killed a girl named Bethany by doing the same thing to her that she was going to do to me. She said the girl tried to steal her boyfriend. She rushed at me and pushed me into that ravine. I don't remember anything else after that."

Jared and Charlie were stunned by Lauren's revelations. Jared felt stupid for allowing himself to fall for Kim's manipulations. She was good. Very good.

"Lauren, I know this had been hard for you, but thanks for this. We're going to have to look into Kim's confession of murder. See if we can follow her life, find out about her past relationships and look into accidental deaths in the places she lived that might parallel what you've told us. Jared, I think this could be in your cold case wheelhouse. How about helping me out?"

'Charlie, I think you've got this. I'm going to be a little busy," he said as he sat on Lauren's bed and held her in his arms.

Chapter 70

Twenty years earlier…

Ed Tyler felt blessed. He was an ex-pat in Costa Rica and since his wife had died, he'd been living the good life. His reason for going on after Bella's diagnosis was his angelic and exceptionally beautiful 16-year-old daughter. She'd been reluctant to move to Costa Rica, but had grown to love it. She was a runner, and had introduced him to the many mountainous trails she'd discovered. They'd even ziplined near a couple of them.

Four weeks ago, he had introduced his daughter to the woman he hoped would share the rest of his life with him. She was nothing like his late wife, who had been his college sweetheart. Bella had been quiet, intelligent and devoted to their daughter.

His new love, Grace, was vivacious, funny and outgoing. She loved socializing and kept herself fit and healthy. Ed felt alive every time he was with her. And he was with her a lot, sometimes breaking plans with his daughter to follow one of Grace's great adventures. He'd make it up to his daughter, once they were a family. Ed had wanted to make sure Grace was willing to marry him before he brought her into his daughter's life. After the introduction, they had seemed to hit it off just fine.

His daughter had even instilled in Grace a love of running. Wanting to keep in shape, the two of them had logged over 50 miles together since they'd met. So, he wasn't surprised when earlier this morning, Grace had said she was trying out a new trail that his daughter had recommended. His daughter would be with friends, so Grace would be going alone.

Three hours later, as he sat with his final cup of morning coffee, a sudden whoosh of a rescue helicopter overhead broke his reverie.

He glanced at his watch, mild concern on his face. Grace had been gone longer than he had realized. As he headed outside, his attention was diverted to a view of his daughter. She had returned home from her morning with friends and was now in the backyard, her head raised skyward towards the direction of the helicopter, her hand shielding her eyes from the sun as she followed its flight. As the helicopter left her sight, her head lowered and she dropped her hand. Sensing her father behind her, she turned slowly and smiled.

"How about dinner for just the two of us tonight, Dad? I'm sure Grace won't mind," Kim said, possessively linking her arm in his and walking back into the house.

ABOUT THE AUTHOR

Karen Oliver has always been a lover of books. From walking each weekend as a child to the local library to bring home an armful of her beloved treasures, to majoring in English education in college, to using her writing skills in her chosen profession, advertising, she knew a book or two would someday transition from her brain to words on a page.

She is currently retired and lives in Arizona with her husband, Randy.

Killer Looks

Made in the USA
Las Vegas, NV
23 January 2022

42138850R00184